(1596)

Publications of the Barnabe Riche Society

Volume 17

A Margarite
of America

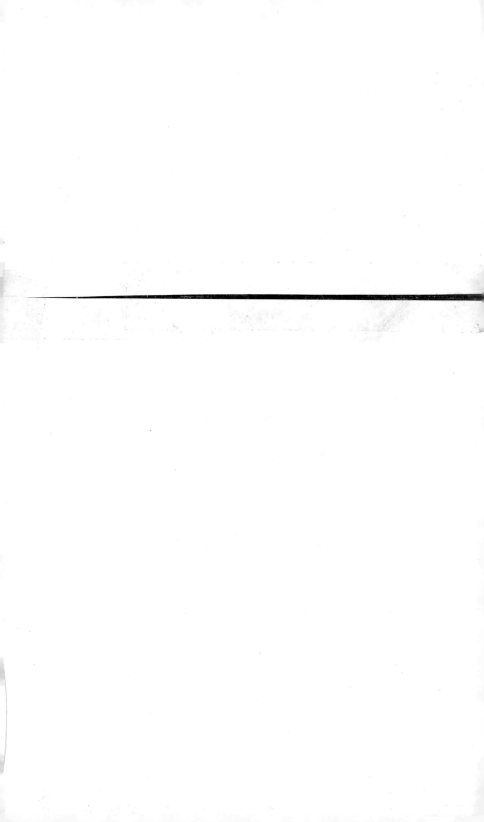

Thomas Lodge

A Margarite of America

(1596)

Introduction
Donald Beecher

Editing and Annotations
Henry D. Janzen

Toronto
Centre for Reformation and Renaissance Studies
2005

Library and Archives Canada Cataloguing in Publication

Lodge, Thomas, 1558?–1625.

A Margarite of America (1596) / Thomas Lodge ; introduction, Donald Beecher ; editing and annotations, Henry D. Janzen.

(Publications of the Barnabe Riche Society ; 17)
Includes bibliographical references.

ISBN 0-7727-2027-4 (paper)

I. Beecher, Donald   II. Janzen, Henry D.   III. Victoria University (Toronto, Ont.).   Centre for Reformation and Renaissance Studies   IV. Title.   V. Series.

PR2297.M37 2005   823'.3   C2005-900029-5

For distribution write to:

Centre for Reformation and Renaissance Studies
Victoria University
University of Toronto
71 Queen's Park Crescent
Toronto, ON M5S 1K7

For information about the series:

The Barnabe Riche Society
c/o The Department of English
Carleton University
1125 Colonel By Drive
Ottawa, Canada, K1S 5B6

Typeset in Canada: Carleton Production Centre
Printed and Bound in Canada

To my daughter Cathy and my son Paul

(HDJ)

To my daughter Sophie and my son François

(DAB)

Preface

The publication series of The Barnabe Riche Society has been established to provide scholarly, modern-spelling editions of works of imaginative literature in prose written in English between 1485 and 1660, with special emphasis on Elizabethan prose fiction. The program allows for works ranging from late medieval fabliaux and Tudor translations of Spanish picaresque tales or ancient Greek romances to seventeenth-century prose pastorals. But the principal goal is to supply much-needed editions of many of the most critically acclaimed works of the period by such authors as Lodge, Greene, Chettle, Riche, and Dekker, and to make them available in formats suitable to libraries, scholars, and students. Editorial policy for the series calls for texts carefully researched in terms of variant sources, and presented in conservatively modernized and repunctuated form in order to make these texts as widely accessible as possible, while respecting the substantive integrity of the originals. Each edition will provide the editor with an opportunity to write a full essay dealing with the author and the historical circumstances surrounding the creation of the work, as well as with its style, themes, conventions, and critical challenges. Each text will also be accompanied by annotations.

The Barnabe Riche Society is based in the English Department of Carleton University in Ottawa, and forms a component of the Carleton Centre for Renaissance Studies and Research. The society invites the informal association of all scholars interested in its goals and activities.

Table of Contents

Acknowledgments

In the preparation of this edition of Thomas Lodge's *A Margarite of America*, I owe debts of gratitude to Max Nelson of the Department of Classical and Modern Languages, Literatures, and Civilizations at the University of Windsor for help with Latin quotations, to Barbara Pagotto for assistance with the Italian, to Don Beecher for insightful comments and criticisms, and to my dear wife Mary for help in textual collation and proof-reading, as well as for loving encouragement.   H.D.J.

Special thanks go to Colette Tracey of Carleton University's Department of English for her careful scrutiny of the introduction.   D.A.B.

Introduction

Horror Fiction for the 1590s

The action of this composite work, perhaps best described as a "romance-turned-revenge-tragedy," begins with a grand tableau of war as the armies of two emperors prepare for yet another engagement in a three-year-long struggle over the city of Mantinea. But at the last available moment, a heroic voice is heard declaiming on the horrors, vanities, and wastes of war, climaxed by a proposal that Arsadachus, the only son of the ruler of Cusco, be married to Margarita, the only daughter of the ruler of Mosco, thereby uniting these hostile kingdoms. Mutual possession of the contested city would follow, together with all the blessings of peace for the "common weal." In this way, Lodge ensconces his story of the hopeful life and brutal death of Margarita within a political framing tale.

Readers may object that such political overtones are far too generic and secondary to be of concern, but for monarchies, political destinies resided largely in the moral integrity of rulers, their courts, and their offspring. In the case of *A Margarite*, peace for both nations was contingent upon the ability of these two royals to mutualize their love and seal it in a dynastic marriage. Margarita accepted her duty with alacrity, blindly and uncompromisingly, in her determination to join with Arsadachus in fulfilling the order of romance. But the latter pursued a mock courtship while following his erotic whims elsewhere, creating

11

events with high political consequences. Arsadachus enrolls the aid of two corrupt courtiers in his attempt to rape Philenia on her wedding night, then finds himself in a vortex of witness-bearing, politic murders, and banishments which eventuate in the destruction of the entire dynasty. Elizabethan readers would associate the trajectory of the antagonist's career with all that had been fixed in their minds concerning political instability caused by wayward and ambitious princes. Chroniclers and playwrights alike had contributed to a rich store of examples, particularly in such representative works as Sackville and Norton's *Gorboduc* or Greene's *James IV*.[1] A *Margarite* is not, in the final analysis, a work of profound political analysis, yet reifies in its circumstances of court and kingdom preoccupations in the forefront of the Tudor mind concerning succession, the instruction of princes, civil war, and tyranny.

Arsadachus is said to be carrying "Machevil's prince in his bosom," but there is no compelling evidence that Arsadachus was created directly out of the writings of Machiavelli (Pollack, "Studies" 150). Rather, he is another manifestation of the popularized "Machiavellian" tyrant then stalking the Elizabethan stage, a character often barely hiding his origins in the folk Vice figure of the Tudor interludes.[2] Lodge adjusts the constitutional

[1] For the parallel between this work and *Gorboduc*, see Margaret Schlauch, 198.

[2] Arsadachus, as the archetypal trickster-egoist, is "Machiavellian" to the extent that his tactics are based on expediency and are entirely devoid of ethical considerations. But these generic traits do not require direct derivation from the works of the Florentine Secretary, nor do they call for a re-examination of the complex questions surrounding the diffusion of Machiavellian thought in Elizabethan England. Machiavelli the political thinker was appreciated by leading Tudor statesmen and intellectuals, and there were, without doubt, copies of his works in Italian in circulation. But the name alone had been taken over in the popular imagination to represent climbers and opportunists in all spheres of social and economic life who proceeded without scruple or moral concern. Such applications had remote and parodic relationships to Machiavelli's teachings in *Realpolitik* for rulers responsible for the life-or-death struggles of their realms. Arsadachus represents a prince in a story framed by political concerns, but this popularized application of hyperbolical

malignity of the stage villain and the Italianate politico to the mimetic level of the romance in which suave courtiers connive and deceive, and princes pursue acts of filial disobedience, lust, self-aggrandizement, and frivolous hedonism on a grandiose scale. Perhaps no sequence in the narrative reveals these traits more clearly than the prince's seduction by the doxy Diana, closely tutored by her wily and unscrupulous father. Arsadachus' desire is manipulated into a state of lovesickness so that, once Diana is in his possession, he worships her as a goddess, commits dastardly deeds in her honour, and indulges her in the excesses of a coronation treated as a triumph in full Roman splendour. The work is never more political than this. Yet, clearly, Elizabethans had a taste for these luxuriating tales masquerading as political homilies in dramatized form.

By the same token, Lodge was clearly in tune with the times in adapting the formulae of revenge tragedy to prose fiction. *A Margarite of America* is not only about courts, their mores and diversions, their corruptions and intrigues, about tyranny and usurpation, but also about murders and mutilations of enemies and parents alike, and about the smoldering revenge that alone can bring stasis to a story of desolation and woe. J.W. Lever profiles the genre in *The Tragedy of State*, taking note, in select plays by Marston, Marlowe, Kyd, and Shakespeare, of a set of common features: court settings, corrupt rulers, intrigue, delayed revenge, and spectacular catastrophes (18). Inevitably, where there

---

traits to the "villain Machiavel" of the sensationalist variety tends to undermine the work as a serious political study. Marlowe, in his prologue to *The Jew of Malta*, provides the same crossing point between a residue of Machiavellian thinking and the advancement of the villain protagonist styled in the name of the bogeyman "Machevil," in all its variant spellings. As early as 1568 William Maitland refers to a scoundrel as "this false Machivilian," indicating how early the folk version had appeared. Mario Praz believes that the idea came to England through Scotland where, as it turns out, *The Prince* had been translated into Scottish long before the English had a translation (94). Such allusions carry the imagination not in the direction of necessary political strategy— Arsadachus had no reasons of state in mind whatsoever before setting himself up as emperor—but to amorality and sensationalism in the social world of the court.

is despotism there are victims, a polarizing of interests, the loss
and recovery of the memory of heinous deeds, and a settling of
accounts, often on a crowded stage where vengeance exceeds its
bounds and turns to havoc and rampage. This, too, became part
of the Elizabethan aesthetic, and a feature of fiction "as they liked
it." In the linking of the hyperbolical "Machiavel" to the Senecan
protagonist (particularly the "furious" Hercules), Lodge and his
contemporaries found a prototype for the malign hero, capable
not only of the most insidious hypocrisies of the accomplished
courtier, but also of the amoral atrocities of the political butcher.
Thus, when the final settling of accounts arrives, Arsadachus
provides us with a spectacle of carnage, stabbings, beatings, and
mutilations, unrivaled in Elizabethan literature — atrocities too
striking to be reconciled to a quid pro quo enactment of justice.

This work, in its tactile details, concentrates on the liquid
and the hard-edged, the gore of dashed-out brains and gnawed
hearts, and the steel of the sword that kills the heroine, playing
upon our primal fears of fluids, mutilations, piercing, "dissolu-
tion or petrifaction" (Levinson 279). The intent can only have
been to shock sensibilities with representations of raw horror.
In this regard, *A Margarite* is the culmination of a succession of
thrillers that includes Nashe's *Unfortunate Traveller* (1594), featur-
ing the rape of Heraclide on her dead husband's body, Greene's
Planetomachia, in which a young woman drinks from the skulls
of her decapitated brothers while repeatedly stabbing the heart
of the villain murderer, and *The Wounds of Civil War*, in which
"torn limbs or severed heads were exhibited on stage" (Cuvelier,
"Horror and Cruelty" 39).

Precisely how the modern reader will be moved by such inventions is a moot question. Clearly, *A Margarite* is a study in
Elizabethan tastes. It is an accomplished example of the composite style of the era with its balance of formal and informal features
mixed with poetic interludes. It carries vestiges of pastoral that
serve to underscore the loss of innocence. It is a lesson in the conventions of romance and revenge, and a study in the conflation
of genres as romance gives way to the imperatives of justice — or
the absurd. But whether the horror pertains merely to the grue-
some details or extends to the fortunes of the characters, there
is nevertheless a thematic and experiential bent apparent in the

egregious manifestations of violence and carnage. One could argue that too much shock effect collapses the finale into parody, that such excess generates indifference at the affective level. Or the claim might be made that the sensations of horror are insufficiently attached to the characters themselves. Thus, at the level of human empathy, the work may be underestimated. It is by no means difficult to fault the lack of character interiority by novelistic standards, or to criticize the formulaic design of events, the over-structured modes of discourse, or the topical insets that appear to get in the way of feeling. A.C. Hamilton agreed that modern readers have resisted the romance formula in general as an imposition upon their sensibilities, yet he reminds us that in the romance-reading age "the intensity of passion associated with sex and violence possess[ed] the reader immediately, powerfully, and profoundly" (28). In the final analysis, *A Margarite* may seek to arouse such qualities of felt experience. Not only does it recreate a court milieu of great variety and subtlety in a closely plotted and suspenseful sequence of episodes, but Margarita's desires remain the centre of our well-wishing throughout the work, even as we see her chances for happiness compromised and eventually erased. The culmination of the narrative is her death: the heroine still deceived by her naïveté, the reader only too aware of the meeting of finality and futility. The gloom holds not only for Margarita, but, by thematic extension, for the prospects of human happiness in such "worlds" of unrelieved hypocrisy.

Subsequent discussions, in metaconscious fashion (i.e. thinking about ourselves thinking), will point out how reticent we are, in hermeneutic terms, to remain in the maelstrom of abjection. Inevitably, with so much of the order of a failed romance still intact, there are structural intimations that allow for symbolic ascent. Margarita, as one of Northrop Frye's "beleaguered virgins" (87), is the epitome of chaste feminine merit.[3] Her sisters in

---

[3]Certain of Frye's analyses of romance in *The Secular Scripture* suggest themselves here, namely that Arsadachus, in the context of the underlying *agon*, is the destroyer of the agent of redemption and renewal. He is the god of the waning year who brings nature to her nadir in death and desolation. In *A Margarite*, Lodge elects to tell only the

suffering include Griselda, famed for her patience in adversity, and Castania in Greene's *Gwydonius*. Death, to be sure, is final, yet memory of virtue lingers, potentially transforming her life and death into the stuff of myth.[4] The reflexive mind, to survivalist ends, may prove adept in reconstructing hope: lives conducted with dignity, though blindly through a vale of tears, must possess something still of value and redemption. Paul Ricoeur, in his study of evil, remains convinced that we always end up by allegorizing our moral antinomies as a refuge from the kind of blank nihilism with which Lodge confronts us, by

first half of this story, as though it had no sequel. It is a tale of warring realms whose future well-being depends upon the ritual mating of these princely children—one which never comes to pass. Master passions thus define the hedonist, the beleaguered and suffering virgin, and the hermit magician and revenger. Each passion in turn determines the literary mode in which the character operates, each one seeking to imprint the order of closure. As a marguerite/margarite, the heroine is both the green and white flower of fertility and purity and the pearl of great cost, which Anne Falke allegorizes as the Christian soul trapped in the sinful body and imprisoned in a world of spiritual darkness. Hence Margarita's persistent "unknowing" of evil. She is at the same time, as Falke points out, a sun image, a Diana (in spite of the wicked pseudo-Diana who captures the prince's heart in Margarita's place), a creature dressed in the colours of May. Such allegorizing can be taken too far, to the cost of the vision of horror at a lower mimetic level. Nevertheless, it is these many potential readings around the emblematic dimensions of the heroine that leave the story with its richest intimations of the archetypal.

[4]Salzman would make a homily out of her inability to learn not to trust in appearances (80), and he would not be entirely wrong. Surely, Arsinous had such a lesson in mind in furnishing her with a magic illusion of her beloved during their passage through the countryside. Even Arsadachus sought to instruct her concerning his true state of mind in the poems he sent to her before his final departure; they are not so much exercises in dissimulation and subterfuge as they are revelations of Margarita's self-deceiving powers of positive thinking, in spite of her distant recognition of the truth. In this there is a utility of sorts. But to lay blame on her "unspotted simplicity" in love is to moralize in gratuitous fashion. Margarita's naïveté does not bankrupt the value of love (Selzer 176, 188), and it does not detract from her role as the *pharmakos* in transactional payment for the sins of others.

fixing deeds of darkness within a larger myth of fall and redemption, the evil components of which we anthropomorphize
as agents loosed upon the world of human endeavours (307).
Lodge goes far in making Arsadachus such a demonic agent,
and Margarita such a redemptive spirit. Their world almost becomes a comfortable struggle between good and evil within safe
and distanced confines.

But without those familiar antinomies, *A Margarite* remains
a fiction of abjection, characterized by an ethos of despair. Its
levels of feeling are created around ineffectual and abused saintliness and unrelenting depravity. That is a strong-minded kind
of experiment in which the return to stasis and order resides in
a lone surviving revenger following the massacre of all in whom
we have taken a narrative interest. The atrocities committed by
Arsadachus in disregard of ethical values or human empathy in a
state of uncontrolled emotion generate a *frisson* of horror, both of
a limbic as well as of a cognitive kind. Lodge may have been out
to prove, as his first goal, that such mind states — those in which
the nerves are made taut and thoughts frozen by the hopeless
and the deplorable — lie within the scope of narrative effect. Yet,
how the mind deals with the innuendoes of devastation is unresolved, whether abjection takes affective control, at least until
consciousness supplies its own escape through differential concerns, or whether the story itself is transmuted to a less blighted
version through symbolization.

Romance and Revenge Tragedy

Romance is a genre driven by the imaginative excitement of
its episodes and by the fulfilment of erotic expectations in its
closure. Typically, romance readers are turned into well-wishers
for lovers in a menacing world. By a change of events, however,
the genre can be inverted, turning virgin heroines into virgin
martyrs and uncooperative lovers into villains, producing the
horror already described. In this variation on the romance *telos*,
readers come to understand, well before the heroine herself, that
counter forces will frustrate the conventional closure in union
and renewal. In romance, the lovers can be cruelly tried, but
one of them cannot simultaneously be responsible for abhorrent

crimes crying out for retribution. If Lodge takes this direction in *A Margarite*, it represents no failure in his understanding of the genre, or a thematically oriented abandonment of that genre, but rather a deliberate choice to cross one order of plot with another, setting up a kind of double order, namely that of commiseration for the victims, and of tragic justice for the villain. Such a design has a jarring effect, for not only does it turn romance into revenge tragedy, as in the contemporary theatre, but it turns pastoral landscape, intimated in the garden scenes, into a wasteland of havoc and ruin.

The question of why Lodge would wish to culminate his career as an imaginative writer with a shocking derailment of romance expectations is perhaps best answered in terms of structural and aesthetic opportunities: Lodge hit upon the "idea" that such a design was possible through a mannerist reconfiguration of motifs most likely drawn from his own former works. Such an account gives short shrift to reasons of personal discouragement or the despondent times — explanations that can never be more than selectively and circumstantially true. Dark literary visions do not, of necessity, reflect a doomed society or a despondent author, although such constructions, with very little effort, can be imposed upon the 1590s. During the last decade of the century, plague had come and gone, young men from the universities were without professional prospects, the Queen was ageing and crotchety, her court less than gay, the Catholic question remained unsettled, merchant ventures had failed, the poets had turned satirists and harped endlessly upon decadence and corrupt mores, while the new science threatened with its decentred universe. Lodge's personal disappointments could also be credited with leading him to the melancholy arts. But the question remains whether the bleak tableau of carnage at the end of *A Margarite* can be lifted out of its narrative context and made to stand as an emblem for the mood of an age or the temperament of the author. All that can be said with certainty is that *A Margarite* represents the last of Lodge's efforts to compel his muse to scale the depths of the diabolical, now in the form of a prose revenge tragedy.[5]

---

[5]In this vein Katharine Wilson sees Arsadachus as the "author's surrogate" in demonstrating the "inadequacies of romance" (15). It is her

thesis that *A Margarite* is an all-out assault on the entire genre as the result of Lodge's disillusionment with his own writing career. This is based on the presupposition that the metamorphosis of a genre indicates a critique of the original form, and that literary structures invariably encode information about the author's personal and affective life. One might argue, contrariwise, that even in conflation with other genres, the order of romance remains operative as the measure of all that is destroyed by lust and rapine. An even more complex argument of this kind is advanced by Joan Pong Linton in *The Romance of the New World* (1998) wherein she seeks to demonstrate by subtle "deconstructionist" arguments a critique of mercantile colonialism implicit in the unfulfilled romance structure. She begins by assigning to the author a personal disillusionment that "must" have resulted from writing *A Margarite* while sailing with Cavendish in the icy waters off the southern tip of South America, simply because the venture itself was a failure. For Linton, that Lodge left no memoirs about the trip can only mean that his political views are buried in the romance he wrote aboard; that is the grounds for her entire thesis. More clues are contained in naming his heroine Margarita, and in making the antagonist, Arsadachus, an Incan prince from Cusco. These together compound into a dark vision of the English colonializing intentions in the New World (albeit barely imagined at the time of the Cavendish expedition, which was bent merely on plunder and discomforting the Spanish fleet). In this "pre-colonial" reading, Arsadachus (from arsedine — a kind of false gold) becomes the object of Margarita's now misplaced and irresponsible attentions (overlooking her original duty as a princess to marry for the sake of peace). This argument requires a strategic use of irony to reassign the characters' positions. By extension, Margarita becomes a representative of Una, the Protestant Church in Spenser's *Faerie Queene*, and Elizabeth I, the exploitative mercantile queen, thereby representing the colonial subjugation of helpless peoples, as well as something of a parody of chastity. Lodge's disenchantment with the program of Elizabethan imperialism, for Linton, becomes manifest.

One must appreciate in this the desire to render Lodge's work more thematically engaging to readers in the gendered, post-colonial world of New Historicist criticism. To be sure, there are alternate readings to much of the supporting evidence. As future discussions will reiterate, the "margarite" is merely the romance brought back from America because found or written there, but not the heroine herself, who is Margarita. Moreover, she is not from America, but from Mosco, within walking distance of Cusco, and there is no hint of an Incan association for any of the characters. There are other ways of seeing the Cavendish

Already outlined is the fusion of genres, the romance world of Margarita, with its overtones of courtship aligned with the seasonal cycles of sterility in tribulation and fertility in the union of lovers, and the order of the *lex talionis*, of punishment for crimes in kind and degree through a motivated counter-agent. Arsadachus gives birth to that order, beginning as the prodigal son who flings away after hearing the paternal words of wisdom that should have been his guide.[6] His compulsion to know no restraints in his quest for illicit pleasures is augmented by a sense

adventure than as a "picture of a violent world in which greed and necessity overtake any pretension to spiritual ideals and knightly goals" (49). That "a calculated indecorum" in the style of *A Margarite* becomes evidence for "a veiled critique of empire" (51) remains open to demonstration, and that Lodge's modification of the genre "mocks the period's use of romance in glorifying the mercenary acts of empire" (52) depends upon establishing an historical alignment between romance structures and the promotion of empire. The thesis also depends upon building a thematic symmetry between Old and New World negotiations and the one-sidedness of the relationship between the principals in Lodge's story. The details about these characters may be too imprecise and too specific at once to reduce them to political allegory. Finally, in this reading, it is not clear that there was a gem in the probative box that Margarita presents to Arsadachus, or if there were, that it was her virginity, which, upon seeing, would drive him to frenzy. Arsadachus does not seduce her, as is suggested, nor does Mosco conquer Cusco at the end of the story (61). Nevertheless, there are readers who will find these associations important attempts to place Lodge's writing within this modern frame of critical discourse. Given Margarita's very vulnerable position in Lodge's highly emblematic representation of sexual relations, this work will surely incarnate multiple views of human nature and inspire engaging polemics. There are issues of power and innocence that, in the representational field of romance, functioning as it does between novelistic mimetic levels and the patterns of myth, will continue to invite thematic interpretations by extrapolation from meaningful structures and implicit authorial intentions — because art is someone's intentional state, and because it is our business in the social world to read those intentional states in others in accordance with their gestures, and in accordance with our own needs in "reading" the world.

[6]The most famous example in English literature of the advice of a father given to a child at the moment of departure is the speech Polonius makes to Laertes in *Hamlet,* but there were many others of an earlier date

of princely prerogative and complemented by a ruthless streak in managing his entourage. His lechery leads him to murder, for which he shows no remorse. By the end, the prodigal has transformed himself into a tyrannical hedonist whose program of self-gratification includes the usurpation of his father's kingdom, lavish processions, and the enactment of his most erotic fantasies. Until then, he endorses the politic necessity of courting Margarita for reasons of state, thereby becoming the perfect hypocrite in the guise of the perfect courtier. His most sustained endeavour is to deceive Margarita with a false love that leads her to destruction. This would seem a mere peccadillo by comparison with his other crimes, but in fact, such betrayal is the work's central motif. Arsadachus may well be, simultaneously, another of Lodge's amoral berserkers, potentially as apt for conversion to sainthood as Robert the Devil.[7] Yet his conversion does not arrive in time, and his deeds call out for compensation. In this economy, he is the overreacher, laying himself open to the devices of a revenger eager to play upon his self-confidence.

Braden observes that Arsadachus has too much of the Senecan "selfhood" of the popular revenge plays not to link him to the theatrical tradition (214). In this there would seem to be little doubt. His method of eliminating his accomplices in crime while assuring them of their safety is a technique that enjoyed paradigmatic success in both Kyd's *A Spanish Tragedy* (as Pedringano fools his life away on false promises) and *The Jew of Malta* (as Ithamore toys himself to destruction). *Titus Andronicus* likewise manifests a telling number of corresponding traits: tongues carved out,

which Lodge could have employed as models, including the paradigmatic speech by Eubulus in Lyly's *Euphues*, Clerophontes in Greene's *Gwydonius*, and in Lodge's own works, Anthenor in *Euphues' Shadow*, and Sir John of Bordeaux at the beginning of *Rosalind*. It may have had its origins in the tragedies of Seneca, as discussed below.

[7] *Robert, Second Duke of Normandy* is a kind of pseudo-historical romance in which a medieval villain trickster, ostensibly beyond redemption, ultimately finds conversion to a life of saintliness. This design allows the author to dwell on both the protagonist's incorrigible depravity and perverse inventiveness as well as the remarkable transition to a heightened moral awakening. Addison has no doubts that Robert "is the prototype for Arsadachus" (21).

hands lopped off, rapes or intended rapes followed by murder, the gleeful mockery of maimed victims, fathers who curse then cuddle daughters, criminals who finagle to destroy the evidence against them, violent banquet scenes, pastoral interludes and encounters in forests, hypocrite courtiers, hermit figures who study revenge for slain children, rulers who refuse to examine evidence and condemn the innocent, and rage leading to the murder of family members. So many correspondences do not a source make, necessarily, but they offer confirmation that Lodge and Shakespeare were at least selecting related narrative and thematic parts from a general cupboard of common elements particularly proper to the milieu of sensational revenge plots. To these might be added motifs from the plays of Seneca, such as the concluding rage of Arsadachus in relation to the deeds of Hercules in *Hercules Oeteus* and *Hercules Furens* (Wilson 9ff).

The revival of Senecan revenge drama in England belongs to the late 1580s when *The Spanish Tragedy* first came to the boards. This is not to discount an acquaintance with Seneca during preceding decades in the form of critical comment, translations, and academic performances. But it was Kyd who brought to the "popular" imagination of theatre-goers the dramatic force of retributive justice, together with the agonies of the revenger who devises the "fraud" necessary to lure offenders to their punishments. A similar Senecan revival, however, had already taken place in Ferrara in the early 1540s in the work of Giambattista Giraldi, known as Cinthio, and the point is moot whether English Senecan tragedy owes more or less to Cinthio than it does to the ancient writer. In either case, Cinthio's work remains instructive in any assessment of the mode. He had been a close student of Seneca's *Thyestes* before writing his *Orbecche* — a seminal work in the founding of Italian erudite tragedy. Aristotelian criteria for Cinthio, Sperone, and fellow writers were never far from consideration, and particularly Aristotle's description of the concluding emotions aroused in the spectators as the markers of the tragic ethos. The two words from the *Poetics*, today most frequently glossed as "pity" and "fear," Guddi, in the mid-sixteenth century, identified as "compassion" and "terror." The nuances were to have important repercussions, for Cinthio could bring them into common cause by creating not a single response, but a response

split between feelings of solicitude and amazement. These no-
tions were most readily applied, respectively, to the paralysed
heroine, helpless in her self-deception, and to the deeds of the
active Neo-Senecan tyrant (Horne 150). That is to say, Cinthio
separated the emotional responses, now contrasting those applying to the sufferers with those applying to the perpetrators
of evil.

Another of the markers of this theatrical mode was the long
inaugural didactic discourse delivered by a wise counsellor that
sets the moral field for the entire work. Lodge observes the
formula in the sermon Arsadachus receives from his father at the
point of his departure into the world as a young prince. Lodge
had used the motif on former occasions, most notably in *Rosalind*
in the deathbed advice given by John of Bordeaux to his two
sons. In Cinthio's works, these scenes are directly redolent of
those in Seneca: Satelles and Atreus in *Thyestes*; Pyrrhus and
Agamemnon in *Troades*; or Seneca and Nero in *Octavia*. Lodge's
employment of the motif as a narrative and thematic device,
and as a preliminary essay on the shortcomings of the hero, is a
further marker of *A Margarit*'s affiliations with a literary tradition
pointing back to Seneca.

The inventive cruelty, the butchery and mutilations, formerly
attributed to the Italian horror *novelle*, can be traced as effectively
to this Senecan mode. But there is no particular need to choose
between them insofar as Cinthio himself was active as a writer
of such prose tales (the plot for Shakespeare's *Othello* originates
in Cinthio's *Hecatommithi*, 1566). The exchange of characteristics
between the two genres was extensive. One such motif was that
of the "precious gift," an object or person of inestimable value
disfigured or slain in order to torture the recipient, as when, in *A
Margarite*, Artosogon slays Diana's father, quarters his body, and
sends the parts to her. In this episode, there is a distinct echo of
the tactics employed by Orbecche's father to spite her for the marriage she had contracted against his will. In Cinthio's tragedy,
both husband and children are seized and slain, her husband's
head placed in a vase and sent to her as a gift at the time of an
enforced wedding to another. The "precious gift" motif gathers
resonances from ancient myth in the story of Procne, who slays
her own son Itys and serves him at a banquet to her lecherous

and cruel husband in revenge for raping her sister Philomela. One thinks too of the story of the Duchess of Amalfi, dramatized by Webster, wherein the duchess is tormented by a tableau of her dead husband and children. (In a parallel version by Lope de Vega, Antonio's head is served on a platter at a banquet.[8]) Cinthio strove to amaze with the sinister and macabre inventions of cruelty featured in his plays: the severing of limbs, the excision of hearts, the fondling of the heads of the dead, as well as the tell-tale sword play about the midriffs of the heroines. At the same time he strove for a lachrymose commiseration with the suffering victims. The Cinthian vocabulary of motifs, the compound ethos, the contest between tyrants and helpless heroines, the Senecan revenge patterns, all serve as a handbook to Lodge's final fictive creation.

Yet there is no particular case to be made for Lodge as an avid reader of the Ferraran. Cinthio pioneered a formula that left its generic mark upon an age. There had been controversies of a critical and ethical nature that arose around his *Orbecche*, much as there had been around Sperone Speroni's *Canace*, in which a father also discovers a daughter's illicit marriage, this time to her twin brother, resulting in outrage and a bloodbath. Imitators and commentators remained active down to the end of the century, with ripples potentially travelling as far as England. Meanwhile, the English had generated their own Senecan tradition. Gascoigne had translated *Jocasta* as early as 1566. Thirty years later the English had learned how to render Seneca in more extravagant ways with double and triple plots, larger casts, sexual motifs, and additional horrors presented to the eyes of the spectators—such as they are seen in *Titus Andronicus*—with or without the help of the Italians. From this composite tradition, Lodge drew motifs that clearly signal an incorporation of Senecan modes into the conception of *A Margarite*. He needed outrage,

---

[8]See *The Duchess of Amalfi's Steward* (El mayordomo de la duquesa de Amalfi), translated by Cynthia Rodriguez-Badendyck (Ottawa: Dovehouse Editions, 1985).

horrors, an avenger, and a mechanism of reversal to complete the formula.[9]

The final marker is, of course, the revenger himself, whose role it is to arrange the circumstances whereby those who have violated life and honour, and have placed themselves beyond the reach of common justice, are brought to the bar of tragic reversal. The action is good when the malefactor circulates unopposed, surpassing himself in heinous deeds, while the revenger broods and temporizes. However, in later works in the tradition, nature or the civil order is doubly outraged by the excesses of both the antagonist and the agent who pursues him, encouraging us to expect, in Braden's words, that "even the most defensible exercise of private justice recoils upon its agent" (201). But that turns out not to be the case for Arsinous, who alone survives to provide rule and order for the devastated realms. Lodge's Arsinous is not a deep study of revenge consciousness. He is a man whose self-evident suffering over the loss of his daughter is sufficient pretext to account for his withdrawal from society and his dedication to the powers of magic. Moreover, through

---

[9]The resonances between *A Margarite* and *Titus Andronicus* seem particularly clear, but there are other plays in the Senecan revenge tradition that offer comparisons and that may have supplied Lodge with ideas. Hercules in Seneca's *Hercules Oetaeus* is not a criminal character, yet while wearing the treacherous poisoned shirt of Nessus given him by Deianira in order to win him back, he kills Lichas in his tormenting agony. A similar model for Arsadachus' violent rage may be seen in *Hercules Furens*. Among the plays of the 1590s *The Lamentable Tragedy of Locrine* (ca. 1591) stands out as an English history with strong Senecan elements in which, in the last two acts, the lust of the protagonist ruler for the concubine of the conquered hero leads to the destruction of the nation and the suicide of both Estrild and Locrine. The play, importantly, combines concerns with ambition and civil war and the disruptions caused by lust and the betrayal of loyal partners, leading the hero to self-incrimination and self-retribution. The anonymous author (thought by several to have been Peele, by Irving Ribner to have been Greene, and by even earlier observers to have been Shakespeare) may have borrowed from Lodge's *Complaint of Elstred* (published 1593). While the correlations remain too general to establish a formal alliance, there is relevance in establishing the degree to which these themes and motifs were part of the late Elizabethan *Zeitgeist*.

Lodge's choice of the folklore motif of the magic coffer as the mechanism of *peripeteia*, Arsinous is distanced even more from the revenger as a criminal usurper of the law. He provides Margarita with the coffer to present to her beloved, one which, in itself, is both judge and executioner, for it is a probative device that operates by its own laws to determine guilt or innocence. So remote does he seem from the obsessive revenger that Josephine Roberts manages to describe Arsinous as "the traditional seer of pastoral romance" (411). But that may be somewhat misleading, for revenger he is, bearing with him all the imperatives of the mode, which is not only to see justice carried out proportionately to the perceived violation of the moral order, but to witness the momentum that sometimes carries vengeance well beyond the confines of that order. In that regard, the reader is called upon to respond to an economy of growing crimes and outrages that demands reciprocity. The probative box is prepared deliberately to that end by the magus-revenger. A father's duty, compelled by a daughter's death, cuts across the vestiges of romance, instituting all the elements of a complete revenge tragedy that sweep away the innocent along with the guilty.[10]

---

[10]This spirit of revenge, often embodied in the ghosts that walk the English stage, as in Kyd's *Spanish Tragedy* or Shakespeare's *Hamlet*, is transferred in *A Margarite* to the mind and memory of the slain girl's father. Plato, in discussing a fable of yore in *Laws*, suggested that the ghost of the murdered man had powers sufficient to drive the murderer to a state of madness. In Lodge's story this is conveyed through the box prepared by the revenger to drive Arsadachus to frenzy. Arsinous represents the anger of a natural order destabilized by a vicious crime. This, according to Jane Harrison in *Prolegomena to the Study of Greek Religion* (214–15), led the Greeks to the notion of Erinyes, the angry ghosts of the slain crying out for vengeance — a very particular form of anthropomorphism that became one of the conventions of ancient Greek tragedy (cited in Hallett 20). All this intensely felt necessity, in Elizabethan drama, is invested in the person who first inherits the knowledge of the outrage and the certitude of the identity of the malefactor. His life is thenceforth absorbed by a driving moral obligation which, like Hieronimo for his son, Arsinous assumes for his daughter.

The Patchwork Romance:
A Margarite Through its Sources

Both for ethos and motif, *A Margarite* has its closest affinities in the tradition of the revenge tragedy epitomized by *Titus Andronicus*. But this was not Lodge's only source of inspiration. There are potential analogues if not sources in a significant number of works in prose and in verse both from the contemporary period and from antiquity. The reading undertaken here to locate a selection of those episodes has not been conducted in an attempt to impoverish Lodge's originality, but to reveal the extent to which the Renaissance creative imagination generated novelty through adaptation and imitation. The effect is a symphony of resonances, of intertextual and archetypal overtones.

Clearly, Lodge made a habit of reading, both intensively and extensively, in those kinds of fiction most apt to incite his own creative imagination. But more than this, in keeping with the practices of his age, he read with an eye for styles to imitate, for episodes to meld and modify, and for orders of action and ethos to appropriate as his own. He had read Sidney thoroughly before writing *Forbonius*, and there can be no question that he continued to imitate him for general atmosphere in subsequent works, replicating the pastoral-romance formula right down to the rhythms and spirit of his "Arcadian" style. At the outset, Lodge intended *Rosalind* to be nothing more than a retelling of a medieval outlaw tale; even as the work drifted toward pastoral, he was unwilling to eliminate the traces of his inaugural endeavour. That Lodge was attracted to such medieval tales and chronicles is confirmed by the sources he employed in *Robert the Devil*, derived from the twelfth-century French *Robert le Diable* through the prose romance version published by Wynkyn de Worde early in the sixteenth century, and in *William Longbeard*, which he derived from Robert Fabyen's *Concordance of History* (1515). That he claims to have written *A Margarite* in the same way, following a Spanish narrative, is seductively credible, given that he had worked in that fashion so often before. But whereas in these earlier works we have a clear sense of reading and transforming specifically chosen sources, in the case of *A Margarite* there is less certainty that Lodge goes beyond a pastiche-like employment of his own former works, for nearly every motif—from parlour games to probative lions—and character type, including the villain-turned-saint, have counterparts in his own fiction as well as in creations by Sidney, Lyly, and Greene, and in writers in translation from Bandello and Boccaccio to Heliodorus and Ovid. Such an employment of the collective literary patrimony, if only secondarily through one's own former works, was endemic to the artistry of the sixteenth-century maker.

Lodge claims in his "To the Gentlemen Readers" that he found the Spanish "history" in Santos, and that in reading it he was so enchanted that he decided to "write it." Such a clear declaration is difficult to ignore entirely, even though, in manner and matter, this work is so quintessentially Lodge's own. Eliane Cuvelier, one of Lodge's closest readers, agrees that the work resembles nothing she has found in the Spanish romance literature of the age, although she allows that such a Spanish original might have existed in some form (*Thomas Lodge* 303). In *The Golden Tapestry: A Critical Survey of Non-Chivalric Spanish Fiction in English Translation (1543–1657)*, however, D.B.J. Randall denies even this possibility (244).[11] Cuvelier herself admits, in the final analysis, that Lodge's subterfuge could have been a "publicity stunt" destined to attract the readership of the kind of works then in vogue, such as the chivalric romances of Montalvo (*Thomas Lodge* 303). In any case, if one were to subtract from an imagined Spanish original all the many English and Italian components of *A Margarite*, that original would be a bare document indeed.[12]

---

[11] For more information on the library in Santos and the prospects of a Spanish source, see the "Life" in Appendix I.

[12] Just why Lodge resorted to this description of his source is open to conjecture. Is there something about *A Margarite* that Lodge might seek to attribute to a Spanish author rather than advance in his own name? Would the work pass more readily as "history" by having a Spanish provenance? Are the violence and cruelty so untypically English that Lodge perceived a need to style his book as foreign in its origins? Does the attribution allow Lodge a greater freedom to explore the darker side of his own creative imagination? Or was the Spanish connection intended to misdirect readers into believing that Margarita carried emblematic connections to America? Misled by the title, Josephine Roberts assumed as much in linking the suffering heroine, by analogy, to the

An example of such a component is the episode of the probative lion, one cast in a more "fabulous" mode than the surrounding events. As Margarita and her maid Fawnia approach
Cusco in their final search for Arsadachus, a lion emerges to attack them. Readers will recall first the passage in Book I, canto
iii of *The Faerie Queene*, where a "ramping Lyon" sees the royal
virgin alone and attempts to devour her, for just as Spenser's
lion abandoned his furious nature, fawned upon the maid, and
"lickt her lilly hands" (stanzas 5–6), so too Lodge's lion, after
killing her unchaste companion, honours Margarita's purity by
licking her "milk-white hand." Yet Spenser's lion lacks the truth-
testing role of those in Lodge's fiction and in Painter's "A Lady
Falsely Accused," wherein the beast has no other purpose but to
prove the lady's innocence by "licking and fawning upon her"
(I.215). Without irony or parody, this episode can only serve to
confirm the heroine's spotless nature for the most transparent of
emblematic reasons.

violation of a pristine and virginal New World by Old World conquis-
tadors and capitalists (412). But the margarite "of America" is nothing
more than the book itself, a literary flower or pearl, still protesting in
its title that it was brought back from America. That Margarita herself
is from America, as implied in the city named Cusco, is a slip of attention, for she is from Mosco, and the name of Cusco will prove to have
other than Peruvian connections. Katharine Wilson went even further
to claim that *A Margarite* reveals "the author's apparent loss of faith in
the New World" (9) on the assumption that it is a failed New World
romance, an idea carried to even greater lengths by Joan Pong Linton.
This idea flows from a series of loose analogies linking the misery of
the voyage, the colonializing overtones of the mission, and the abandonment of romance, thereby leading Wilson to the conclusion that "his
fictional landscapes can be interpreted as a record of disenchantment
with the corrupt powers of colonialism which he had witnessed at first
hand with Cavendish" (8). But Lodge does not speak about the politics
of the mission, nor can the revenge romance itself be a reflection of New
World colonial circumstances because it is not set in the New World.
Nor does his conflation of genres (which Wilson also treats as a form
of stylistic colonialism) reveal an anti-colonial philosophical stance. If
Lodge did his drafting aboard ship, as he boasts, this work is, presumably, the first piece of English fiction from America. But further claims
appear to be unfounded.

Clearly such lions are linked to the tradition of mythical beasts emblematizing chastity, as in Pliny's report of the unicorn that sleeps only in the laps of virgins. Given that Painter's story of the falsely accused lady originates in Bandello, as conveyed through the translation of Belleforest, the question of sources generalizes into a question of motifs. The larger issue is why Lodge would introduce this probative lion as a means for underscoring the heroine's virgin nature—as if we had cause for doubt. Is the sequence linked in his mind to the episode in *Rosalind* wherein a lion appears before the sleeping Saladyne, Rosader's hated brother, and threatens to slay him? That episode, too, is probative, for the lion tests Rosader to determine whether he will forgive and thus save his brother, or leave him to his fate. In *A Margarite*, the supernatural animal prefigures the supernatural coffer with its power to search minds and to produce the effects of poetic justice. Lodge's symmetry is clear, for Margarita, in her chastity and faith, passes the test of the lion, while Arsadachus, for his betrayal, fails the test of the coffer.[13]

One of the most striking features of *A Margarite* is the "motiveless malignity" of the wicked characters, and an ethos of violence and depravity that has few parallels in English literature. In this regard, Bandello's Italianate tales of imaginative trickery and unconscionable cruelty provide more than a few narrative motifs. They stand as full partners with the revenge tragedy and medieval villain tales in the genesis of the fiction

---

[13]Acamas, returning from the Trojan War, stopped in Thrace and there married Phyllis. Promising to return, he sailed away without her, whereupon she gave him a box containing an object sacred to the goddess Rhea—a box he was under oath never to open until he knew in his heart that his vow would never be kept. And so it proved that once in Cyprus, Acamus put her out of his thoughts. In time, Phyllis despaired, cursed him, and hanged herself. But the course of fate was fulfilled only when the box was remembered and opened, for it contained something so frightening to behold that Acamus, in an attempt to flee on horseback, was thrown upon his own sword and slain (Tripp 2). The story came to the West in the "Epitome" of Apollodorus and the *Fabulae* of Hyginus, and may have served as the prototype for all subsequent tales in which probative boxes exercised the magic property of reading the intentions of secretive minds and inaugurating appropriate destinies.

of horror. The Italian story-tellers were experts in representing the sinister crimes committed by people of the civil classes, who hid their craft behind hypocritical words and social ceremony. *A Margarite* is an anthology of such devices. Arsadachus, in his attempt to seduce Philenia, kills her husband on their wedding night after ambushing them on the road. Fearful of what his accomplices might report, he has them slain or mutilated one by one. Further maiming follows when Arsadachus has his own father's right hand lopped off and his tongue cut out. In the sixth of Bandello's *Tragical Tales*, ready-to-hand in the Fenton translation, the vicious abbot Gonsaldo becomes so besotted by love for the innocent and virtuous daughter of the goldsmith that, when all means fail to win her, he creates a band of conspirators to assault her at sword's point while *en route* with her parents toward their country house near Naples. This brave girl, Parolina, feigns compliance by offering to slay her own protesting father. Once in possession of a weapon, however, she turns it upon the abbot, wounding him in the melee that follows before leaping into the Sebetho River. It is a tale of a villainous hypocrite and a spotless virgin, of ambush and the girl's willingness to die rather than forfeit her virginity — one of several potential models for the attempted rape of Philenia by ambush, and of self-inflicted death. Of equal note is Bandello's description of the vale with its river "descending from certain rocks, giving necessary moisture to the valley near the town, which the poet Sannazaro in his *Arcadia* calleth Sebetho" (278), and how the maid passes through the setting like a nymph. This conversion of the *locus amoenus* of pastoral into a theatre for atrocities is a prominent feature of Lodge's creation.[14]

The list of potential inspirations from Fenton's Bandello is easily extended. In the third of the *Tragical Tales*, "Pandora of Milan," a woman of uncontrollable passions, on the brink of madness, kills her own child by smashing him against a wall, thereafter painting the surfaces with his blood, extracting and eating his heart, and feeding the remainders to the dogs. Her

---

[14]Lodge, in sending Arsinous to a melancholy cave surrounded by a sublime and wild nature, may have taken something from the example of Timon, who seeks out the green world to nurse his revenge.

deed is carried out with a frenzy redolent of the madness that drives Arsadachus to slay his own son by beating his brains out on a wall. Pandora, as a prelude to the deed, sends to the vale of Cainonica for magical potions and drugs to effect her will, while seeking others from a wicked grey friar. When the potions fail to abort the hated child, she resorts to violence upon her own womb. We are reminded, then, that Arsadachus slits open Diana, spreading her entrails on the floor, before tearing her heart in pieces with his teeth.[15] Claudette Pollack was certain that the Italian novel accounts for "the cult of the atrocious" in Lodge ("Studies" 62). The stealth and devious plans, the poisonings and crafted murders, the mutilations, the compulsive desires and uncontrollable emotions, the jealousy and abandonment, and many similar motifs provide strong support for her thesis.

In one sense this borrowing of motifs from author to author is a process of literary larceny, leading to Margaret Schlauch's impression that *A Margarite* was "only convention thrice shopworn" (199), while for John McAleer, such cultural ventriloquism was an indication that Lodge could not decide what kind of a writer he wanted to be (83). But such procedures are not proof of a paucity of imagination. These motifs are a form of cumulative memory, even in their specific structures. The recombinant process represents the very essence of the "Renaissance" imagination at work in building up new narratives out of the received conventions and materials of the past. Lodge's mind was a workshop of analogy whereby old parts could be renewed through transfer and adaptation, bringing forward intimations of things known and felt, such as the quality of myth that lingers in the struggle of the life and death forces invested in the principal characters.

In the final analysis, however, it is Lodge's own collected works of imaginative fiction that form the most complete compendium of motifs present in *A Margarite*. As stated earlier, his *Robert, Second Duke of Normandy* surely made a contribution. There is an ethos of horror as the duke, in his unredeemed

---

[15]There are useful criteria for establishing the critical number of similarities necessary to posit a source relationship: the parallels with Bandello's tales may just pass that test (Beecher "Symbolic Forms" 230–31).

state, progresses from raping nuns and cutting off their breasts to ambushing Lord Beaumont and his bride as they return to their castle. Comparison with the proposed rape of Philenia is self-evident, for after imprisoning the husband, Robert employs every means of coercion imaginable to win Ermine to his will. Failing in this, he brings back the husband to be mutilated limb by limb until the lady consents or her tormented husband compels her to submit. Lord Beaumont then bites off his own tongue to preclude all chance of so instructing his wife. When he dies, Robert runs the woman through the entrails with his sword in the precise manner that Arsadachus runs Margarita through the abdomen. Here in close configuration is the ambush, the bitten tongue, and death by the thrilling sword. Lodge's *Euphues' Shadow* provides yet another case in point, for it is a story of suffering caused by broken promises. After failing in love and slaughtering his friend, whom he had mistakenly taken for a rival, Philamus becomes a hermit necromancer in a pastoral-like retreat, redolent of Arsinous, father to the slain Philenia, who takes to his melancholy cave to study the goetic arts whereby he intends to work his revenge. Just as Arsinous tests Margarita with a vision of Arsadachus, Climachas comforts Philamour with a vision of his beloved, suggesting that for inspiration, Lodge needed only consult his former works, in perfect keeping with the humanist cut-and-paste mode for making the old into the new.

Romance Topography

The half-geographical, half-literary landscape of romance is a distinct part of the liminal space this genre inhabits between myth and mimetic realism; it hovers on the line that separates probability from the barely possible. That is precisely where it must function in order that the imagination can project itself into a real and substantial world, yet roam through the emblematic and fantastical. Thus we are treated to a unique construction of setting that is designedly anachronistic and far-fetched, yet tosses our imaginations to remote parts of the world confirmed as geographical realities. There, exotic descriptions enter into the amazing events — places where deserts and palm trees join

Arcadian vales, while northern forests remain within a half-hour's walk. Presumably, we can take a last critical leave of the notion that "the American continent . . . seems as the background to the action of the tale" (Roberts 407–08), for the action begins in Arcadia. This is a clear nod to Sidney and a first allusion to the pastoral, given that the battle lines drawn between the armies of Mosco and Cusco are near Mantinea, the capital of this classical region. Margarita is of Mosco, Arsadachus of Cusco, more credibly identified by Philip Edwards as the Slovenian city of Kosice, Kaschou, or Kassa (48). Lodge invites us to understand, as a bare criterion of orientation, that these two cities share the same continent, and that travel from one to the other can be carried out on foot. Other allusions to place include Arsinous as Duke of Volgradia, Argias of Tamirae, and Plicatus of Macarah. Lodge mentions the "deserts of Russia," using as well the form "Moscovia," and describes the pikemen in battle as members of the "Macedonian phalanx."

For the English reader of the late sixteenth century, these names carried impressions that we can only imagine. The Muscovy trade was on the minds of Elizabethans particularly after the dramatic attempts to sail the seas above Russia in search of a Northeast passage to China. The merchant venturers were mapping and exploring, but the exploits of Pet and Jackman, for example, were also voyages of the imagination. Vagueness and the indeterminacy of things "oriental" were part of the romance formula. *A Margarite* is thus fashioned as a form of pseudo-news from realms beyond the Danube, beyond the Austro-Hungarian shield, but outside the territory of the Ottomans. It was a Bohemian-Russian-Greek romance.

Lodge had begun his *Euphues' Shadow* with a geography lesson on the rivers of central Europe, following the model set by Barnabe Riche in *Brusanus of Hungary*. Lodge, in fact, mentions "Hungaria," spelled in the same way, as well as Moravia, Passan,[16] Bohemia, and the mountains of Sticia. Almost concurrently with Lodge, Emanuel Ford was writing his *A Pleasant History of Ornatus and Artesia*, which he places in the Asia Minor

---

[16]Passan could suggest Passau on the Danube, although Passan is located in Austria in *Euphues' Shadow*.

of Phrygia and Natolia, such as they were variously and ambiguously represented on contemporary maps (Stanivukovic in Ford, 27). The same polarity of political places occurs in *A Margarite*, much as it appears in the Bohemia and Sicilia of Shakespeare's *Winter's Tale*, the latter rich in pastoral ambience. They all evince the same fusion of a present world imbued with a literary past; they are places where the natural and the supernatural exist side by side, places where mysteries go unresolved as part of the natural state of things, yet where social groups participate in precisely the kinds of activities familiar to the readers of contemporary English courts and salons.

Given these affiliations with the pastoral romance in design and allusion, some observers have aligned the entire work with this mode. Ian Watt concludes that it is the last example of pastoral romance in Elizabethan fiction (125), while Claudette Pollack states that "the atmosphere of *A Margarite* — its locality and place in time — is entirely pastoral" ("Lodge" 7) in the mistaken belief that the complete action was situated somewhere in Arcadia. But Margaret Schlauch is surely closer to the mark in her view that "the pastoral strain is minimal and is besides formally introduced" (198) insofar as the safety and innocence of pastoral as a refuge from the machinations of courts and cities is completely violated. The green retreat of Arsinous, as the secret abode of the magician revenger, is barely pastoral, while the gathering in the gardens at Asaphus' estate (described in the following section) where the lovers engage in the social ceremonies of the day is pure deception. This pastoral-seeming interlude should not be taken for the genuine retreat that Addison sees in it: "a Saturnalian where Love rules along with Nature and where Fortune and Degree, omnipotent in the world outside, are powerless . . . ." (27). This would hardly seem possible when the villain himself leads the performance. Alert readers will recognize, rather, that Lodge turns the entire sequence into a ceremony of dark foreshadowing — readers more astute than Margarita herself. There is to be no strategic escape into an idealized *locus* where the corrupt outside world finds reform through the amorous alignments established through innocent play, disguises, picnicking, and the mutualizing of minds afforded by a place of natural beauty and protection. Rather, just as the *telos* of romance, invested in the heroine's private longings, provides the background to her martyrdom, so the forestalled and compromised pastoral interludes of the ostensibly protected social retreats in *A Margarite* underscore the hypocrisy and eventual horror. In Lodge's final arrangement of genres, the pastoral setting doubles as a theatre of violence, while the poetry of the shepherds is appropriated by urban poseurs like Mincius, and by the arch-hypocrite Arsadachus — the leading poet of *A Margarite*. The invocations of an Arcadian setting in the spirit of Sidney are but vestiges at best of the idyllic world destroyed by evil.

The Fiction of Social Gaming: The "Questioni d'amore"

Following the exile of Arsinous to his melancholy cave, both courts make their way to Mosco. There, magnificent jousts take place in which Arsadachus acquits himself a hero, followed by lavish festivities full of pageantry, and a retreat to the house of Asaphus, where the lovers and their friends pass the time away in banqueting, gallant conversation, and the playing of fashionable games, themselves extensions of love banter and courtship. All of these activities were to have been inducements to the principals to avow their love over and above the formal betrothal that had been imposed upon them. The sequence is significant, for it amounts to nearly twenty percent of the entire work, furnishing Lodge once again with the occasion to show his skill in writing out a "questioni d'amore." This game was played in "a fair arbour covered with roses and honeysuckles, paved with camomile, pinks, and violets, guarded with two pretty crystal fountains on every side, which made the place more cool and the soil more fruitful."

If *A Margarite* is designed to manifest its referential parts as a component of the pleasures of the text, the game of "love questions" must be considered a salient contribution, for Elizabethan readers would have known something of this activity and of the polite parlour gaming that had been adopted from Italian models, typically through French imitations, and that had become fashionable in English aristocratic circles. Asaphus announces the "colloquium" as a means for inciting those present to engage in witty conversation upon a chosen topic. The ploys of courtship and pleasant social exchanges are not interrupted by such formalities, but simply channelled through the rituals and contents of the game. Moreover, through these structured activities, Lodge introduces *topoi* that pertain directly to the psychodrama unfolding between Margarita and Arsadachus. The topic set was a familiar one, whether love "but worketh by the eye, the touch, or the ear." Asaphus is chosen by acclamation for the position of governor or games-master, whose duty it is to pose the questions, determine the order of play, maintain decorum, and pronounce the winners and losers, in accordance with the rules set out in the conduct books. Lodge does not carry his representation through to a judgment, often involving further recitations on the part of the losers as a means for redeeming such forfeits as articles of jewellery and the like. But true to form, Lodge's players are separated by gender and made to face their respective partners.

The purpose of the question was not so much to search after truth as it was to reveal wit. As for the topic, by tradition the eye is the point of love's entry and also the most reliable of the senses, for what is seen is most assuredly true. Following an array of arguments favouring both touch and hearing, Margarita's assessment chimes with that of Arsadachus in defending the primacy of the eye in matters of love, only to underscore the degree to which she is deceived by all she presumes to have seen and hence take for truth. As the dark irony of the story will have it, seeing is no defence against hypocrisy.

In following the debate, Lodge's readers would have been mindful of other contexts in which such "questioni d'amore" had been described. This "polite" game can be traced back to the medieval love courts where courtiers and their ladies discussed the fine points of chivalric courtesy and honour. Love provided the most entertaining of paradoxes, inspiring endless debate and illustration. Collectors of sixteenth-century court and academy games, such as Innocenzo Ringhieri and Girolamo Bargagli, attest to the survival of the tradition of love debates in their compendia. Bargagli, one-time member of the Sienese Academy of the Intronati, wrote a nostalgic account of the games that used to be played in Siena before the invading Florentines

closed their academy. In his book of *Giuochi* (1572), "Delle quis-
tioni" (the game of questions) appears as Number 47. Girolamo's
brother Scipione, in his *Trattenimenti* (1587), describes the order
of play: the young men first debate the "doubt" or objection
concerning the nature of love proposed by the games-master,
followed by the young ladies, who pose counter positions. (Skill
in such games entailed an ability to debate either side with equal
conviction!) When all have taken their turns, the men reiterate
their positions, and the judge chooses the winner. The questions
included whether the true lover devotes himself to arms or to letters, whether art or nature holds sway in determining the quality
of love, whether beauty of the body or of the mind is more pow-
erful in inciting love (a variation on the debate concerning the
primacy of the senses), or whether it is best to love secretly or
in the open. One sees at a glance the extent to which Lodge follows the Italian paradigm. He had invoked the entire tradition
in *Euphues' Shadow* where the question posed was whether it is
better to deserve and not to have friendship than to have it, or to
offend the friend and then to be forgiven.[17]

---

[17] The salon game sequence in *A Margarite* may account for Lodge's os-
tensible promise made in the preliminary section "To the noble, learned,
and virtuous Lady, the Lady Russell" that "your memory shall acquaint
you with my diligence." He may have been suggesting merely that the
magnitude of his endeavours should remain in her memory, but some
readers see in this a hint that the work contains a surprise for Lady Russell linked to something embedded in her memory. Claudette Pollack
assures us that Lodge can only be referring to Baldesar Castiglione's
Il cortegiano, because it had been famously translated into English by
Lady Russell's first husband, Sir Thomas Hoby. We should expect then
to find matters of a specifically referential kind to *The Book of the Courtier*,
although in the final analysis neither the styling of Arsadachus as a false
courtier need depend upon the conditions and definitions of the perfect
courtier presented by Castiglione, nor need the gaming device of the
questions depend upon the gaming structures through which the court
of Urbino established its debating format. Lodge may have intended
only that she recall the service he had offered to her son, Edward, when
they were both students at Trinity College. Lodge had dedicated several
of his earlier works to prominent Catholics and had been criticized for
it severely. Here he seems to be calling upon that "memory" as the basis
for a dedication to a prominent member of the Protestant establishment

Significantly, however, Lodge need not have resorted to Italian originals for the games (although he had all the linguistic qualifications to do so). He could have turned to any of the several works through which Italian social culture was introduced into England, such as the English translation of Ortensio Lando's *Quattro libri de' dubbi*, which had been translated as early as 1566 under the title *Delectable demands, and pleasant Questions, with their several Answers, in matter of Love, Natural causes, with Moral and politic devises*. This work also reappeared in print the year of the publication of *A Margarite*. Or he could have relied upon George Whetstone's *An Heptameron of Civil Discourses* (1587). Whetstone had been to Italy in 1580 and could legitimately claim that the contents were first-hand acquisitions from the period he spent in Ravenna. The parts of the civil life he underscores include story-telling, dancing, dining, debates, games, riddles, music-making, and the specific game of devices (improvising mottoes), all of which were studied manifestations of the grace, wit, and decorum of the ideal courtier. Finally, Lodge could have turned to the translation begun by George Pettie (his part published in 1581) and completed in 1586 by Bartholomew Young, of Stefano Guazzo's *Civil Conversation* — a work first appearing in Brescia in 1574. Guazzo, in the fourth book, describes a banquet at which six noblemen and four ladies are present. They too, according to tradition, choose from among themselves a queen by drawing lots (as in Whetstone), and engage in elaborate games of wit on the topic of love. Of particular note, they play the game "whether the eyes or the tongue are of more force to gain the good will or love of the person beloved" (Guazzo 176).[18] Cavalero, in fact, anticipates Margarita in his view that the eyes "openly disclose the hidden and secret passions of our hearts" (177), giving away all that is hidden, while only the tongue remains deceitful. Lady Jane, by contrast, argues that the eyes are lowest on the ladder of love, for they serve only to admit impressions of physical

who, as a sister-in-law to the Lord Treasurer, Sir William Cecil, enjoyed influential connections to the highest echelons of Tudor society.

[18] For further details on the power of lovers' eyes and the terms of the debate, see Appendix II.

beauty. Only through the speaking that follows seeing can there be a close enjoyment of love.

Then again, Lodge need not have relied upon such books directly, because Gascoigne, before him, had employed the "questions" motif to characterize the salon life in *The Adventures of Master F.J.* (1573), and Lyly adopted the form as a means for testing the sentiments held by Fidus and Iffida in *Euphues and his England* (1580). Even closer to Lodge, Greene employed the device in *Morando* (1587) as "doubtful questions of Love, most pithily and pleasantly discussed," a game which takes up much of the narrative, the contents of which are calibrated to events and issues in the framing story. Lodge's group in the arbour engages in exactly this kind of banter. With so many models to choose from, the issue is no longer a matter of sources, but of the prominence of salon gaming in Elizabethan cultural consciousness. This institution, so widely known to them, found its natural place in their fiction both as a form of social representation and as a means for investing the amorous circumstances with contextual ideas.

The Poetic Insets

As with all of Lodge's imaginative fiction, *A Margarite* is prosimetric in format. The poems serve as architectural decorations, gestures of courtship, and, in this work, as epitaphs for all three women who perish in the course of the action: Philenia, Margarita, and Diana. In all, there are twenty-four poems, exceeding *Rosalind* by three. The ten that appear as a group toward the end of the narrative, presented by Arsadachus to his goddess-fiancée Diana, represent a final glut of lyric effusion more opportunistic than dramatically justified. Margarita, throughout all the preceding pages, receives but two from him — both calculated efforts to speak the unflattering truth in riddles. Minecius provides four such pastoral performances in courting Philenia earlier in the work. The very first poem to appear, in fact, is found on a tester in Arsinous' castle, the eighth is placed over the entrance to his melancholy cave, while the ninth is a long lament that Arsinous murmurs only to himself. Among the authors translated are Ludovico Paschale, Ludovico Martelli, and Philippe Desportes, the last of whom is generously represented in *Rosalind*.[19] In the pastoral poem "With Ganymede now joins the shining sun," sung by Minecius to his beloved, Lodge, translating from the Italian of Paschale, presents an Italian sestina in English — a form that goes back to Dante and Arnaut Daniel, and that appears both in its single and double forms in the manuscript and printed versions of Sidney's *Arcadia*.

Lodge was gifted as a poet, but uneven. Often he was content merely to translate the works of French and Italian poets. Some of his own creations are formulaic or strangely fanciful in their forms. At his best, however, in the words of a trustworthy critic, Lodge was surpassed only by Spenser in the writing of lyric (McAleer 89). That *A Margarite* contains the greatest number of such insets among his prosimetric works defies expectations. *Rosalind*, with its cast of singing shepherds and a lovesick scribbler of verses on trees, is an altogether more accommodating environment. Presumably Sidney's *Countess of Pembroke's Arcadia* was Lodge's principal model for the prosimetric style; Lodge may have come to the practice even ahead of his friend Robert Greene (McAleer 86). The fusion of prose and verse goes back to the ancients, but the Tudor manifestations look back principally to the pastorals of Montemayor and Sannazaro.

Pastoral conventions alone, it may be argued, permit the introduction of spontaneous poetic discourse as a mode of natural social expression. Lodge was determined to carry on with the prosimetric style in his final romance, despite the revenge milieu, allowing that Arsadachus "would recount such passions as gave certain signs in him of an excellent wit, but matched with

---

[19]Lodge, in stating that several of the poems in *A Margarite* were written "in imitation of Dolce the Italian," was taken at his word until Alice Walker actually attempted to locate them. Failing to find them there, she pressed on until she located them in the poets mentioned above. Whether Lodge intended to mislead readers is a moot point, for when he stated Dolce he meant Paschale, in whose *Rime* he found the inspiration for at least seven of the twenty-four. These are listed in Appendix B of N. Burton Paradise's *Thomas Lodge* (228–30). Those by Paschale from the *Rime volgari* (1549) are Nos. 1–4, 12, 15, and 19. Sonnet 20 is by Lodovico Martelli, No. 61 of his *Opere poetiche* (1548), and No. 21 is from the *Diana* of Philippe Desportes.

exceeding wickedness." Such a disparity between the corruption of the performer and the postures of sincerity in the lyrics
cannot be explained away; the divergence of sensibilities must
stand, even though Arsadachus manifests all the symptoms of
genuine lovesickness for Diana. But in the final analysis, we may
have to reconcile ourselves to the fact that Lodge was in search
of whatever pretext he could find to include the poems he had
prepared for the work.

In general, these poems tend merely to interrupt the action
to decorative ends. Characters employ them not to reflect the
passions of their interior lives, but as social graces, or as gestures
in the game of courtship. As a poem, "Heap frown on frown"
is suffused with the passion of loss, despite the stoic resolve to
speak well of the lady even from the grave. This is surely one
of the finest lyrics in the collection. But is it not also Lodge's
final adieu to all that is Petrarchan, gilded, and courtly because
it issues from the mouth of Arsadachus? Selzer believes as much
in urging that a distrust of "courtly Love" is "voiced in all his
fiction" (181). Readers are further removed from the mimetic
contract by the intrusions of the narrator-critic. He presents
the last two poems by Arsadachus as aesthetic performances to
be judged by his lady readers, after which, he assures them,
the story will resume. Literally, his intercalation is tantamount
to a confession that the poems are unrelated to the intrigue or
to the reciter for that matter. In presenting the "Complaint-
Answer" group, Lodge's narrator breaks in to explain that the
verse makes good sense "howsoever you turn it backward or
forward" with matching lines and cadences "the curiousness and
cunning whereof the learned may judge." At such moments, it
is clear that Lodge is providing verse for connoisseur readers
in no way made ironic by its context; the characterization of
Arsadachus is remote from his considerations.

Style

In the words of Eliane Cuvelier, "*A Margarite of America* among
the writings of Lodge remains the most readable for the twentieth-
century non-specialist" (*Thomas Lodge* 313). In general, prose
stylists were turning away from the more rhetorical and symmet-

rical styles of earlier years to explore modes of utterance less artificial and contrived; such "progress" could only contribute to the transparency of these works for the "common reader." M.G.B. Harrison concurs, suggesting that *Menaphon* and *A Margarite* are the first readable Elizabethan prose romances, and that one should even perform them aloud, savouring the style, preferably on summer days when the spirit of pastoral would seem most immediate (qtd. Pruvost 2). That Lodge's style is something to be savoured, however, is a reminder that his gravitation toward "plainness" was by no means absolute. In fact, *A Margarite* preserves vestiges of a range of styles including Lyly's euphuism with its erudite allusions and balanced phrasing, together with an extended employment of Sidney's delicately descriptive "arcadianisms."

One incentive for Lodge's break with the formalities of euphuism was Sidney's personal dislike for its artifice. In his *Apology for Poetry* he calls Lyly's gatherings of similitudes "as absurd a surfeit to the ears as possible" and without power to inform the judgment (139). In the place of euphuism he offers a cumulative or additive style, open to detours, forays, and parenthetic asides, to be sure, but a style that, nevertheless, orders information as required for arriving at naturally discursive conclusions. By no means did this entail an elimination of all rhetorical embellishments of sound and sense, all allusions to ancient myth or natural lore. But Sidney liberated his writing from the isocolons and antitheses of euphuism that unnaturally forced all thought into formal oppositions. From the anaphora and alliteration favoured by Lyly, he extended his figures of sound to include many more, such as they were described by Aristotle, Cicero, and Quintilian. Above all, however, he preferred clarity of ideas and weight of matter over stylistic copiousness for its own sake. Works rebalanced stylistically in favour of the new modes epitomized by Sidney achieved a transparency that could only seem more "readable" to modern eyes.

Paradoxical to this "revolution" is the degree to which writers continued to work as imitative stylists, choosing according to context from an active repertory of models and motifs, as opposed to merely transcribing daily speech. The argument is circular, in any case, for the language spoken was itself structured upon models chosen according to occasions—learned models made to appear as improvisatory as the speaker's wits could make them.   Thus, *imitatio* in speech or writing remained an operative concept—one of the *idées forces* of the Renaissance—so that while aesthetic preferences might change, the habit of reflecting signature traits inscribed in the writings of the best stylists would not disappear.   For this reason nearly every sentence by Lodge can still be assessed for its allegiance to the touchstone styles at his command.

The full measure of Lodge's supple performance cannot be examined here.   But for our purposes, euphuistic, arcadian, and plain may be said to constitute the strongest points along the continuum of stylistic choices.   A certain prominence is given to descriptive writing involving the houses, arbours, caves, pageants, jousts, games, and ceremonies that fill the pages of *A Margarite*. This writing is redolent of the "additive" descriptive style made famous (and authoritative) by Sidney.   Consider as a touchstone the following:

> for it being set upon such an unsensible rising of the ground, as you are come to a pretty height before almost you perceive that you ascend, it gives the eye lordship over a good large circuit, which according to the nature of the country, being diversified between hills and dales, woods and plains, one place more clear, and the other more darksome, it seems a pleasant picture of nature, with lovely lightsomeness and artificial shadows. (*Arcadia* 91)

Here are the delicate modifiers, the cumulative procedures, and the progression of details that lead to a complete picture, together with the quaint paradox that allows the material landscape to play its equivocal role in the aesthetics of romance.   Or consider the lament of Leucippe, abandoned by Pamphilus: "How oft didst thou swear unto me, that the Sun should loose his light, and the rocks run up and down like little kids, before thou wouldst falsify thy faith to me?   Sun therefore put out thy shining, & rocks run mad for sorrow, for *Pamphilus* is false" (*Arcadia* 289). Arguably, the Sidneyan lament comes closer than euphuism to an expression of accusation and self-pity insofar as the utterance itself approximates an outpouring of high emotion mixed with self-imposed restraint.

These arcadian features abound in *A Margarite*, as when Arsinous' fortress is fixed in nature "situate by a gracious and silver floating river, environed with curious planted trees to minister shade and sweet-smelling flowers to recreate the senses, besides the curious knots, the dainty garden plots, the rich tapestry, the royal attendance . . . ." From detail to detail the sentence grows to a representation of a pastoral place fitted to the requirements of romance. Margarita's art of lament is likewise pitched in the Sidneyan spirit: "What then shall remain with me to keep me in life, but my sorrow? Being the bequest of misery shall assist me in my melancholy. Ah dear Arsadachus, since thou must leave me, remember thou leavest me without soul, remember thou leavest me heartless . . . ." It is the forward movement of her speech that is telling, each idea emerging from the preceding, not by careful planning, but as the mind adds feature to feature in words of felt experience: "farewell, dear Lord, farewell, ever dear Lord, but I beseech thee, not for ever, dear Lord." With that realization of hopelessness, she begins to rebuild in her mind's eye the fulfilment of the union to which she has committed herself.

Euphuism in Lodge, more fully visible in the titled formal speeches in *Rosalind*, goes underground, to reappear as the chosen mode for select moments of public expression, as when, in Arsinous' final speech, he pronounces his satisfaction with the workings of revenge. Suddenly the operative words regroup themselves into balanced opposition, to which are added the tell-tale allusions to natural history.

> But the just gods have suffered me to behold the revenge *with mine eyes*, which I have long wished for *with my heart*. Truly, ye Cuscans, ye are not to marvel at these chances *if ye be wise*, neither to wonder at your emperor's troubles *if you have discretion*; for *as unity*, according to Pythagoras, is the father of number, *so is vice* the original of many sorrows. When the *fish tenthis* appeareth above the water, there followeth a tempest: when evils are grown to head, there must needly follow punishment; for as the gods in mercy *delay*, so at last in justice they *punish*.

The passage is worth citing in full, for it shows the Lylyan manner in action, full of balance and a semblance of perfect argumentation, if the conduct of fish and the assurances of the punishment of evil can be brought into a common circle of causation. The passage thereby reveals all that Jonas Barish and others have objected to in the style as an effective vehicle of reasoning and argumentation. In that regard, euphuism becomes the perfect vehicle for exposing the pretensions of the false orator who hides sophistries under the facade of stylistic order and control. Nevertheless, with Arsinous as eulogist and chorus to the entire action, we are less certain that Lodge meant to satirize the man most sinned against through the death of his daughter. His manner of speech is manifest evidence, either way, that euphuism remained an operative part of Lodge's aesthetics to the close of his career as a writer of fiction.

What Harrison meant by "readable" he left to common judgment, and just those aspects of style he most relished in reading aloud he took as self-evident. Perhaps it is the integration of the embellished with the plain that engages without tiring the attention. What strikes the reader, at the same time, are Lodge's less laboured moments of simple utterance having all the charms of a natural style, as when "Protomachus, somewhat urged by these tears, roused himself on his pillow and began more intently to listen, asking her what had happened." After Margarita recounts her "grievous dream," her father replies, "And so you waked and found all false. . . . Tut, dote not on dreams; they are but fancies: and since I see, sweet daughter, that you are so troubled by night, I will shortly find out a young prince to watch you, who shall drive away these night-sprights by his prowess." Here, the copious style is exchanged for intimacy, humour, and simple phrasing. There is no name for this style, yet its contrast with the formal styles is marked, and, in itself, represents Lodge's progress toward the plainer styles, while at the same time it renders less axiomatic the notion that "since there are no private or unique aspects to the characters of Tudor romances, all speeches are a kind of oratory" (Gubar 35).

Between these three points of reference, Lodge's discriminations merge into one another. He had read the Italians framed by Fenton and Painter, as well as Spenser, and the chivalric romances. When he chooses to describe the allegorical trappings of the rooms, the tapestries and testers, the jousts and chivalric events, or the order of events in the lengthy coronation inset, the matter is difficult to separate from the style. There is a kind of imitative form in the segments of the procession separated by the cumulative designations "after them," "next them," or "next unto them," ten-fold in a single sentence. Lodge, in this, reaches after an oriental sumptuousness: "After them there came a chariot drawn by elephants and attended by six and thirty elephants, with eight hundred young men attending them as their keepers, attired with ornaments of gold and having their temples encompassed with wreaths of roses and silver bends." In the cumulative images there is opulence, but in the order of prose there is the precision of the recording eye. No writing could be more ordered. Yet on select occasions, Lodge bypasses the plain to arrive at the curt and elliptical.

> Fawnia, that first spied him [the lion], was soon surprised, then she cried and was rent in pieces, in that she had tasted too much of fleshly love, before she feared. Margarita, that saw the massacre, sat still attending her own tragedy, for nothing was more welcome to her than death, having lost her friend, nor nothing more expected.

Could death by a lion or the heroine's reaction be more cryptic? Such appendages as "before she feared" and "nor nothing more expected" are riddle-like in their brevity and obliqueness.

In following the modulations of the age, Lodge had removed something of the erudite and formal from his writing, whether in deference to the tastes of his readers, or in keeping with his own aesthetic choices, suggesting a place for *A Margarite* on the emerging continuum between Ciceronian and Senecan styles. This is not to be construed as liberation from imitative stylistics, however, for Lodge continues to acknowledge his allegiances, although he alters his registers as his reading of contexts dictated. Laments, formal challenges, pastoral landscape, allegorical descriptions as set topics relayed their own stylistic traditions. These passages, together with the decorum of the dialogue, the moments of formality, and the poetic insets create a program of accomplished aesthetic effects. During the twelve-year period separating *Forbonius and Prisceria* from *A Margarite* (1584 to 1596), Lodge had developed his own writing style, beginning with a "straightforward conventional romance" and concluding with a hybrid form that is "dark, ironic, and disturbing" (Addison 14).

Part of that achievement was a more self-confident, integrated manner of writing marked by more supple transitions among imitative choices.

D.A.B. Ottawa

Bibliographical and Editorial Matters

The book was published in 1596 in quarto format, with a letterpress title-page printed as follows:

> [within a compartment of separate cast type ornaments built up to form a border, within which is another border of single rules] *A Margarite of* / *America* / [rule] / *By T. Lodge* / [rule] / [ornament] / Printed for *Iohn Busbie,* and are to be / *sold in S. Dunstons church-yard in* / Fleet-street, at the little shop / *next Cliffords Inne.* / 1596

The collational formula for the book is 4°: A^2, B-M^4, N^2; the pages are unnumbered, and the running title is *A Margarite / of America*. The text occupies signatures B through N and is printed in black letter in a continuous block without chapter divisions.

The dedicatory epistle to Lady Russell is dated May 4, 1596. The work was never entered into the Stationers' Register. A quarto of 48 unnumbered leaves, this edition survives in only three copies: one in the Bodleian, and two in the British Library. They are differentiated by some thirty-five press variants corrected by the printer or his compositor, presumably in consultation with the original but without benefit of the author's presence, who apologizes in the dedication for the errors that had slipped through: "those faults . . . escaped by the printer in not being acquainted with my hand, and the book printed in my absence." There is no indication whether he was looking at a copy early or late in the run, or whether there are errors to his eye persisting in the corrected copies. J.O. Halliwell Phillips prepared the first "modern" edition in 1859, based on one of the British Library copies, which he liberally altered according to his own best understanding of the text. Edmund Gosse followed in 1883 with his version in *The Complete Works of Thomas Lodge,* more wisely based on the copy in the Bodleian, the so-called "Malone Quarto," which contains the greatest number of corrected formes. Even though it is the best single control copy, I have nevertheless collated all three copies for this edition, and have provided a comprehensive record of the substantive variants. John Busbie, the printer, conducted his operations in St. Dunstan's Churchyard in Fleet Street on the west side of the City. This was the sixth of Lodge's works he had seen into print. Busbie, in a dedication to Sir John Hart which he appended to *Catheros*, refers to Lodge as "a Gentleman my deare friend" (Johnson 6).

In the treatment of the text, I have taken a conservative approach, modernizing spelling while retaining certain obsolete and archaic forms, with glosses, and providing appropriate paragraph division and punctuation where necessary, particularly in sections of dialogue where Lodge has habitually run narrative/description and direct speech together. I have given each speaker his or her own paragraph, enclosing direct speech within quotation marks according to modern convention. Throughout, I have generally left sentence structures as in the original, except in cases where a change in comma, semicolon, or colon was called for in order to preserve clarity of expression. Where I have emended the text or have had to select a variant an asterisk marks the spot, with an explanation appearing in the Textual Notes at the back.

The Commentary on this edition is comprised of annotations placed in a separate section at the end of the volume. Corresponding to the superscript numbers in the text, these annotations attempt to explain, as far as possible, Lodge's numerous references and allusions to matters historical, geographical, mythological, literary, and scientific; and they identify proverbial expressions. In many of the annotations, references to ancient and modern sources are designed to encourage further reading.

H.D.J. Windsor

Appendices

I. A Life of Thomas Lodge

This account of Lodge's life and career is a somewhat abbreviated version of the "Life" published as an appendix to the critical edition of *Rosalind* appearing in this series in 1997, but filled out here with a much lengthier account of the voyage to Brazil and the Strait of Magellan — the period during which Lodge claims to have written *A Margarite*. So rich and varied a career has not escaped the attention of biographers. The following résumé of Lodge's life is particularly indebted to the work of N. Burton Paradise (1931), Alice Walker (1933), Charles Sisson (1933), E.A. Tenney (1935), Wesley Rae (1967), and Eliane Cuvelier (1984) — this latest biography being unsurpassed for its careful research and judicious evaluation of the materials. Nearly all of the factual material presented here has been derived from these sources and reassembled, with the greatest debt to Eliane Cuvelier. I am also indebted to the article on Lodge prepared by Charles Whitworth for *The Dictionary of Literary Biography* (which I was privileged to read in a pre-published version). For the factual material in the new section on the voyage to South America I relied entirely on the edition of Cavendish's journal, *The Last Voyage of Thomas Cavendish, 1591–1592*, and the introductory essay by David Beers Quinn, as well as *The Last Voyages of Cavendish, Hudson, Ralegh: The Original Narratives*, edited by Philip Edwards — also containing parts of the account of the voyage written by Antony

Knivet—again merged into a single narrative. A substantial amount of information has come to light concerning Lodge's life, but of a factual kind that only hints at the daring and drama we must otherwise imagine. For not only was Lodge a gentleman soldier aboard the *Leicester* during one of the most arduous voyages of the Elizabethan era, but a doctor who remained in the City of London to practise during two of the worst plagues, as well as a recusant forced into exile on several occasions.

Thomas was the fourth of nine children born to Anne, the second wife of Sir Thomas Lodge (Paradise [9] says seven children). The year was 1558, that of Elizabeth I's coronation. His mother was the daughter of Sir William Laxon, "a grocer, Master of the Grocers' Company, and Lord Mayor, just as his son-in-law was destined to be after him" (Paradise 8). His father was a leading member of the grocer's guild who worked his way up to Lord Mayor of London, and to knighthood. In the family there were men of standing, one a sheriff, another a city councilor, a third an ambassador to Spain, a fourth a governor of the Company of Merchant Adventurers (Cuvelier, *Thomas Lodge* 22). But the prosperity of Thomas' youth would not last. Plague, war, and mismanagement of affairs conspired to ruin the family's finances. By 1563, when Thomas was only five years old, his father was sent to debtors' prison. Nevertheless, by 1568 means were found to send the boy to school in an aristocratic household, that of Henry Stanley, fourth Earl of Derby ("Lodge," *Spenser Encyclopedia*; although Lodge, in his dedication to *A Fig for Momus*, calls him "Right Honorable and thrice renowned Lord, William Earl of Darby"), and three years later (1571) he would manage to secure a place in the prestigious Merchant Taylors' School as a pauper student.[1] There he would have known the celebrated humanist master, Richard Mulcaster, and have been exposed to his Protestant neo-classicism. Cuvelier speculates that he may also have encountered the future playwright Thomas Kyd as well as Ralph Crane, later clerk of the Privy Council and scrivener to the King's Players, although Kyd entered the school as early as 1565 and

---

[1]Paradise points out the anomaly of seeing him among the 50 sons of the poor, but perhaps Lodge's father had not yet recovered his losses of former years that had forced him into bankruptcy (13).

may have departed by 1571 (*Thomas Lodge* 41). At fifteen (1573), Lodge continued his studies at Trinity College, Oxford, where he developed important friendships with Sir Edward Hoby (to whose mother, Lady Russell, *A Margarite* is dedicated), and with the two sons of Henry Carey, Lord Hunsdon (to whom he later dedicated his pastoral romance *Rosalind*).[2] Very likely, too, it was through the Careys that Lodge was recommended for duty as a gentleman venturer on two voyages, the first commanded by Captain Clarke, during which he wrote *Rosalind*, the second by Sir Thomas Cavendish, during which he claims to have written *A Margarite* (Cuvelier, *Thomas Lodge* 49). In spite of his staunch Protestant upbringing, Thomas developed an affinity for Catholicism that originated during his Oxford years, an interest that would eventually align him with the English recusants and force him into several periods of exile.

Lodge made his way back to London in 1578 where he took up residence at Lincoln's Inn, undoubtedly to work toward professional qualifications in law — as his parents expected — but in reality perhaps merely to enjoy the company of the city wits, many of whom kept residence in the Inns of Court.[3] What we do know, as reported by all of Lodge's biographers, is that by 1579, at the time of his mother's death, there was doubt among family members that Thomas had pursued his studies in an acceptable way. By that date, he had, in any case, severed all ties with the family and with the world of mercantile aspirations. Thus it was that his mother stipulated in her will that Thomas would come into his inheritance only four years later, at age twenty five, and only if he remained diligent in his law studies.[4] The measure of

---

[2]Tenney sees these as critical years during which Lodge acquired his Catholic leanings, pointing out the many recusants associated with Trinity College. "Here . . . Lodge probably breathed in the germ of Catholicism which later carried him away from the religion of his family and nation" (59).

[3]Tenney provides a full account of the years 1578–84 during his residence at Lincoln's (64–91).

[4]This and related documents pertaining to Lodge's life are reprinted in the biography by Paradise, in Appendix A, his mother's two wills appearing on pages 193–207.

his performance was left to the determination of his father and her executors. Should they decide against him, his part was to be forfeited to his brothers. That was a perfect formula for family feuding, back-stabbing, and favouritism. The arrangement would, in fact, lead to years of penury for the young writer, not to mention conflicts with his brothers that involved lawsuits and assault with intent to have Thomas murdered.

Lodge, meanwhile, placed himself in double jeopardy by borrowing against his expected inheritance. When the money was not paid out, he was sent, in his turn, to debtors' prison. His father's will of 1584 had been the cause, for, in effect, old Thomas had disinherited his son because of his "disordered course of life," a phrase certain to disqualify him according to the terms of his mother's will. At face value, the statement is proof of the young man's dissolute life, but under the circumstances we can never be certain, given the mean-spiritedness of his brothers and the degree to which disapproval of his Catholic tendencies, or his indifference to the mercantile traditions of the family, could have swayed his father's mind. In fact, by 1581 Lodge had already been called before the Privy Council to account for acts of civil disobedience or recusancy, an indictment resulting in three months in prison (Cuvelier, *Thomas Lodge* 68). His father may have resorted to the tell-tale phrase in his will merely to avoid paying out money that would have otherwise been taken by creditors or confiscated by the Crown in the form of fines. In the interim, writing for the commercial presses may have been the only solution to his penury that Lodge could find. But his involvement in various pamphlet wars, the first piece in defense of the players, the second an assault on usury, could only have contributed to the loss of his father's approbation (Barish 204).

Even in broader social terms, his timing could not have been worse, for in 1580 the London magistrates were seeking to close the theatres permanently for fear that the close proximity of the spectators would lead to the spreading of the plague (Barish 89). In those same years the controversy over Catholicism was equally intense, given the presence on English soil of the imprisoned Mary, Queen of Scots, and the fear of uprisings in her name. On the front page of *Plays Confuted*—Stephen Gosson's reply to

Lodge's theatre pamphlet—the author not only named his ad-
versary, but conspicuously dedicated the piece to the Queen's
chief intelligencer and prosecutor of Catholics, Sir Francis Walsingham. Conjecture suggests that Lodge understood this ploy
as an attack upon his Catholic sympathies, inducing him to
strike back by dedicating to Sir Philip Sidney his *Alarm against
Usurers* refuting Gosson, followed by his first prose romance,
The Delectable History of Forbonius and Prisceria (1584). Sidney's
acceptance of the tribute would afford Lodge a degree of protection. In all these activities, Lodge was engaging in risks with
repercussions, one of which was that he would never come into
his inheritance until all of his brothers were dead (this episode
of Lodge's life is recounted in far greater detail in the biography
by Paradise 66–77).

   The publication date of Lodge's first foray into prose fiction
was 1584. Thereafter, he followed the tastes of the age from
project to project. There were, at the same time, two creations
for the theatre: a play, *A Looking-Glass for London and England*,
written in collaboration with Robert Greene, about the mores of
contemporary city life; and *The Wounds of Civil War*, concerning
events in ancient Rome. In 1589, he published an Ovidian epic
in verse entitled *Scilla's Metamorphosis*, along with satirical and
pastoral poems, and translations from the poems of Philippe
Desportes. In the year following, he published *Rosalind* (the
source for Shakespeare's *As You Like It*), a work widely agreed to
be the finest pastoral romance in English after Sidney's *Arcadia*
(Salzman 72); it would go through some ten editions by 1642.
Thereafter, works appeared in print in rapid succession: *The Life
of Robert Second Duke of Normandy* (1591); *Catharos: Diogenes in
his Singularity* (1591); *Euphues' Shadow: The Battle of the Senses*
(1592); the sonnet cycle *Phillis* (1593); *William Longbeard* (1593);
his play co-authored with Greene, *A Looking-Glass for London
and England* (1594); and several shorter works in 1595 and 1596
including satires, a collection of verse, and a pro-Catholic treatise.
These were followed by his last work of imaginative writing, *A
Margarite of America* (1596).[5]

----

[5]For a complete bibliographical listing of Lodge's works, see Para-

There is a sense in which this final work was also a retrospective, for it contains not only the romance foundations of his earlier fiction, but verse translations, pastoral episodes, and a villain hero redolent of earlier antagonists derived from medieval legend. Successively, in his former works, there had been a darkening of spirit — whether as a reflection of literary fashions or as a by-product of his own hardships (for which there is no proof either way). It would appear that by mid-decade his life as a gentleman author was turning sour: he was unable to repeat the success of *Rosalind*, and he remained plagued by debt. Philip Henslowe was the guarantor of a loan made to Lodge in 1594–95, and he borrowed further from the actor Edward Alleyn — facts that indicate his good standing with the players, but his ongoing financial distress. Nothing had been resolved with his brother William over the inheritance, and Lodge probably faced more time in debtors' prison in those years as well. *A Margarite*, with its abject views of humanity, may be a kind of bitter testament — although the tastes of the age for tales of horror and revenge may alone be responsible for its tone.

In the intervening years, Lodge had not only taken up authoring to mend his fortunes, but privateering on the high seas. Given the extraordinary nature of those voyages, towards which he could not have been an indifferent observer, we can only regret that he did not write his travel memoirs. Nevertheless, two very different eye-witness accounts survive of that ill-fated second voyage, one by Cavendish himself, compiled up to the time of his death at sea on the return voyage, and one by Antony Knivet, who found himself abandoned on shore in Brazil, but who managed to find his way back to England many months later. Lodge's "life" is recounted in these events by dint of his participation, and presented here not merely for the sake of the record, but for purposes of contextualizing the origins of *A Margarite*, which he claims to be derived from Spanish sources located in Brazil on the out-bound voyage, and to have been written during the voyage.[6]

---

dise, Appendix C, "A Chronological List of the Writings of Thomas Lodge" (231–43).

[6] I am amused to discover, after writing the composite account given here, that Tenney (in 1935) carried out a similar exercise in a strangely

Concerning the first expedition, Captain Clarke set out on piracy missions with gentleman venturers aboard in 1585, in 1587, and again early in 1590, the year in which *Rosalind* was published. The question remains moot as to which voyage Lodge joined, each date having different implications for the drafting of the book and the revisions it received following his return. Those matters are taken up in greater detail in the introduction to the *Rosalind* published in this series (16–19). The date of his second venture is beyond all doubt, for Sir Thomas Cavendish set sail from Plymouth Harbor, August 26, 1591. That Lodge was actually aboard (as he claims in *A Margarite*) is confirmed by Robert Greene, who stated of Lodge in his preface to *Euphues' Shadow* that the author had gone to sea "upon a long voyage" and that he was anxious to see "what labours his sea studies" would afford. Even Greene knew that it would be a lengthy venture, for Cavendish intended no less than to repeat his first circumnavigation of the globe, going this time to Japan, China, and Manila, where he was to have rooted out the Spanish presence. As a gentleman, Lodge would have had no duties involving ropes and sails, hence time on his hands for writing. There is reason to think, moreover, that he had the *Rime volgari* (1549) of Paschale in his duffel bag because his sonnet sequence *Phillis*, much indebted to Paschale, appeared soon after his return. That he presumably translated the further seven by Paschale to appear in *A Margarite* while at sea may be some justification for his claim that the work was formulated during their attempt to sail through the Strait of Magellan to the Pacific.

A more contentious issue is that Lodge claims to have found the narrative source for *A Margarite* in the form of a Spanish romance in a Jesuit monastery in Santos, Brazil. However, to date, research undertaken by several specialists in early Spanish literature has produced nothing even similar — and is unlikely

pseudo-historical document entitled "Master Thomas Lodge his Disastrous Voyage towards the South Sea with Sir Thomas Cavendish, with his many Disadventures in the Magellan Straits and other Places: Written by Several Hands" (114–25). In a note he explains that the "hands" are those of Sir Thomas Cavendish, *Purchas His Pilgrims* (Hakluyt Society No. 16); Antony Knivet, *ibid.*; and John Jane, in Hakluyt's *Principal Navigations* (Hakluyt Society No. 11).

to do so, given the entirely Italianate nature of Lodge's creation. In fact, a close scrutiny of *A Margarite* suggests that every facet of the work is in direct line with Lodge's own former styles and narrative preoccupations, conflation of genres, and character types. There is nothing about it that suggests narrative sources outside of the Italian horror novellas translated by Fenton and Painter, the works of Greene, Lyly, and Sidney, the popular courtesy books in English translation, Elizabethan revenge tragedies, and above all, Lodge's own former works. The claim, nevertheless, remains part of the reception strategy that Lodge provided for the work, and hence an insight into the tastes he presumed for his readers.

Taking that claim literally, he would have found the work of Spanish provenance in a small Portuguese religious establishment at the edge of civilization where, in fact, the exportation of such secular materials had been forbidden by the Portuguese government (Pollack, "Studies" 134). That there were books in Santos, however, is out of doubt, for Lodge returned with one and possibly several. The one certain to have come from Brazil survives today in the Bodleian Library in Oxford (MS Bodley 617) entitled *Doutrina Christana na lingua Brasilica* — a book on Christian doctrine in the language of the local natives. It bears the dedication *Ex dono Thomae Lodge D.M. Oxoniensis, qui sua manu e brasilia deduxit* (material proof that he made the voyage), and given to the library, presumably in 1602 when the university accredited his continental medical degree so that he could practise as a physician in England (Edwards 47). There is reason to think, moreover, in light of the frequent citation of Luis de Granada and Joseph Angelés in later works, that Lodge found their work on that same occasion. But it is useless to speculate that if Lodge returned with books, he would have brought the mysterious Spanish romance as well. *A Margarite* is too patently made of other stuff.

As for his parallel claim, that he wrote the work while in the Strait of Magellan, we can only acquiesce in wonder. Lodge alludes to the cold and privation, but these hints fall far short of the reality of those weeks as recounted by others. For a full appreciation of the circumstances, the story must be sketched from the beginning. Lodge was aboard the galleon *Leicester* with

Cavendish, a ship of 400 tonnes that would prove cumbersome and unwieldy. With the *Leicester* there were four other ships of lighter tonnage, including the *Daintie*, belonging to John Davis, whose mishaps during the voyage led Cavendish to think of him not only as a traitor, but as the nemesis of the entire expedition.[7] Cavendish may have been doomed from the start because he did not supervise the outfitting and supplying of the ships; they were short of materials and provisions not long after leaving port, and throughout the voyage, they were constantly beleaguered by want. More fatally, Cavendish miscalculated the seasons, dawdling along the Brazilian coast to pillage settlements under pretext of revictualling his ships; as a result both storms and doldrums depleted stores and washed valuable equipment overboard. Undoubtedly the stay in Santos was the most agreeable part of the voyage; one can imagine their reluctance to leave, despite the advancing season. The gentleman members of the expedition had the Jesuit monastery for lodgings from the time of their arrival on December 26, 1591 to February 3, 1592—five critical weeks during which they should have sailed on toward Patagonia (Cavendish 23). While Cavendish was out pillaging in the countryside, Lodge was meeting the locals and going through the library. Knivet—whose memoirs of the trip read like pure fantasy, but whose facts have nevertheless been corroborated—boasts of having found "170 rials of eight" in the monastery and of hiding them in his lodging (Edwards 84). John King, an English trader, resident there for some fifteen years, was one of Lodge's new acquaintances, together with Giuseppe Adorno of Genoa. Adorno had a sugar plantation and refinery, and his daughter had married the merchant John Whitehall (Edwards 48). Lodge, in a letter of 1609, remembers the old gentleman, his many kindnesses, and his farewell when the fleet set sail: "*Vale, mi fili, Deus te salvum reducat in domum tuam.*" And indeed

---

[7]By comparison, Drake had set out with five ships and 170 men on his famous voyage around the world in the Golden Hind, none of them over 120 tonnes (Giggal 29). Aboard his own ship, Drake had only nine gentleman venturers, and in emergencies he put them to work as common seamen. Drake was much more efficient, moreover, in victualling his ships before departure.

He did, proving at the same time that school Latin along with a knowledge of Italian — on the part of the translator of Paschale and Dolce — also served Lodge during his travels.

After the stay in Santos, one of the ships, laden with sugar, crept away for home, leaving the remaining four to make for the south — Davis, among them, intent upon leaving the expedition in California to make his way north in search of a Northwest Passage from the Pacific side. Fourteen days out, the *Leicester* and her companion ships ran into a ferocious storm that not only damaged rigging and sails, but temporarily divided the fleet. More seriously, most of their deck boats were lost. They did not meet up again until March 16. The winter season was drawing nigh, and the mood aboard the *Leicester* was growing so menacing to Cavendish that he escaped it only by transferring himself to the *Desire*. By April 18, they were at Cape Froward, the southernmost point of the voyage, but could make no further progress against the winds. Only one longboat remained to go ashore, and there the men found only mussels, winter's bark, and seaweed. Within seven or eight days, forty men aboard the *Leicester* had died of exposure and frostbite, and seventy more were sick. Toes were lost to the cold, and one man professed to having twisted off his own frozen nose by mistake and thrown it into the fire. Lodge was among those remaining men, only fifty of them able-bodied, perhaps in a state of near starvation — and he was writing *A Margarite*?

Cavendish finally returned to the *Leicester* to negotiate their future plans. His men elected to return to the Brazilian coast in search of provisions, secretly intending nevermore to return to the south. The coast was in a state of alert, however, following the events in Santos, making raiding less feasible. Many of the rivers were, in any case, inaccessible to the lumbering *Leicester* (Cavendish 28). Davis wanted to press on to the west, but grudgingly he agreed to accompany Cavendish. When they were again separated and without a planned rendezvous point, Cavendish became paranoid and impetuous. The men refused to come up for duty, and he began to beat them with ropes. When the shore raids resumed, twenty-five good men were killed in an ambush; they had remained ashore against orders. Cavendish then wanted revenge, and in that process sacrificed another twenty-five men, though for the first time in weeks they were again in possession of cassavas, potatoes, plantains, and pineapples. When all other hopes of completing his mission began to fade, Cavendish again fell to scheming, this time to strip one of his own vessels, the *Roebuck*, by taking the best men, the provisions, and the doctors, leaving the ship hulk and the sick men to their fates. But his intentions leaked out to those aboard the *Roebuck*, by word or intuition, and they began to play cat-and-mouse games with their own commander. More raids were attempted, leaving fifty-five of an eighty-member scouting party dead or wounded. Lodge had to have been involved in some of these actions. By this time, the *Leicester* had fewer than fifty of its original numbers left. Then the *Roebuck*, having the only two fleet doctors aboard among the forty-six of its crew who remained, as well as most of the unspoiled provisions, struck off on her own for home. That was the final straw. Cavendish had no choice but to limp after with his miserable provisions, consisting largely of salted penguins that had turned rotten and were full of maggots and worms. Three of the five ships eventually struggled back with only ninety or one hundred of the original complement of 350 men (Cavendish 38). Cavendish was not among them, having determined, for reasons of shame, honour, or frustration, to die at sea — which he did — but not without penning a full account of the entire expedition, complete with all manner of frenzied recriminations, and a final testament that would deprive all of the mariners and gentlemen who had shared in the voyage of any of the profits to ensue from the sale of the ships and the small amount of booty. Once again, Lodge the venturer would return without improving his fortunes (Cavendish 32).

Lodge may have been back as early as November 1592, some fourteen months after setting out. That he was back by early 1593 is certain, because he left for the north country in February to visit his brother William, who had abandoned London with his family on account of the plague. But not only did William refuse him hospitality, he hired ruffians to assault Thomas on his way south. The attack failed, leading to a hearing before the Court of Chancery in 1594 which left Lodge with a settlement of 200 pounds sterling (Sisson 90–100). By 1596 it would seem that he had also gained access to a house rightfully his in Leyton, Essex (Paradise 51). The critical issue by then was his status as a Catholic, for *The Act Against Popish Recusants* of 1593 stipulated that Papists were not allowed to stray more than five miles from their domiciles.

Whether for financial or religious reasons, by 1597 Lodge had given up on England, and on his profession as a writer, determining instead to become a physician. He chose to study in Avignon, where he received his diploma in 1598, after which time he practised abroad, returning to England only in 1600 (Cuvelier, *Thomas Lodge* 149ff). At that time he married Jane Aldred, who remained with him many years thereafter, a loyal wife, a nurse in the clinic, and a Catholic. She was twelve years his elder, and had been formerly married to a man who was a double agent for the Pope and for Walsingham. Lodge may have known her from a meeting in 1595, and perhaps it was her influence that caused him to change professions (Paradise 54–56).

Their life in London could not have been an easy one, for Lodge, only months after his return, re-exiled himself for a time to practise medicine in Liège. In 1602 he returned, intent upon completing a translation of the works of Josephus. Throughout the plague year of 1603, at great risk to himself, Lodge remained in the city tending the sick.[8] Anti-Catholic sentiments began to run high again following the Gunpowder Plot. Among the new measures, Catholic physicians were prohibited from practising by legislation. Once again Lodge made his way to the continent, this time to follow the Irish troops fighting in the service of Spain. Only in 1609 did he make application for the documentation needed to return free from the threat of spies and informers. By 1610, the Royal College of Physicians granted him the right to practise, and in January 1611 he swore an oath of allegiance to the king (Paradise 56–57). When the last of his brothers died in 1612, Thomas received his long-withheld inheritance. By 1614 he had completed his monumental translation of the prose works

---

[8]There is some documentary evidence about Lodge's career as a doctor during this period (see Paradise 54–56). He was then living in Warwick Lane, where he wrote his *Treatise of the Plague*, dated August 16, 1603.

of Seneca. His final literary project was the translation of Simon Goulart's commentary on the works of the Huguenot poet Du Bartas.[9] Lodge's long and active life ended in 1625 when plague again swept through London, taking another 35,000 victims; his personal sacrifice for his patients on this occasion was acknowledged by the city. He was born the year that Elizabeth came to the throne, and died in the same year as King James I. He lived his youth intensely and dangerously, suffered for his religious convictions, and died in the service of humanity. His literary works include a rich variety of genres. His best works, of their kind, are among the best of the age. And while little attention is paid to his later works today, they too are outstanding achievements of a weightier nature, known and appreciated by specialists.

D.A.B.

II. On the Power of Lovers' Eyes

The *topos* of the hierarchy of the senses in love itself has an established pedigree in intellectual history. The power of the eyes in inciting love is prominent in the poems of Guido Cavalcanti, who in turn drew upon the medieval medical treatises in which love is diagnosed as a disease of the eyes. Perhaps the most influential vehicle for this confluence of ideas was Marsilio Ficino's *Commentary on Plato's Symposium on Love* (1484), in which he discusses the eyes as the conductors of love. The most novel of his asseverations arises in the Seventh Oration, namely that, in keeping with the medieval theories of sight, the eyes emit blood vapours, still material in nature, that are capable not only of conveying to the beholder a simulacrum of the beheld, but of poisoning the blood through the toxic qualities of the alien spirits. Ficino thereby brought into medical parlance all that had been attributed by the poets to Cupid's darts and to the power of

---

[9]There is reason to think that Lodge made his choice because of King James I's early interest in the works of the French poet. The *Judith* of Du Bartas had been Englished and published by Thomas Hudson as early as 1584, and Sidney himself at one point had projected a translation of some of his works (Paradise 172). Joshua Sylvester took up the challenge in a publication of 1590 followed by others. As a Huguenot, Du Bartas was deemed a great moral as well as poetic force in England.

beautiful eyes to cast spells. At the same time, Ficino ennobled sight as a non-concupiscent sense apt for conveying images upon which the lover might exercise his imagination and memory in order to move toward a more spiritual contemplation of pure Beauty. Touch, above all, was ignoble for Ficino, because it led to sensuality and carnality. These matters began their descent into the polite conversation and idle banter of the salons through the dialogic circumstances introduced by Cardinal Bembo in *Gli Asolani* (1505), and through the love treatises that began to appear with Mario Equicola's *Libro de natura de amore* (1525). Lodge's interlocutors perform pieces of the old Neo-Platonic debate that included a reflection on the magic powers of sight epitomized in the stare of the basilisk.

The *topos* of the lovers' eyes also had ties to the *Nicomachean Ethics*, where Aristotle states that "no one falls in love without being first pleased with the personal appearance of the beloved object" (1167a). The semi-magic powers of sight had been recognized by the earliest poets, as in the tragic tale of Hero and Leander in which Musaeus blames the eyes for the injuries of love. Cavalcanti knew the language of hearts wounded by glances and how foolish eyes permitted to gaze could expect nothing but death. Nearly all of these points were teased out of his poem "Dona me prega" by the physician-commentator Dino del Garbo. In Lodge's treatment of the topic, the medical, philosophical, and poetic perspectives are trimmed down to the aphorisms that appear in the respective "turns" of the players. Yet all the positions are represented: whether the eye curses or blesses with its compelling species, whether it is a trustworthy vehicle for the evaluation of beauty, inner character, or hidden intentions. Critical for the modern reader is the double realization that the scene in the arbour is neither a social fantasy nor a rehearsal of obscure *topoi*, but the enactment of a contemporary social practice involving a topic in which the court wits were expected to be versed.

D.A.B.

Bibliography

Addison, James C. Jr. "A Textual Error in Thomas Lodge's *A Margarite of America* (1596)". *The Library*, 6th series, 3 (1981): 142–43.

Baker, Ernest A. *The History of the English Novel*. Vol. II: *The Elizabethan Age and After*. 10 vols. New York: Barnes and Noble, 1968. [1936]

Bandello, Matteo. *Tragical Tales*. Trans. Geoffrey Fenton (*Certain Tragicall Discourses*, 1567). Ed. Robert Langton Douglas and Hugh Harris. London: George Routledge and Sons [1925].

Bargagli, Girolamo. *Dialogo de' Giuochi che nelle Vegghie Sanesi si Usano di Fare*. Ed. Patrizia D'Incalci Ermini. Siena: Accademia Senese degli Intronati, 1982.

Barish, Jonas A. *The Antithetical Prejudice*. Berkeley: University of California Press, 1981.

——. "The Prose Style of John Lyly." *ELH* 23 (1956): 14–35.

Beaty, Frederick. "The Novels of Thomas Lodge." Ph.D. Diss., Harvard, 1952.

Beecher, Donald. "The Fiction of Symbolic Forms: Mythological Drifting in *A Margarite of America*." *Critical Approaches to English Prose Fiction 1520–1640*. Ed. Donald Beecher. Ottawa: Dovehouse Editions, 1998. 219–39.

Beilin, Elaine. *The Uses of Mythology in Elizabethan Prose Romance*. New York: Garland Publishing, 1988.

Boccaccio, Giovanni. *The Most Pleasant and Delectable Questions of Love*. New York: Illustrated Editions, 1931.

Braden, Gordon. *Renaissance Tragedy and the Senecan Tradition: Anger's Privilege*. New Haven: Yale University Press, 1985.

Cantar, Brenda. "Monstrous Conceptions in Lodge's *Robin the Devil*." *Studies in English Literature 1500–1900* 37 (1997): 39–53.

Carroll, Noël. *The Philosophy of Horror, or Paradoxes of the Heart.* New York: Routledge, Chapman, and Hall, 1990.

Cavendish, Thomas. *The Last Voyage of Thomas Cavendish, 1591–1592.* Ed. David Beers Quinn. Chicago: University of Chicago Press, 1975.

Couton, Marie. "Didactisme et romanesque dans le roman élisabéthain." Ph.D. Diss., University of Lyon II, 1982.

Crane, Thomas F. *Italian Social Customs of the Sixteenth Century and their Influences on the Literatures of Europe.* New Haven: Yale University Press, 1920.

Cuvelier, Eliane. "Horror and Cruelty in the Works of Three Elizabethan Novelists." *Cahiers élisabéthains* 19 (1981): 39–51.

———. *Thomas Lodge: Témoin de son temps (ca. 1558–1625). Études anglaises* 85. Publications de la Sorbonne: Littérature 11. Paris: Didier, 1984.

Davis, Walter, R. *Idea and Act in Elizabethan Fiction.* Princeton: Princeton University Press, 1969.

Durham, Charles W. III. "Character and Characterization in Elizabethan Prose Fiction." Ph.D. Diss., Ohio University, 1969.

Edwards, Philip, ed. *The Last Voyages of Cavendish, Hudson, Ralegh: The Original Narratives.* Oxford: Clarendon Press, 1988.

Falke, Anne. "The 'Marguerite' and the 'Margarita' in Thomas Lodge's *A Margarite of America.*" *Neophilologus* 70 (1986): 142–54.

Ford, Emanuel. *The Most Pleasant History of Ornatus and Artesia.* Ed. Goran Stanivukovic. Ottawa: Dovehouse Editions, 2003.

Frye, Northrop. *The Secular Scripture: A Study of the Structure of Romance.* Cambridge, Mass.: Harvard University Press, 1976.

Giggal, Kenneth. *Classic Sailing Ships.* New York: Norton, 1988.

Gorge, J. "Additional Materials on the Life of Thomas Lodge between 1604 and 1613." *Papers, mainly Shakespearean.* Collected by George I. Duthie. *Aberdeen University Studies* 147. Edinburgh: Oliver and Boyd, 1964. 90–105.

Guazzo, Stefano. *The Civile Conversation of M. Steeven Guazzo.* Trans. George Pettie (1581) and Bartholomew Yonge (1586). Intro. Sir Edward Sullivan. 2 vols. New York: AMS Press, 1967.

Gubar, Susan David. "Tudor Romance and Eighteenth-Century Fiction." Ph.D. Diss., University of Iowa, 1972.

Hallett, Charles A.,and Elaine S. Hallett. *The Revenger's Madness: A Study of Revenge Tragedy Motifs.* Lincoln: University of Nebraska Press, 1980.

Hamilton, A.C. "Elizabethan Prose Fiction and Some Trends in Recent Criticism." *Renaissance Quarterly* 37 (1984): 21–33.

Hamilton, Donna, B. "Some Romance Sources for *King Lear*, *Robert of Sicily* and *Robert the Devil*." *Studies in Philology* 71 (1974): 173–91.

Helgerson, Richard. *The Elizabethan Prodigals*. Berkeley: University of California Press, 1976.

Herpich, Charles A. "The Source of the 'Seven Ages'." *Notes and Queries* 105 (1902): 46–47.

Horne, P.R. *The Tragedies of Giambattista Cinthio Giraldi*. Oxford: Oxford University Press, 1962.

Hunter, G.K. "Isocrates' Precepts and Polonius' Character." *Shakespeare Quarterly* 9 (1957): 501–06.

Izard, Thomas C. *George Whetstone: Mid-Elizabethan Gentleman of Letters*. New York: Columbia University Press, 1942.

Johnson, Gerald D. "John Busby and the Stationers Trade, 1590–1612." *The Library*, 6th series, 7 (1985): 1–11.

Jones-Davies, Marie Thérèse. *Victimes et rebelles: L'écrivain dans la société élisabéthaine*. Paris: Aubier Montaigne, 1980.

Jusserand, Jean-Jules. *The English Novel in the Time of Shakespeare*. London: T. Fisher Unwin, 1890.

Kastner, L.E. "Thomas Lodge as an Imitator of the Italian Poets." *The Modern Language Review* 2 (1963): 155–61.

Keefer, Michael. "Violence and Extremity: Nashe's *Unfortunate Traveller* as an Anatomy of Abjection." *Critical Approaches to English Prose Fiction 1520–1640*. Ed. Donald Beecher. Ottawa: Dovehouse Editions, 1998. 183–218.

Kermode, Frank. "Secrets and Narrative Sequences." *On Narrative*. Ed. W.J.T. Mitchell, Chicago: University of Chicago Press, 1981. 79–97.

Kinney, Arthur. *Humanist Poetics: Thought, Rhetoric, and Fiction in Sixteenth-century England*. Amherst: University of Massachusetts Press, 1986.

Lando, Ortensio. *Delectable Demaundes and Pleasaunt Questions, with their severall Answers in Matters of Love, Natural Causes, with Morall and Politique Devices*. London: John Cawood for Nicholas Englande, 1566.

Leite, Serafim, S.J. *Historia de Companhia de Jesus no Brasil. Sécolo SVI. Estabelecimento*. Lisboa: Livraria Portugalia, 1938.

Lever, J.W. *The Tragedy of State*. London: Methuen, 1971.

Levinson, Jerrold, "Horrible Fictions." *The Pleasures of Aesthetics: Philosophical Essays*. Ithaca: Cornell University Press, 1996. 277–86.

Lievsay, John Leon. *Stefano Guazzo and the English Renaissance, 1575–1675*. Chapel Hill: University of North Carolina Press, 1961.

Linton, Joan Pong. *The Romance of the New World*. Cambridge: Cambridge University Press, 1998.

Lodge, Thomas. "*A Margarite of America*" with "*Menaphon*" by Robert Greene. Ed. G.B. Harrison. Oxford: Blackwell, 1927.

————. And [sic] Old-Spelling Critical Edition of Thomas Lodge's "A Margarite of America (1596)." Ed. James Clyde Addison, Jr. Elizabethan Studies 96. Salzburg: Institut für Anglistik und Amerikanistik, 1980.

————. *Rosalind*. Ed. Donald Beecher. Ottawa: Dovehouse Editions, 1997.

Lytton Sells, A. *The Italian Influence on English Poetry from Chaucer to Southwell*. London: George Allen and Unwin, 1955.

Mack, Peter. "Rhetoric in Use: Three Romances by Greene and Lodge." *Renaissance Rhetoric*. Ed. Peter Mack. New York: St. Martin's Press, 1994. 119–39.

Margolies, David. *Novel and Society in Elizabethan England*. Totowa: Barnes and Noble, 1985.

McAleer, John J. "Thomas Lodge's Verse Interludes." *The College Language Association Journal* 6 (1962): 83–89.

Orr, David. *Italian Renaissance Drama in England Before 1625*. Chapel Hill: University of North Carolina Press, 1970.

Painter, William, trans. *The Palace of Pleasure*. Ed. Joseph Jacobs. 3 vols. New York: Dover, 1966. [1890]

Paradise, Nathaniel Burton. *Thomas Lodge: The History of an Elizabethan*. New Haven: Yale University Press, 1931.

Paschale, Ludovico. *Rime volgari*. Vinegia: Stoffant Battista, 1549.

Pollack, Claudette. "Lodge's *A Margarite of America*: An Elizabethan Medley." *Renaissance and Reformation* 12 (1976): 1–11.

————. "Studies in the Novels of Thomas Lodge." Ph.D. Diss., Yale University, 1969.

Praz, Mario. *The Flaming Heart*. Gloucester, Mass.: Peter Smith, 1966.

————. "Machiavelli and the Elizabethans." *Proceedings of the British Academy* XIII. London: Milford, 1928.

Pruvost, Réné. "Réflexions sur l'euphuisme à propos de deux romans élisabéthains." *Revue Anglo-Américaine* 8 (1931): 1–18.

Raab, Felix. *The English Face of Machiavelli: A Changing Interpretation 1500–1700*. London: Routledge and Kegan Paul, 1964.

Rae, Wesley D. *Thomas Lodge*. Twayne's English Authors Series 59. New York: Twayne, 1967.

Randall, D.B.J. *The Golden Tapestry: A Critical Survey of Non-chivalric Spanish Fiction in English Translation (1543–1657)*. Durham: Duke University Press, 1963.

Relihan, Constance. *Fashioning Authority: The Development of Elizabethan Novelistic Discourse*. Kent, Ohio: Kent State University Press, 1994.

Ricoeur, Paul. *The Symbolism of Evil*. Boston: Beacon Press 1969. [1967]

Roberts, Josephine A. "Lodge's *A Margarite of America*: A Dystopian Vision of the New World." *Studies in Short Fiction* 17 (1980): 407–14.

Ryan, Pat M. Jr. *Thomas Lodge, Gentleman*. Hamden, Conn.: Shoe String Press, 1958.

Salzman, Paul. *English Prose Fiction 1558–1700: A Critical History*. Oxford: Clarendon, 1986.

Schlauch, Margaret. *Antecedents of the English Novel 1400–1600*. London: Oxford University Press, 1963.

Scott, Janet. *Les sonnets élizabéthains: Les sources et l'apport personnel*. Paris: Champion, 1929.

Selzer, John Lawrence. "A Critical Study of the Fiction of Thomas Lodge." Ph.D. Diss., Miami University, Ohio, 1978.

Seronsy, Cecil C. "The Seven Ages of Man Again." *Shakespeare Quarterly* 4 (1953): 364–65.

Shakespeare, William. *Titus Andronicus*. Ed. Gustav Cross. Baltimore: Penguin Books, 1967.

Sidney, Sir Philip. *An Apology for Poetry*. Ed. Geoffrey Shepherd. London: Thomas Nelson and Sons, 1965.

——. *The Prose Works*. Vol. I: *The Countess of Pembroke's Arcadia*. Ed. Albert Feuillerat. 4 vols. Cambridge: Cambridge University Press, 1965.

Sisson, Charles J. *Thomas Lodge and Other Elizabethans*. Cambridge, Mass.: Harvard University Press, 1933.

Spenser Encyclopedia, The. Gen. ed. A.C. Hamilton. Toronto: University of Toronto Press, 1990.

Spivack, Bernard. *Shakespeare and the Allegory of Evil*. New York: Columbia University Press, 1958.

Stallybrass, Peter, and Allan White. *The Politics and Poetics of Transgression*. Ithaca: Cornell University Press, 1986.

Tenney, Edward Andrews. *Thomas Lodge*. Cornell Studies in English 26. Ithaca: Cornell University Press, 1935.

Tripp, Edward. *The Meridian Handbook of Classical Mythology*. New York: Meridian, 1970.

Walker, Alice. "Italian Sources of Lyrics of Thomas Lodge." *Modern Language Review* 22 (1927): 75–79.

——. *The Life of Thomas Lodge*. Folcroft, Penn.: Folcroft Press, 1969. [1933]

Watt, Ian. "Elizabethan Light Reading." *The Age of Shakespeare*. Ed. Boris Ford. Baltimore: Penguin, 1955.

Whitworth, Charles W. "Thomas Lodge: Elizabethan Pioneer." *Cahiers élisabéthains* 3 (1973): 5–15.

Wilson, Katharine. "From Arcadia to America: Thomas Lodge's Literary Landscapes." *Imaginaire* 5 (2000): 7–19.

Wind, Edgar. *Pagan Mysteries of the Renaissance*. New York: W.W. Norton, 1968. [1958]

A Margarite of America

By T. Lodge

[ornament]

Printed for *Iohn Busbie*, and are to be
sold in S. Dunstons church-yard in
Fleet-street, at the little shop
next Cliffords Inne.
1596

[Preliminary Pieces]

To the noble, learned, and virtuous Lady, the Lady Russell,[1] T.L. wisheth affluence on earth and felicity in heaven.

Madame, your deep and considerate judgment, your admired honour and happy readings have drawn me to present this labour of mine to your gracious hands and favourable patronage, wherein, though you shall find nothing to admire, yet doubt I not but you may meet many things that deserve cherishing. Touching the subject, though of itself it seem historical, yet if it please you, like our English Sappho,[2] to look into that which I have slenderly written, I doubt not but that your memory shall acquaint you with my diligence, and my diligence may deserve your applause. Touching the place where I wrote this, it was in those straits christened by Magellan,[3] in which place to the southward many wondrous isles, many strange fishes, many monstrous Patagones[4] withdrew my senses; briefly, many bitter and extreme frosts at midsummer continually clothed* and clad the discomfortable mountains, so that as there was great wonder in the place wherein I writ this, so likewise might it be marvelled that in such scanty fare, such causes of fear, so mighty discouragements, and many crosses, I should deserve or eternize anything. Yet what I have done, good Madame, judge and hope this felicity from my pen, that whilst the memory thereof shall live in any age, your charity, learning, nobility, and virtues shall be eternized. Oppian writing to Theodosius[5] was as famous by the person to whom he consecrated his study, as fortunate in his labours, which as yet are not mastered by oblivion; so hope I, Madame, on the wing of your sacred name to be borne to the temple of Eternity, where, though Envy bark at me, the Muses[6]

shall cherish, love, and happy me. Thus hoping your Lady-
ship will supply my boldness with your bounty and affability, I
humbly kiss your most delicate hands, shutting up my English
duty under an Italian copy of humanity and courtesy. From my
house this 4. of May, 1596,

Your honours in all zeal,
T. LODGE.

To the Gentlemen Readers.

Gentlemen, I am prevented in mine own hopes, in seconding thrift's forward desires. Some four years since, being at sea with M. Candish,[7] whose memory if I repent not, I lament not, it was my chance in the library of the Jesuits in Sanctum[8] to find this history in the Spanish tongue, which as I read delighted me, and delighting me, won me, and winning me, made me write it. The place where I began my work was a ship, where many soldiers of good reckoning finding disturbed stomachs, it cannot but stand with your discretions to pardon an undiscreet and unstayed pen, for hands may vary where stomachs miscarry. The time I wrote in was when I had rather will to get my dinner than to win my fame. The order I wrote in was past order, where I rather observed men's hands lest they should strike me, than curious reason of men to condemn me. In a word, I wrote under hope rather the fish should eat both me writing and my paper written, than fame should know me, hope should acquaint her with me, or any but misery should hear mine ending. For those faults, Gentlemen, escaped by the printer in not being acquainted with my hand, and the book printed in my absence, I must crave you with favour to judge of, and with your wonted courtesies to correct, and, according to ecclesiastical law, give us on our confession absolution. If you will not, remember this, that a country lass for ladies may tell them they curl too much; and for gentlemen, that they are unfashioned by their fashions. To be short, who lives in this world, let him wink°in the world; for either men prove too blind in seeing too little, or too presumptuous in condemning that they should not.

Yours, T. Lodge.

wink close eyes.

A Margarite of America
for Ladies' delight, and Ladies' honour.

The blushing morning gan no sooner appear from the desired bed of her old paramour, and remembering her of her Cephalus,[9] watered the bosom of sweet flowers with the crystal of her tears, but both the armies, awaked by the harmony of the birds that recorded° their melody in every bush, began to arm them in their tents and speedily visit their trenches. Among the rest, the two emperors — the one, Protomachus of Mosco, the other, Artosogon of Cusco — considering with themselves the care princes ought to have that command multitudes, the prefixed hour of their fight already arrived, suddenly armed themselves, commanding their corronels° by sound of trumpet to draw out their companies into the plain. Then marched forth each squadron, deaffing the air with their cries, dimming the sun with the reflexion of their costly curets;° their high looks promised happy forwardness,° and their haughty hearts were portrayed in their dreadless demean° At the last embattled in due order, the pikemen in a Macedonian phalanx, the horsemen in their out-wings, the shot°as guards to the pikes, all as protectors of their colours, the fatal charge was sounded, and both the armies marched forward to encounter. When suddenly an old man, whose sober looks betokened his severe thoughts, whose mournful garments shadowed his melancholy mind, bearing the image of the gods, whom he most honoured, between his arms, and the homage a true subject ought to have in his heart, thrust himself between both the armies. When sending many sighs from his breast to famous° pity and tears from his eyes to move compassion, he fixed both his hands on their knees, who were nearly encountered to enter combat, and began in their terms to persuade both

---

recorded sang.   **corronels** colonels.   **curets** cuirasses: combination armour of breast-plate and back-plate.   **forwardness** advancement to successful completion.   **demean** demeanour.   **shot** soldiers armed with muskets or other firearms (*OED*).   **famous** "make famous"; "earn celebrity for" (*OED*).

the monarchs, whilst both the armies withdrew their weapons, to give diligent attention to his words.

"Stay your unbridled furies, O you Princes, and let not the world say that you, who were born to be the defenders of the monarchies, are through your ill-governed furies become the destroyers of mankind. Whereto tendeth this your unjust arms? If for your private grudges, oh how fond° are you, that to revenge your mislikes are the murtherers of many innocents. If to enlarge your seigniories,° oh how vain are you, that seek to attain that with blood which you must keep with care, that labour to sell that with stripes° which you have bought with peace, that travail°* to lose your own estates and seigniories for a little name of sovereignty! Hear me, O you Princes, nay rather be advised by me: you have spent huge treasures, made many widows, lost three years, and for what, I pray you? For the right of one city, the whole confines and revenues whereof are* not sufficient to acquit for one month of your charges. O unhappy Mantinea,[10] the cause of such heart-burning. O lawless° name of seigniory,° the occasion of such sorrows. Hear what Plutarch saith: 'Ye potentates, there is no war that taketh head amongst men, but of vice: for either the love of pleasure, either covetousness, ambition or desire of rule, provoketh the same.'[11] If this be true, as it is most certain, why blush you not, Princes, to behold your own follies? Why reconcile you not to amend your misdeeds? If you say there are more pleasures in Mantinea than in your several countries, you detract from whole provinces to make proud one poor city; and if it were, what a vain thing is it that such as are in authority should purchase a private delight by public danger! Plato, being demanded why he praised the Lydians so much and dispraised the Lacedemonians so highly, answered thus: 'If I commend the Lydians, it is for that they were never occupied but in tilling the field; and if I do reprove the Lacedemonians, it is because they knew nothing else but to conquer realms.'[12]

fond foolish.   **seigniories** territories.   **stripes** blows, strokes.
travail labour, toil.   **lawless** above the law.   **seigniory** domination, sovereignty.

So virtuous a thing hath it been held by the learned to maintain peace and to shun occasions of contention.   If you will be held virtuous and monarchies, as I wish you should be, desire nothing to the damage of your common weals, lest in satisfying your own humours ye subvert your subjects' happiness.   If for covetousness ye hunt after conquests, how vain are you, labouring like mad men to lay more straw on your houses to burn them and cast more water on the sea to drown it?[13] Covetousness is an affection◊ that hath no end, an extreme that hath no mean, a profit full of prejudice.   Well said Aristotle in his *Politics* there is no extreme poverty but that of covetousness.[14] If for ambition, well may ye weep with Alexander[15] to be laughed at, practise with Zeno[16] to repent with him; for in desiring beyond your reach, you fall besides your hopes.   But if all these evils be grown to one head, if your incontinency in desire, your excessive thirst after pleasure, your covetous longing after riches, your ambitious hunting after seigniority◊ have occasioned this war, subdue these errors in yourselves for your subjects' sakes.   And sith◊ Protomachus hath one daughter and no more to inherit Mosco, and Artosogon one son and heir to succeed in the empire of Cusco, let both these be joined together in happy matrimony.   So shall the cause of this difference* be quickly decided, yourselves* may root out your ingrafted errors, your subjects enjoy their desired peace, and finally, your children shall have greater cause to praise their fathers' foresight than to repent hereafter their unjust fury.   Hereunto I conjure you, O you Princes, by these holy gods whom you honour, by these hoary hairs which you should reverence, lest your subjects hereafter ruinated through your rashness have rather occasion to curse you than commend you.   In Octavius Caesar's time,[17] each one thought himself fortunate to be born under his empery,◊ and him happy that maintained his province in peace.   So let it be said of you, good Princes, and leave you

affection passion, state of mind.   **seigniority** lordship, governance.
sith since.   **empery** dominion of an emperor.

such memory to your succession: then shall I think myself happy in my persuasions, and you shall be famous to all posterity."

No sooner had he ended his oration, but both the emperors resolved by his reasons and pacified by the persuasions of their nobility, who after long debate and consultation and cheer behooveful,◊ drew to an accord, wherein it was concluded that Arsadachus, the youthful heir of Cusco, should be sent to the emperor of Mosco, where, considering the worthiness of his court, he should find fit companions and apply himself to fancy,◊ being continually in the presence of his fair Margarita. Finally, after the decease of both the princes, it was enacted that both Mantinea and the whole empire should remain to Arsadachus and Margarita and their heirs forever. These articles thus concluded upon, both the camps brake up; the brave knights, who toforetime delighted in tossing of lances, now have no other pleasure but in talking with fair ladies; the soldier's sword was changed to a husbandman's scythe; his gay curets to a grey frock; the gates which beforetime were shut against foes were now opened to all sorts as unsuspected friends. Such liberty followeth peace exempted from the tyranny of war. Artosogon withdrew his followers to his own frontiers, and returning to his court, made honourable provision for his son Arsadachus to send him to Moscovia. Protomachus, after he had rewarded each soldier according to his desert,◊ withdrew himself to the castle of that aged father who had so faithfully counselled him,[18] yielding him for reward the dukedom of Volgradia, the chiefest place of honour through all Moscovy, whither, as to the open theatre of all delights, the nobility and ladies resorted, among the which the chiefest, fairest, and chastest, Margarita, presented herself, rejoicing at the happy reconcilement. Where being resolved by her father of the contract that was concluded upon, with blushes at first showed her modesty, and with obedience at last condescended to his mind.

cheer behooveful disposition proper or fitting.   **fancy** pursuits of love.   **desert** worthy or meritorious action or quality.

In this rare fortress of Arsinous, situate by a gracious and silver floating◇ river, environed with curious planted trees to minister shade and sweet-smelling flowers to recreate the senses, besides the curious knots,◇ the dainty garden plots, the rich tapestry, the royal attendance,◇ Protomachus found as evident signs of high spirit as of huge expense. At the entrance of his chamber, which had a prospect into a delicious garden in which all sorts of birds enclosed in a cage of crystal recorded◇ their harmonies, whilst the gentle fall of a bubbling fountain seemed to yield a sweet and murmuring consent◇ to their music, was placed that sentence of Drusus Germanicus which he carried always engraved in his ring:

Illis est gravis fortuna quibus est repentina.◇[19]

About the walls of the chamber in curious imagery were the seven sages of Greece,[20] set forth with their several virtues eloquently discovered◇ in Arabic verses. The bed appointed for the prince to rest himself was of black ebony enchased◇ with* rubies, diamonds, and carbuncles◇ made in form of an arch, on which by degrees man's state from infancy to his old age was plainly depictured, and on the testern◇ of the bed the whole contents of the same most sagely deciphered in these verses.

Humanae Miseriae discursus.◇

O whereof boasteth man, or by what reason
Is filthy clay so much ambitious?
Whose thoughts are vain, and alter every season,
Whose deeds are damned, base, and vicious,

floating ebbing and flowing. **knots** flower-beds laid out in fanciful or intricate designs (*OED*). **attendance** attendants, servants. **recorded** sang. **consent** harmony of sounds. *Illis est . . . repentina* Fortune is harsh to those upon whom it falls without warning. **discovered** revealed. **enchased** inlaid. **carbuncles** gems of a red colour. **testern** tester, a canopy over a bed or the tall headboard which ascends to the canopy and helps support it. **Humanae Miseriae discursus** a discourse on human misery..

Who in his cradle by his childish crying
Presageth his mishaps and sorrows nighing.

An infant first from nurse's teat he sucketh
With nutriment corruption of his nature:
And from the root of endless error plucketh
That taste of sin that waits on every creature,
And as his sinews firm his sin increaseth,
And but till death his sorrow never ceaseth.

In riper years when youthly courage reigneth,*
A winter's blast of fortune's louring changes
A flattering hope wherein no trust remaineth,
A fleeting love his forward joy estranges:
Achieve he wealth, with wasteful woe he bought it,
Let substance fail, he grieves, and yet he sought it.

In stayed years whenas he seeks the gleanings
Of those his times in studious arts bestowed,
In sum, he oft misconstrueth wise-men's meanings,
Soiling the spring from whence his science flowed;
In all he gains by perfect judgment gained,
A hate of life that hath so long remained.

From height of throne to abject wretchedness,
From wondrous skill to servile ignorance:
From court to cart, from rich to recklessness,
The joys of life have no continuance:
The king, the caitiff wretch, the lay, the learned,
Their crowns, woes, wants, and wits with grief have earned.

The judgment seat hath brawls, honour is hated,
The soldier's life is daily thrall to danger,
The merchant's bag by tempests is abated,
His stock still serves for prey to every stranger,
The scholar with his knowledge learns repent,
Thus each estate in life hath discontent.

And in these trades and choice estates of living,
Youth steals on manly state, and it on age,

And age with weakened limbs, and mind misgiving,
With trembling tongue repenteth youthly rage,
And ere he full hath learned his life to govern,
He dies, and dying doth to dust return.

His greatest good is to report the trouble
Which he in prime of youth hath overpassed,
How for his grains of good he reaped but stubble,
How lost by love, by follies' hew[◊] disgraced,
Which whilst he counts, his son perhaps attendeth,
And yet his days in self-like follies endeth.

Thus mortal life on sudden vanisheth,
All like a dream, or as the shadow fleeteth
When sun his beam from substance banisheth,
Or like the snow at once that dries and sleeteth,
Or as the rainbow which by her condition
Lives by the sun's reflect and opposition.

Thus life in name is but a death in being,
A burthen to the soul by earth entangled:
Then put thou off that veil that lets[◊] thy seeing,
O wretched man with many torments mangled,
Since neither child, nor youth, nor stayed, nor aged,
The storms of wretched life may be assuaged.

And with the Egyptian midst thy delicates
Present the shape of death in every member,
To make thee know the name of all estates:
And midst thy pomp thy nighing grave remember,
Which if thou dost, thy pride shall be repressed,
Since none before he dies is perfect blessed.

Thus sumptuous was the lodging of Protomachus, but far more glorious the chamber of Margarita, which seemed from the first day to be fashioned to her affections, for over the entrance

hew cut, gash; or hue: form, appearance. Perhaps *hew* is a misprint for *how*, in which case the phrase would read "by follies how disgraced."
lets hinders,obstructs.

of the doors was drawn and carved out of curious white marble the fair goddess of chastity[21] blushing at the sudden interception of Acteon[22] and her naked nymphs, who with the one hand covering their own secret pleasures with blushes, with the other cast a beautiful veil over their mistress's dainty nakedness. The two pillars of the door were beautified with the two Cupids of Anacreon,[23] which well-shaped Modesty often seemed to whip lest they should grow over-wanton. No sooner were* the inward beauties of the chamber discovered, but the work wrought his wonder, and the wonder itself was equalled by the work, for all the chaste ladies of the world, enchased out of silver, looking through fair mirrors of chrysolites,◊ carbuncles, sapphires, and green emeralds, fixed their eyes on the picture of Eternity, which, fixed on the tops of a testern, seemed with a golden trumpet[24] to applaud to them all.   In the tapestry, beautified with gold and pearl, were the nine Muses curiously wrought, who from a thicket beheld amorous Orpheus[25] making the trees leap through his laments, and as he warbled his songs the floods of Hebrus[26] stayed their sources, and the birds that beheld their comfort began likewise to carol. It was strange to think, and more strange to behold, in what order Art matched with Nature, and how the limning painter had almost exceeded Nature in life, saving that the beauteous faces wanted breath to make them alive, not cunning to prove them lively. Thus were* both the emperor and his daughter lodged, wanting neither delights of hunting nor other princely pleasures to entertain them: so curious◊ was the good old man in pleasing his emperor and master.

But among all other courtly delights Margarita met not the least, who in this castle found a companion to accompany her in life and a chaste maid to attend her in love, who, beside her education, which was excellent, her virtues such as equalled ex-cellence, her beauty so rare as exceeded both, was beloved by a noble lord of Moscovy, who for his singularities◊ in poetry and

chrysolites gems of a green colour.   **curious** careful as to stan-dard of excellence, particular about details.   **singularities** special excellences.

science in feats of arms, was rather the seignior than second of
all the empire. The interchange of which affections was so con-
formable to the fancies of the princess that she, who was ordained
to be the miracle of love, learned by them and their manners the
true method of the same; for when Minecius courted his Philenia, Margarita conceited◇ her Arsadachus; and by perceiving the
true heart of the one, supposed the perfect habit of the other.
If at any time cause of discourtesy grew betwixt Philenia and
her friend, Margarita salved it, hoping by that means to sacrifice
to Love, to gratify him in her fortunes, which were to succeed.
How often would she make Minecius' deserts excellent by her
praise, and he his Philenia famous by his poetry? It was a world
to see in them, that when love waxed warm, those lovers waxed
witty, the one to command, the other to consent. If at any time
Minecius wrote an amorous sonnet, Margarita should see it; and
if at any time Margarita read a sonnet, she would commend it
to satisfy Philenia. And in that Arsinous, the father, through the
good opinion of Protomachus, the emperor, thought not amiss of
the marriage between his daughter and the Moscovite, he rather
furthered than frowned on their pastimes. And Minecius, having
achieved◇ her father and entangled the daughter in fancy, sought
all means possible to satisfy her delights; sometimes therefore,
under a pastoral habit, he would hide him in the groves and
woods where the ladies were accustomed to walk, where recording a ruthful◇ lay as they passed by, he through his harmony
caused them believe that the tree tattled love, and such was his
method in his melancholy fancies that his coat was accordant to
his conceit◇ and his conceit the miracle of conceits. Among the
rest, these of no small regard I have thought good in this place to
register, which though but few in number are worthy the noting.
First, being on a time melancholy by reason of some mislikes
of his mistress, he wrote these sonnets in imitation of Dolce the

conceited imagined.   **achieved** gained the favour of.   **ruthful**
sorrowful.   **coat was accordant to his conceit** dress matched his
imagined role.

Italian,[27] and presented them in presence of the Princess Margarita, who highly commended them, over the top whereof he wrote this in great Roman letters.

PIETATI.◊

If so those flames I vent whenas I sigh,
Amidst these lowly valleys where I lie,
Might find some means by swift address to fly
Unto those alpine topless mountains high.

Thou shouldst behold their icy burthens thaw,
And crimson flowers adorn their naked backs,
Sweet roses should enrich their winter wracks,
Against the course of kind and nature's law.

But you, fair Lady, see the furious flame,
That through your will destroys me beyond measure,
Yet in my pains methinks you take great pleasure,
Loath to redeem or else redress the same.

Nor hath your heart compassion of mine ills,
More cold than snow, more hard than alpine hills.

The other was this, which seemed to be written with more vehemency of spirit and far greater melancholy, which in a shepherd's habit, sitting under a myrtle tree, he had mournfully recorded in the presence of his mistress.

PIETATI.

O deserts, be you peopled by my plaints,
And let your plants by my pure tears be watered,
And let the birds whom my sad moan acquaint,
To hear my hymns have harmony in hatred.

Let all your savage citizens refrain
To haunt those bowers where I my woes bewray,◊

PIETATI for duty/piety.   **bewray** reveal, declare.

Let none but deep Despair with me remain,
To haste my death when Hope doth will me stay.

Let rocks remove for fear they melt to hear me,
Let Echo[28] whist° for dread she die to answer:
So living thus where no delights come near me,
My many moans more moving may appear.
And in the depth of all when I am climbing,
Let Love come by, see, sigh, and fall a-crying.

This mourning passion pleased the ladies very highly, especially Philenia, who thought herself no little blessed to be thus beloved. Among the rest, they gave this that follows his deserved commendation; for being written in the desolate season of the year, and the desperate success of his earnings° being so applied to his affects,° and accordant with the year's effects, in my mind deserveth no small good liking.

With Ganymede[29] now joins the shining sun,
And through the world displays his chiller flame,
Cold, frost, and snow, the meadows and the mountains
Do wholly blend, the waters waxen ice:
The meads want flowers, the trees have parched leaves,
Such is the dolie° season of the year.

And I in coldest season of the year,
Like to a naked man before the sun,
Whilst drought thus dwells in herbs and dried leaves,
Consume myself, and in affection's flame
To cinders fall: ne helps me frost or ice
That falls from off these snow-clad cloudy mountains.

But whenas shades new clothe again the mountains,
And days wax long, and warmer is the year,
Then in my soul fierce love congeals an ice,
Which nor the force of fierce enflamed sun

whist keep silence.   **earnings** longing desires.   **affects** feelings, mental states.   **dolie** doleful, sad.

May thaw, nor may be moult° with mighty flames,
Which frost doth make me quake like aspen leaves.[30]

Such time the winds are whist, and trembling leaves,
And beasts* grow mute reposing on the mountains,
Then when aslaked been the heavenly flames,
Both in the wane° and prime tide° of the year:
I watch, I ward, until the new-sprung sun,
And hope, and fear, and feel both cold and ice.

But when again her morrow-gathered ice
The morn displays, and frostieth drooping leaves,
And day renews with rising of the sun,
Then wailful forth I wend through vales and mountains:
Ne other thought have I day, month, and year,
But of my first the fatal inward flames.

Thus love consumes me in his lively flames,
Thus love doth freeze me with his chilly ice,
So that no time remains me through the year
To make me blithe: ne are there any leaves
Through all the trees that are upon the mountains,
That may conceal me from my sweetest sun.

First shall the sun be seen without his flame,
The wintered mountains without frost or ice,
Leaves on the stones, ere I content one year.

This written in an amorous and more plausible vein, as that
which most pleased the ladies and was not of least worth, I have
set down last.

O curious gem, how I envy each while
To see thee play upon my lady's paps,
And hear those orbs where Cupid lays his traps
From whence a gracious April still doth smile.

And now thou playst thee in that garden gentle,
Twixt golden fruit and near her heart receivest

moult melted.   **wane** autumn.   **prime tide** spring.

Thy rest, and all her secret thoughts conceivest
Under a veil fair, white, divine, and subtile.

Ye gentle pearls, where ere did nature make you?
Or whether in Indian shores you found your mould,
Or in those lands where spices serve for fuel:
Oh if I might from out your essence take you,
And turn myself to shape what ere I would,
How gladly would I be my lady's jewel!

Many such like were devised by Minecius and allowed by
Philenia, through which Love, that had new burgeoned his wings,
began to fly, and being shut in close embers, brake out to open
fire. So that, like the alcatras[31] that scenteth far, Philenia consented to yield him favour who sought it, knowing that his wit
like the rose, being more sweet in the bud than in the flower,
would best fit her: and, as the herb ephemerus[32] that hath in his
spring a sweet and purple flower, but being of ten days' growth
conceiveth nothing of beauty but is replenished with barrenness,
so course of time would change him. She made choice of him,
since in that estate of life wherein he then lived was fashioned
to all pleasures and disfurnished of no perfection, she knew him
most meetest◊ to enjoy his beauty, and most accordant to possess
her marriage bed.

But leave we Philenia delighted in her Minecius, Margarita
applauding them both, Protomachus conversing with Arsinous,
and the whole courtly train of Mosco living in their content. And
let us have an eye to Cusco and the emperor thereof, who no
sooner arrived in this court, but like the good gardener knowing
his time to plant, like the fortunate husband well trained to yoke
and plough, learned of trifolium,[33] who lifteth up her leaves
against tempest, and the emmet,◊ who by her provision and
travel foretelleth a shower and trouble that followeth, thought
good, having been taught by experience to take the opportunity,
knowing that princes' and monarchs' minds are most subject to
alterations according to the humours of their counsels, to send

meetest fit, suitable.   **emmet** ant.

his son Arsadachus to Mosco. Whereupon, furnishing him with princely attendance and great treasures, he set him forward on his way, and at his last farewell took his leave of him in this fatherly and kingly manner.

"My son, as thou art young in years, so hast thou young thoughts, which if thou govern not with discretion, it will be the cause of thy destruction. Thou art leaving thy country for another court, thy familiars for new friends, where the least mite of folly in thee will show a mountain, the least blemish a great blot. Since therefore thine inclination is corrupt, and the faults which I smother in that I am thy father others will smite at, being thy foes, I will counsel thee to foresee before thou fall and to have regard before thy ruin. Thou art born a prince, which being a benefit sent from heaven is likewise an estate subject to all unhappiness. For, whereas much dirt is, thither come many carrions;◇ where high fortunes, many flatterers; where the huge cedar grows, the thistle springeth; where the ford is deepest, the fish are plentiest; and whereas sovereignty is, there are many seducers. Be thou therefore wary like the unicorn,[34] which, for fear she should taste poison, toucheth with her horn before she lap it with her lip. So seem thou in feigning credit to those who mean to fawn on thee in thy error, to discover them in their sleights, as the fowl anthias[35] doth the locust, and prevent them in their subtilties, as the fish nibias[36] doth the sea dragon. In choosing thy friends, learn of Augustus, the Roman emperor,[37] who was strange and scrupulous in accepting friends, but changeless and resolute in keeping them. Choose not such companions, I pray thee, as will be drunk with thee for good fellowship, and double with thee in thine affairs; but use such as the thriftier sort do by their threadbare coats, which being without wool, they cast off as things unfit for their wearing. And especially remember these short lessons, which the shortness of time maketh me utter by a word, where indeed they require a whole day's work; beware of over-trust, lest you commit the sweetest of your life to the credit of an uncertain tongue. Use all

carrions vermin.

such courtiers as visit you in like manner as goldsmiths do their metal, who try it by the touchstone if it be forthall,◊ and melt it in the fire, before they vouchsafe it the fashion; so do thou, and if they be counterfeit, they will soon leave thee; if faithful, they will the more love thee. Trust not too much to the ear, for it beguileth many; nor to the tongue, for it bewitcheth more. Strive not with time in thy affairs, but take leisure; for a thing hastily enterprised is more hastily repented. In your counsels, beware of too much affection; and in your actions, be not too proud; for the one will prove your little regard of conscience, the other the corruption of your nature. And since thou art going into a foreign court and must follow the direction of a second father whose favour if thou keep, thou mayst hap to be most famous. Look to thyself, for as Plato saith: 'To be a king and to reign, to serve and be in favour, to fight and overcome are three impossible things, and are only distributed by Fortune and disturbed by her frowardness in following.'38 Therefore, Protomachus◊ seek in all things to follow his humour, for opinion is the chief step to preferment, and to be thought well of by the prince is no small profit; and if so be thou wilt please him, do him many services and give him few words. In thy speech, be deliberate without bashfulness; in thy behaviour courtly without pride; in thy apparel princely without excess; in thy revenges bold but not too bloody; in thy love be courteous and not troublesome, and rather deserve a beck◊ by bashfulness than a check by overboldness; for many which for good nurture have by ladies at first been stroked with the hand, have for their impudency afterwards been kicked out with the heel, or at leastwise thrust out by the head. Let it not be said of thee as it was of Hannibal39 among the Carthaginians, that thou neither give that which thou promisest to thy friends, neither keepest any covenant with thine enemies, lest through the one thou be accounted without faith, through the other unworthy

forthall not to be trusted, spurious (Gosse). **Therefore, Protomachus** i.e., Therefore, seek in all things to follow Protomachus his humour. **beck** gesture, like a nod, expressive of salutation or respect.

life. Fain◊ would I speak more, my son, but time suffereth me not: wherefore I pray thee by our gods, who gave thee me, have respect unto my counsels, lest thou grieve me; for better is a son lost in the cradle than lewd and dissolute in the kingdom."

This said, the old emperor Artosogon with piteous tears watered the cheeks of his corrupt son Arsadachus, and committing him to the conduct of his followers and his presence to the hands of the chief peers, he carefully, suspecting the worst, returned to his court.

Arsadachus, being thus delivered of his father, fed himself with his own natural follies; and as the bird lenca[40] flying toward the south foretelleth storms, even so his lewd thoughts aimed at nothing but wickedness were the evident signs of his sinister behaviour. For being well shaped by nature, there was not any man more estranged from nurture; so that it was to be feared that he should sooner want matter to execute his dishonest mind upon, than a dishonest mind to execute any lewd matter. For among the train appointed by his father to attend him, he took no delight but in those who were most lascivious, who ministering the occasions bred in him an earnest desire to do ill. His cruelty he shadowed with a kind of courtly severity, his lust under the title of love, his treasons under the pretext of true meaning. So like the fair lily he cloaked his stinking scent with his white leaf; and like the bird acanthis[41] living among thorns, he took no other pleasure than to converse among unthrifts. The grave counsellors appointed him by his father he set light by; and like a second Catiline[42] rather honoured him that did invent new mischief than countenance those who did persuade him from his corrupt manners. From this so sour a stock what fruit may be expected but crabs;◊ from so lewd beginnings, how lamentable issues?

At last, arriving in Mosco, he was informed of the emperor's being in the castle of Arsinous: whereupon addressing himself thither according to the mightiness of his estate, he was by Protomachus entertained royally, who, receiving the presents of

Fain gladly.   **crabs** crab-apples.

Artosogon, returned them back who brought them with high rewards, choosing among all the princely gentlemen of his court those for to accompany Arsadachus who were virtuously disposed and well indued.◇ Among the rest, Minecius was appointed chief, whom Margarita highly trusted by reason of the trial Philenia had made of him. But among all other subtile demeanours in court, this one was most to be admired, that Arsadachus should make signs of great devotion toward Margarita, and delude* her with most hateful doubleness. It was wonderful to see him counterfeit sighs, to feign love, dissemble tears, to work treasons, vow much, perform little; in brief, vow all faith and perform nothing but falsehood. Margarita, poor princess, thinking all that gold which glistered;[43] the stone precious by reason of his fair foil;[44] the water shallow by reason of his mild silence,[45] trusted so long until she perished in her trust, wholly ignorant that love is like the sea-star,◇ which whatsoever it toucheth it burneth. For, knowing the resolution of her father, the conclusion of the nobility, she began to strain her thoughts to the highest reach, fancying every motion, wink, beck, and action of the Cuscan prince in such sort as that, assisted by the virtuous, constant, and unspotted simplicity of her nature, she seemed not to suspect whatever she saw, nor to count it wrong howsoever she endured. Among all other the counsellors of this young and untoward heir, about that time the flame of his folly, long time smothered, began to smoke, besides his own countrymen, which were Brasidas, Capaneus, and others,* there lived a great prince in the court of Protomachus, who delighted rather to flatter than counsel, to feed corruptions than purge them, who had Machevil's prince[46] in his bosom to give instance and mother Nana, the Italian bawd,[47] in his pocket to show his artificial villainies. This Thebion, being in high account with the emperor for his ripe wit, was quickly entertained by this ungracious prince for his cunning wickedness; who, where

indued brought up, educated.   sea-star starfish.

Arsadachus was prone by nature to do ill, never ceased to minister him an occasion of doing ill. For, perceiving one day how with over-lustful eyes the young prince beheld Philenia, egged him onward which had too sharp an edge, using old proverbs to confirm his odious discourses and purposes: to be brief, Arsadachus, perceiving Philenia and Margarita always conversant, resorted often to them, giving the emperor's daughter the hand for a fashion whilst Arsinous' darling had the heart for a favour. And the better to cloak this corruption, he used Minecius with more than accustomed familiarity, seeming to be very importunate in his behalf with Philenia, where indeed he only sought opportunity to discover his own love. Whereupon being one day desired by Minecius to work a reconcilement between him and his mistress, by reason he knew him to be both eloquent and learned, he taking the occasion at a certain festival, whilst Minecius courted Margarita, to withdraw Philenia to a bay window in the castle, which overlooked the fair fields on every side; where taking her by the hand he began thus.

"Beautiful Philenia, if I knew you as secret as you are sage, I would discover that to you in words which I cover in my heart with sighs."

"If it be love, great Prince," said Philenia, little suspecting his treachery, "you may commend it to my ear, in that it is settled in this heart; as for silence, it is lovers' science, who are as curious to conceal as cunning to conceive. And as hunters carry the feather of an eagle against thunder,[48] so lovers bear the herb therbis[49] in their mouths, which hath the virtue to stay the tongue from discourse whilst it detaineth the heart with incredible pleasure."

"If it be so," said Arsadachus, blushing very vehemently, for nature's sparks of hope were not as yet altogether ruinated, "I will hold ladies' weakness for worth and disclose that secret which I thought to keep close."

"And what is that?" quoth Philenia.

"Love," said Arsadachus, "it is love," and there he paused.

"Love, my Lord," quoth the lady, "why, it is a passion full of pleasure, a god full of goodness; and trust me, Margarita hath of late days stolen him from his mother at Paphos[50] to make him her play-fellow in Mosco. She proineth[◊] his wings every day and curleth his locks every hour; if he cry, she stills him under your name; if he be wanton, she charms him with thinking on you; since then she hath the sickness in her hand that loveth you in her heart, complain not of love, since you command it."

Here Arsadachus, unable to endure the heat of affection or conceal the humour that restrained him, brake off her discourse in this sort: "Ah Philenia, if I did not hope that as the hard oak nourisheth the soft silkworm, the sharp beech bringeth forth the savoury chestnut, the black bdellium[51] sweet gum, so beautiful looks concealed pitiful hearts, I would surfeit in my sorrows to the death rather than satisfy thee in my discourse. But hoping of thy silence, Philenia, I will disclose my mind: I love Philenia; fair Philenia, I love thee. As for Margarita, though she cherish Beauty in her bosom, thou enclosest him in thy beauty; she may have his feathers, but thou his fancies; she may please him well, but thou only appease him."

"You do speak Greek,[52] Arsadachus," said Philenia; "I understand you not."

"I will paraphrase on it then," quoth the prince, "to make it plainer." For now occasion had emboldened him. "I come not to plead a reconcilement for Minecius, as you suppose, but remorse[◊] for myself, sweet Madam, on set purpose, for upon you, fair Madam, dependeth my life, in your hands consisteth my liberty; your looks may deify my delights; your lours dare me with discontents. I pray thee, therefore, dear Philenia, by those chaste eyes, the earnest[◊] of my happiness, by this fair hair, the minister of all favours, take compassion of Arsadachus, who, being a prince, may prefer thee, and an emperor, will love thee. As for Margarita, let Minecius and her accord them, for only I will make thee empress, and she may make Minecius emperor."

Philenia, unable to endure his devilish and damned assaults, flang from him with this bitter and sharp answer: "Did not my

proineth trims, adorns. **remorse** compassion, pity. **earnest** pledge, foretaste.

promise lock up these lips, thou injurious prince, thy doubleness should be as well known in this court as thy name; but since my promises have made thee presumptuous, I will hereafter hear before I answer and try before I trust. Is this the faith thou bearest to Margarita, thy friendship thou vowest to Minecius, to falsify thy faith to one and delude the trust of the other? Hence, poisoned, because I abhor thee; and if hereafter thou haunt me with these lewd and lecherous salutes, trust me, the emperor shall know thy treasons, and others shall be revenged on thee for thy treacheries."

This said, she thrust into the company of other ladies, leaving him altogether confused. Yet being made confident by reason of her promise, he withdrew himself to his chamber, where, tossing his licentious limbs on his soft bed, he fed on his desperate determination, till Thebion and Brasidas, the one a Cuscan and the other a Moscovian, both of his dissolute counsel, entered his chamber; who, after they had sounded the cause of his sorrows and the manner of the disease, quickly ministered the method of curing it. For the day of Minecius' marriage being at hand and the nuptial feast ordained the Monday following, they, seeing the grounded affection of the prince, concluded this: by the death of Minecius to minister Arsadachus his remedy, the complot whereof they laid in this sort. That, where in Mosco it was accustomed that such nobles as married young heirs in their father's house should, after the joining of hands, conduct them to their own castles, there to accomplish the festivals, Arsadachus and they his counsellors, with the assistance of their followers, should lie in wait in the woods of Mesphos, by which Minecius and his bride should needly pass, where they might surprise Philenia and murther Minecius. Arsadachus, too toward in all tyranny, no sooner conceived the manner than consented to the murther: and having a subtile and preventing$^\diamond$ wit, and being very careful how to acquit himself of the matter, he asked Thebion how he should answer Protomachus.

preventing anticipating.

"Tut," said he, "fear not that, for in the enterprise you shall be disguised, and Brasidas here, your true counsellor, shall only take the matter on him and flee into Cusco, where your credit can countenance him against all justice. For yourself, fashion your mind for these few days to please Margarita, to appease Philenia, to further Minecius; seem likewise discontented with your former motions, so shall you rid suspect in them, and be more ready in yourself to effect. Seem now to be more devout to the gods than ever, for this opinion of devotion is a great step to perform any weighty action; for where we offer much to the gods who are most pure, our actions are least suspected; and revenge is better performed in the temple where we pray than in the field where we fight; for the offender in that place trusteth sufficiently to his forces, wherein the defender presumeth too much on his devotion. Tut, the king that nipped Aesculapius[53] by the beard gave instance to those that follow to gripe the enemy by the heart. But, mighty Prince, I must end with etc."

Arsadachus, knowing the cloth by the list,◇ the bill by the item, the steel by the mark,◇ and the work by the words, with a smile commended that which was concluded; and thereupon hasted to court, where finding Margarita, Philenia, and Minecius in the privy◇ garden, he counterfeiting marvellous melancholy, having his coat suitable to his conceit, presented both the ladies with this melancholy,◇ which Minecius overreading most highly commended.

CANZON.◇

My words, my thoughts, my vows,
Have soiled, have forced, have stained,
My tongue, my heart, my brows.

My tongue, my heart, my brows,
Shall speak, shall think, shall smile,
Gainst words, gainst thoughts, gainst vows.

---

list selvage, bordering strip.   **the steel by the mark** the weapon by its manufacturer's stamp or inscription.   **privy** secluded, private.
melancholy a short sad or mournful poem.   *CANZON* song.

For words, for thoughts, for vows,
Have soiled, wronged, and stained,
My tongue, my heart, my brows.

Whereon henceforth I swear.

My words, my thoughts, my vows,
So vain, so vile, so base,
Which brought my tongue, heart, brows
To shame, repulse, disgrace,

Shall evermore forbear
To tempt that brow, that heart, that tongue so holy,
With vows, with thoughts, with words of too great folly.

Margarita, overreading this sonnet, supposed it to be some melancholy report of his pretty, wanton discourses with her, whereupon she spake thus: "Arsadachus, were I the priest to confess you, you should have but small penance, since in love, as Philostratus[54] saith, Cupid dispenseth with an oath, and words are good weapons to win women; but if either of these have defaulted in you, blush not, they shall be borne withal, for as the mole hath four feet and no eyes, so a lover may be borne withal for one mistaking among many* virtues. To be brief, as the logicians say, passion is no more but the effect of action, the one whereof I have gathered in these lines, the other thou must show in thy life."

This said, she ceased, and Philenia blushed. Minecius, to cut off these mute melancholies of his mistress, gave the dagger a new haft,° turning over the leaf to a second discourse, ministering Arsadachus by that means occasion to court Margarita, and himself opportunity to pacify Philenia, who by the carriage of her eye showed the discontent of her mind. In short words, Arsadachus so behaved himself with his mistress, that neither Tiberius[55] for his eye, neither Octavius for his affability, neither Alexander for his scar, nor Cicero[56] for his mole, were so much commended and noted as the young Cuscan was for his behaviour. Lord, how demurely would he look when he thought

haft handle.

most devilishly; how could he fashion himself to haunt there where he did most hate; to smooth choler under colour of friendship, so that Margarita laughed for joy to see his gravity, Minecius admired to behold his demeanour, but Philenia mistrusted his double and sinister subtilties.

In a word, as the day succeedeth the night, and the shutting up of the evening is followed by the serenity of the morning, so time passed so long till the present day approached wherein the marriage was to be solemnized: whereon the emperor, the more to dignify the nuptials, countenanced the marriage with his presence. Thither likewise resembled◊ the flower of the nobility and ladies, among whom Margarita was not least sumptuous, for on that day her apparel was so admirable, her carriage and behaviour so excellent, that had the wisest Cato[57] beheld her, he would have in some part dismissed his stoical severity. Her golden hairs curled in rich knots, and interlaced with rich bands of diamonds and rubies, seemed to stain◊ Apollo's golden bush;[58] environed with her wreath of chrysolites, her eyes like pure carbuncles seemed to smile on the roses of her cheeks, which, consorted with the beauty of the lily, made her beauty more excellent; her eyes, briars like the net of Vulcan[59] polished out of refined threads of fine ebony; her alabaster neck was encompassed with a collar of orient pearl, which seemed to smile on her teeth when she opened her mouth, claiming of them some consanguinity. Her body was apparelled in a fair loose garment of green damask cut upon cloth of tissue, and in every cut was enchased a most curious jewel, wherein all the escapes of Jupiter, the wanton delights of Venus, and the amorous deceits of Cupid were cunningly wrought. Thus attired, she attended the bride, being herself waited on by a troupe of beautiful damsels that day. Arsadachus, though with little devotion, accompanied the emperor, being that day clothed in red cloth of gold, betokening revenge. It were a vain matter to reckon up the order of the bridegroom, the majesty of his favourers, the manner of the

resembled assembled.   **stain** eclipse, deprive of lustre.

lords and ladies, the sumptuousness of the feasts and triumphs, the harmony and music in the temples; sufficeth it, that by the consent of Arsinous, Philenia was betrothed to Minecius, who seeing the day well-nigh spent and the time convenient to depart to his castle, after he had with humble reverence invited the emperor, his daughter, with the other princes the next day to his festival, which he had prepared in his own house, made all things in a readiness and departed, having received by the emperor and Arsinous many rich rewards.

Arsadachus, seeing the long-desired hour of his delights at hand, stole out of the court in great secret to his lodging, where arming himself according as Thebion had given him instructions, and attended by Brasidas and other Cuscans, his trusty followers, he presently◇ posted unto a grove through which the new-married couple should needly pass, where he privily hid himself and his ambush. By that time the bright and glorious light of heaven, abasing himself by degrees, reposed his sweaty steeds in the soft bosom of clear-looking Eurotas;[60] and evening, the fore-messenger of the night, had haled some stars to illuminate the hemisphere, whenas Minecius, in the top of all his felicities, accompanied with his fair Philenia and other followers, without either suspect of treason or other trouble entered the wood, and through the secretness thereof hied them toward their determined abode. But all the way Philenia took no comfort, dreadfully suspecting the subtile dealings of Arsadachus*; and oft she sighed, and often she dropped down lilies on the roses of her face, or rather such sweet tears wherewith the blushing morn enchaseth the soft hyacinth.[61] Minecius, seeing her in these passions, persuaded her unto patience; but even as, according to the opinion of Aristotle,[62] lions, bears, eagles, griffins, and all other birds and beasts whatsoever are then more eager◇ and cruel when they have young ones, so Philenia having now a second care annexed to her own safety, which was for her dear husband, could not cease to perplex herself and to fear for him.

presently immediately.   **eager** fierce.

Long had they not travelled but they discovered the ambush, and the ambush assaulted them: among which Arsadachus greatly disguised, as he that envied the fortunes of Minecius, took hold on the reins of Philenia's palfrey, whilst Thebion and Brasidas, with others, with their naked swords began to assault Minecius and his followers. He that hath seen the falcon seizing his keen talents◇ in the flesh of a silly◇ dove and playing his sharp bill on her soft feathers, might have thought on Arsadachus, who no sooner took hold on her, but pulling the mask from her face, enforced many violent kisses on her soft lips, whilst she exclaiming on the name of Minecius and crying, "Help," repulsed the injuries with her white hands, which were injuriously offered to her delicate face. Minecius, suspecting no more than was true and unable to endure further violence, deemed it greater honour to die in defence of his mistress than behold the impeach of her credit, left his companions who fled and with naked sword smote Arsadachus a mighty blow on the helm, through which he staggered and lost his holdfast; then, renewing his mistress, which was almost dead for fear, he boldly spake thus to Arsadachus.

"Traitor and coward, that in time of peace goest thus armed, and with unjust arms assaultest naked knights; if any spark of honour reign in thee, give me arms and weapons; if thou seek my life, take it from me with courage like a knight, not by treason like a coward; if my love, I pray thee take these eyes from their sight, these hands from their sense, and this tongue from his speech: for whilst the one may see, the other fight, and the third threaten, thou shalt have no part of that wherein my felicity is reposed."

Thus saying, he remounted Philenia; whilst he was thus occupied, Arsadachus, swelling with impatience after he had been animated by his followers, replied thus.

"Soft, amorous Sir, this is no meat for your mowing;[63] you best were rather to fall to your prayers than to use prating, to beseech

talents talons.   **silly** defenceless, helpless.

for life than to seech◇ love: for assure thyself, there is no way with thee but death, nor no love for Philenia but mine."

This said, he gave Minecius a mighty stroke on the head, so that the blood overflowed his costly attire and he fell to the ground. Philenia, half mad with melancholy, leaped from her palfrey to comfort her paramour: and seeing the whole troop of assailants ready to charge her husband, and assured that Arsadachus was the chief of them, with such a piteous look as Venus cast on bleeding Adonis[64] she beheld Minecius, and wiping his wounds with one hand and touching the knees of Arsadachus with the other, she spake thus.

"Ah, Cuscan Prince, though thy face is shadowed, I know thee by these follies; though thy raiments are changed, I judge thee by thy rashness. What seekest thou? If my favour, it is already bequeathed; if revenge, how base is it against a woman; if Minecius' life, how injurious art thou to wrong him that loves thee as his life! Ah, cruel as thou art, yet would thou wert not cruel, thou knowest Chryses' tears could move Achilles,[65] the one proceeding from a seely◇ maid, the other pitied by a princely man; thou knowest that Alexander to Campaspe,[66] Pompey to his prisoner,[67] and other great conquerors have rather showed compassion than victory; and wilt thou, who art equal to all in power, be inferior to all in virtue? Ah, woe is me, poor Philenia, that have planted my affections there where they are watered with warm blood, and heap my compassion there where working tears have no boot. I pray thee, gracious Prince, I pray thee, be gracious; divide not those by murther whom the gods have united by marriage; separate not those souls by death whom the Destinies[68] have appointed to live."

In speaking these words she beheld Minecius, who through the grievousness of his wounds, fell in a swoon; whereupon she, casting off all care of life and hope of comfort, closed her soft lips to his, breathing the balm of her sighs into his breathless body, clapping his pale cheeks with her pretty hands, moisting

seech beg earnestly for.   **seely** innocent, pitiable.

his closed eyes with her crystal tears, so that they who were the very authors of her sorrow gan sigh to see her ceremonies.

"Wilt thou hence," said she, "Minecius? Oh, stay for Philenia; let our souls post together to Elysium[69] that on earth here may not enjoy their happiness; for nothing shall separate me from thee, my love. If thou do banish sight from thine eye, I will drive out blood from my heart; if thy beauty grow pale as nighing death, my cheeks shall pine as seeking death; if thou faint through feebleness of body, I will default through weightiness of discontent; and since we may not live together, we will die together."

With this Minecius roused himself: and Arsadachus, inflamed, replied, "Philenia, there is no ransom of thy husband's life but thy love, nor no means to pacify me but my pleasure of thee. Speak, therefore, and sound the sentence of my delight, or Minecius' destruction."

Which said, he approached to kiss her, whom Minecius, though half dead, began to rescue; and Philenia, half bedlam,◊ enforced herself in these terms: "Traitor disloyal and damned lecher, since neither tears nor terms will satisfy thee, use thy tyranny, for better were it for me to be buried with honour than bedded with infamy. Do therefore thy worst, thou hated of the gods and despised among men, for no sooner shalt thou assail my husband, but thou shalt slay me. Each drop of his blood shall be doubled by mine; and as in life he should have been the shelter of mine honour, so even in death will I be the shield to defend him from the assaults of his enemies. Come therefore, ye murtherers, in growing cruel to me, you will prove pitiful; first take my life, that Minecius, beholding my constancy, may die with more comfort."

Thus cried she out with many tears, and Minecius dissuaded her. But the time passing away, and Arsadachus fearing delays, seeing all hope lost, grew to desperate fury, so that animating his followers, they set on Minecius, who valiantly defended himself. It was a world to see, how during the conflict Philenia bestirred her, letting no blow slip without the ward of her body, lying between the sword of the enemy for her husband's safety,

bedlam mad.

crying out on the heavens till she was well-nigh hoarse with crying. At last Minecius lacking blood, Philenia breath, both of them entangled arm in arm, fell down dead, leaving the memory of their virtues to be eternized in all ages. Arsadachus, seeing the tragedies performed, not without some sighs which compassion extorted from him, as strokes do fire out of hard flint, he presently sent Brasidas away, as it was concluded, attended by those Cuscans that followed him in the enterprise, and he with Thebion speedily posted to their lodging, both undiscovered and unsuspected.

By this, such as attended Minecius to his castle had with speedy flight entered the court of Arsinous, who, certified◊ of his daughter's danger, advised the emperor, and presently with certain armed soldiers posted on to the rescouse.◊ Meanwhile, Protomachus made search through all the court for such as were absent; and they that were appointed to the action, entering Arsadachus' chamber, found him in his fox sleep,◊ wherethrough the emperor being advertised, gan little suspect him. In like sort found they Thebion; only Brasidas was missing. In the meanwhile, Arsinous, having attained the place of the conflict, found both the murthered bodies sweltered in their bloods: whereupon falling from his horse in great fury, he thus exclaimed on Fortune.

"Oh, Fortune, well art thou called the enemy of virtue, since thou neither favourest such as deserve well, nor destroyest those that perform ill; for hadst thou not been partial, my daughter's chastity had prevented her death, and her murtherers' cruelty had been their own confusion. Woe is me that have lost my flower in the bud, my hope in the ear,◊ and my harvest in the blossom. Ah, my dear Philenia, dear wert thou to me, that bought thee with much care and have lost thee with more: dear wert thou unto me, who hast cost me many broken sleeps to bring thee up, many careful thoughts to bestow thee, more fatherly tears to prevent thy overthrow, and now having reared the fortress of my delights, the tempest of injurious Fortune hath destroyed it.

certified informed.   **rescouse** rescue.   **fox sleep** pretended sleep.
the ear i.e., of corn.

Woe is me that am careful to publish my pains and negligent to seek remedy; fond am I to defy Fortune from whom I cannot fly. Ah, Arsinous, weep not her that may not be recalled with tears, but seek to revenge her; show thyself rather fatherly in act than effeminate in tears."

Which said, he governed himself, causing the dead bodies honourably to be covered and conveyed with him to his castle, where within a temple erected to Chastity, he reared a fair tomb of white marble, wherein with the general tears of the emperor and his whole court these two faithful lovers were entombed, and over their graves thus written:

> Virtue is dead, and here she is enshrined,
>> Within two lifeless bodies late deceased:
> Beauty is dead, and here is Faith assigned
>> To weep her wrack, who when these died first ceased,
>>> Pity was dead when Tyranny first slew them,
>>> And Heaven enjoys their souls, tho' Earth doth rue them.

> Since Beauty then and Virtue are departed,
> And Faith grows faint to weep in these their fading,
> And virtuous Pity kind and tender-hearted,
>> Died to behold fierce Furies' fell invading.

>> Vouchsafe, ye Heavens, that Fame may have in keeping
>> Their happy and thrice-blessed names, for whom
>> Both Virtue, Beauty, Pity died with weeping,
>> And Faith is closed in this marble tomb.

This register of his love did Arsinous with many tears write upon the tomb of his deceased son-in-law and daughter, who had no sooner furnished the funerals, but Phidias, a page of Philenia's, who during the mortal debate and bloody massacre had hid himself in a thicket and overheard the whole discourse of Arsadachus, repaired to the court, who calling Arsinous aside, with piteous tears discoursed unto him the whole tragedy in such ruthful manner, as that it was hard to say whether the lad in bewraying◇ it or the father in hearing it were more compassionate. The old man certified the truth, though scarce able yet smothered his griefs till opportunity offered, suffering the emperor, like a wise man, to follow his own course, who the next morning assembling his nobility, forgot not Arsadachus, who, making semblance to have but new intelligence of the murther of Minecius and his love, repaired to the court in mourning apparel and being present when the matter was debated, seemed to weep bitterly, crying out on the emperor for justice, exclaiming on the iniquity of time, the cruelty of men, and tyranny of love. Protomachus was not a little pleased herewith, neither was Margarita aggrieved to hear it, but Arsinous boiled in choler to see it. At last it was found out by a scarf which Brasidas had let fall, and was after taken up by one of those who fled, that he was at the murther, whereupon his absence was sufficient to convict him.

And Arsadachus, called forth to answer for him in that he was his attendant, spake thus: "Noble Emperor, the gods that have placed thee in thy kingdom shall bear me witness how I grieve this accident, and willingly would revenge it, and since my follower to my defame, hath, as it is supposed, been a principal, vouchsafe me, noble Emperor, licence for a time to depart to Cusco, where I will both discharge my choler, purge my grief, and be so revenged of Brasidas, who, as I hear, is fled and by the token is guilty, as all the world shall ring of the justice and rid me of suspicion."

The emperor, not hearing one that dared say his letters should suffice, endeavouring himself to seek the confederates, and because by his looks he perceived some discontents in Arsadachus, he sought all the means he could to please him. And remembering himself that those good deeds which are done to our self beloved are esteemed as to our self, he highly promoted Thebion, thinking thereby to win the heart of Arsadachus, so that he pretermitted◇ no consultations where Thebion was not

bewraying disclosing.   **pretermitted** omitted.

chief, neither bestowed benefits wherein he had no part. The young prince, measuring all this according to the corruption of his nature, supposed these favours were but to sound him and that Thebion, being won by benefits, would easily consent to bewray◇ him, whereupon he conceived a deadly hate against him, and persevered it so long till he effected it in this manner to his death. For knowing that Margarita dearly loved him, aiming all her fashions to his fancies, her behaviours to his humours, he began anew to cloak◇ with her, showing her so undoubted signs of assured affection that she seemed in a paradise of pleasure to see his pliantness, and having with sweet words trained her to his lure, he attended such an occasion, as that he found her alone walking in the privy garden in her meditations, for those that love much meditate oft, where nighing her with a courtly salute, he thus found her affection.

"Fair Princess, if either my unfeigned love have any force or your virtuous nature true compassion, I hope both my sorrows shall be pitied and my discontents succoured."

"Why, what aggrieveth my dear Lord?" said Margarita, and heartily she sighed in saying so. "Is either our court unpleasant, our entertainment unworthy, our ladies unapt to work your delights? Believe me, good Prince, if Mosco cannot suffice to please you, Europe and the world shall be sought to satisfy you."

"Kind words, good Madam," said Arsadachus, "act and silence must content me, which if you will under the faith of a noble and famous princess promise me, I shall be beadsman to pray for your happiness and rest yours unfeigned in all service and loyalty."

Margarita having gotten such an opportunity to please him both vowed and revowed all secrecy, swearing, although it were with the hazard of her life, to do whatsoever him best liked and conceal whatso it please him to discover, so great is the simplicity of women who are soon led where they most like. Arsadachus, finding the iron hot, thought good to strike;[70] the fruit ripe, began

bewray betray.   **cloak** pretend, dissemble.

to gather; the flower springing, ceased not to water: and thus began to work her.

"True it is, Madam, that where love hath supremacy all other affections attend on it, so that neither the eye beholdeth, neither the scent smelleth, nor the ear heareth, neither the tongue speaketh anything but is to the honour of the best beloved. This find I true in myself, who, since I surrendered you the fort of my fancy, find my delights metamorphosed into yours; yea,* so much am I tied unto you, as that danger which either attempteth or toucheth you, or any of yours, wholly attainteth me. The proof whereof you may perceive in this, that having heard through my entire acquaintance with Thebion a certain resolved determination in him to make your father away, by reason of his familiar access to his majesty every morning, I could not choose but discover his drift unto you, sweet Princess, whose dangers must needly second your father's subversion."

"Thebion!" said Margarita. "Alas, my Lord, what reason should move him hereunto, since no one is more favoured by my father than he? Can favour possibly be requited with such falsehood?"

"Doubt you it?" said Arsadachus. "Why, Madam, where is greater treason than there where is least mistrust? Under the clear crystal lurketh the mortal worm,[71] under the green leaf the greedy serpent,[72] and in fairest bosoms are falsest hearts.[73] Think not that liberality hath any power in depraved minds, for whereas the thoughts hant◇ after empery, hemmed are all* supposes,◇ faith dieth, truth is exiled, *nulla fides regni*.◇ If you have read histories, you shall find that they soonest have supplanted their princes who have been least suspected, as may appear by Gyges[74] and others.* Cast therefore hence, my dear Lady, all thought of excuse, and bethink you of prevention; for it is greater wisdom to see and prevent than to hear and neglect. Thebion hath conspired and doth conspire, resolving with himself to usurp the empire,

---

hant seize, grasp.   **hemmed are all supposes** all hopes are obstructed.   *nulla fides regni* royal power distrusted.

murther Protomachus, banish you; all which I have learned of him, dissembling my affections towards you and soothing him in his corruptions; yea, so far have I brought him, and so near have I wrought it, that I can assure you tomorrow morning is the last of your father's life, unless you prevent it."

"Alas, my Lord," said Margarita weeping, "how may this be?"

"Thus, my sweet love, and thus it is concluded," quoth Arsadachus. "You know he hath every morning of late private access unto your father's chamber, where being alone with him and the unsuspected emperor in his bed, he hath resolved with his dagger to stab him to the heart; which secret, since the gods have opened unto me, I think good to discover unto thee, my dear heart, the means to prevent, which shall the more easily be performed if thus you work it. No sooner let the day appear, but in the morning betimes enter you your father's chamber, where, after you have saluted him, you may seem to utter this: that in a dream this night you were mightily troubled about his majesty, and so troubled that you thought Thebion, entering his chamber with a hidden poniard, stabbed him to the heart."

"But what needs these circumlocutions or delays," quoth Margarita, "if the treason be so manifest? My Lord, if it please you, I will discover it presently and plainly."

"The gods forbid," said Arsadachus, "that my desires should be so hindered, for, my noble Princess, the delay I seek, and the order I prescribe you, is rather to ground your father's affection towards me and get the credit of this service than otherwise. Yea, the love I bear thee, sweet Lady" (with that he sighed and sealed it with a kiss) "for having by this means won favour, both our fortunes shall be bettered, our marriage hasted, and our fames magnified."

Margarita, poor princess, supposing all that gold that glistered, yielded easy consent; whereupon, after many amorous promises, the young prince took his leave, willing her to be careful in the morning and to leave the rest of the affairs to his faithfulness, and thus they parted.

But mark the nature of malice, which as the poet describeth is sleepless, restless, and insatiate, for Arsadachus, being departed from Margarita and earnestly bent on his revenge, sought out Thasilides, the page of Thebion, whom he so cunningly wrought with oaths, gifts, and gold, that he made him both promise and practise the means to put a certain schedule◇ into the pocket of his master's gown which he usually wore, the which he himself had written* and wherein he behaved himself with such art, as that he had not only counterfeited Thebion's hand, but also the names of all such as either he thought his favourites or else likely to thwart his proceedings in court, among which he forgot not Ctesides, a grave counsellor of the emperor's, who the day before was very earnest with Protomachus to marry his daughter, showing him evident reasons of Arsadachus' counterfeiting. All these things falling out according to his own devise and fantasy, he sought out Thebion that night, whom he used with the greatest familiarity that might be; and to insinuate the more into his favour, he bestowed on him a poniard, whose pummel◇ was a bright carbuncle, the haft unicorn's horn, a jewel which Thebion had long time greatly desired, praying him of all loves to wear it for his sake, and since he was in such estimation to continue him in the good grace of the emperor. Thebion, made proud to be entreated and presented by so high a prince, promised both to wear his gift and to win him favour. Whereupon, since the night was far spent, Arsadachus repaired to his lodging, Thebion to his rest.

But vain is the hope that dependeth on the next day and those worldly honours that do wait on this life; for the one is prevented oftentimes by injurious Fortune, the other altered by our overweening mistrusting words, actions, and desires, and shall manifestly appear in the sequel of this history. For no sooner gan bright day to chase away black darkness and the stooping stars do homage to the rising sun, but Margarita arose, apparelling herself freshly like May in a gown of green sendal◇

schedule list.   **pummel** pommel.   **sendal** thin rich silken material, fine linen.

embroidered with all kind of flowers in their native colours, and remembering herself of the affair she had in hand, she, under the conduct of Love, who is both a cunning dissembler and nice flatterer, hasted to her father's chamber, and humbly admitted to the presence of the emperor by the grooms that attended him, with a trembling hand and a bashful countenance, spreading the mute oratory of her tears upon her blushing cheeks, she awoke him.

Protomachus, amazed to see his daughter's sudden access and sad countenance, began thus: "How now, my dear Margarita, what, hath Love awaked you this morning, threatening you with some apparent sorrow to make your after-good indeed more savoury? Why hangeth your countenance? Why tremble your limbs? What moveth this your amazedness? Sweet maiden, tell thy father."

"Ah, my Lord," said Margarita, "it is love indeed that disturbs me, but not that love that is painted with feathers, wanton looks, that love that whispereth affections in ladies' ears and whetteth women's wits, making the eye traitor to the heart and the heart betrothed to the eye; but that love which was engendered by nature, ordained by the heavens, attired by reverence and duty and tired with nothing but death, that love" (and so speaking she wept) "hath awaked me to forewarn you."

Protomachus, somewhat urged by these tears, roused himself on his pillow and began more intentively to listen, asking her what had happened.

"Ah, dear Father," said she, "this night that is past I was greatly troubled with a grievous dream; methought I saw Thebion, a man in high authority in your court, attended by many insolent rebels who violently brake open your Majesty's privy chamber, murther* you in your bed and dispossess* me of my heritage. Methought even then you cried unto me, 'Ah, Margarita, help me!' and I with outcries calling for rescouse, Arsadachus came in hastily, who with his sword bereft Thebion of life and me of fear."

"And so you waked and found all false," quoth the emperor. "Tut, dote not on dreams; they are but fancies:[75] and since I see, sweet daughter, that you are so troubled by night, I will shortly find out a young prince to watch you, who shall drive away these night-sprights by his prowess." Thus spake Protomachus smiling, yet smothered he suspect° in his heart: for such as have much suspect much.

No sooner were these discourses finished, but Arsadachus, knowing how to take his time, hastily approached the emperor's chamber, where intimating some occasion of high import, he required to speak with Protomachus, and was presently let in. The emperor, conceiving new suspicions upon this second assault, began to misdeem:° and seeing Arsadachus with ghastly looks entering the chamber, was ready to speak unto him whenas the young Cuscan prevented him saying:

"The gods be blessed, noble Emperor, that have by their foresight rid me of fear and reft you of danger; for sore have I feared lest your Majesty should have perished before you had been advertised.° Alas, why in such dangers are you unattended upon, when the foe is at the door? Why is not the guard in a readiness? Ah, royal Moscovite, rouse thee and arise, and honour the sequel° of the greatest treason that ever was contrived."

"Why, what tidings bringeth Arsadachus?" said Protomachus.

"Thus, mighty Prince," said he, "yesternight very late when I entered Thebion's chamber unawares, I found his page, his master being absent, laying certain waste papers out of his pocket upon his table, perusing which, as I was accustomed by reason of the near* familiarity between us, I found one among the rest where, alas that subjects should be so seditious, there was a conspiracy signed by Thebion, Ctesides, and others whose names I remember not, to make your Mightiness away, and Thebion to enjoy the crown. The manner to execute their stratagem was when you least suspected, this morning, at which time Thebion, by reason of his near familiarity and access to you, should enter

suspect suspicion.   **misdeem** suspect, mistrust.   **advertised** warned.   **honour the sequel** regard the consequence or conclusion.

your chamber and murther you. This paper, when I had over-read, I laid aside, making semblance of no suspicion, resolving this morning early to signify the whole unto your Majesty, whose life is my liberty, whose happiness is my honour, whose death were my utter ruin and detriment."

"Thebion a traitor?" quoth Protomachus. "Are my favours then so smally regarded? Is my courtesy rewarded with such cursedness? Well, Arsadachus," said he, "happy art thou in bewraying it, and unfortunate he and his confederates in attempting it, for they all shall die."

This said, he presently attired himself, laying certain of his trustiest gentlemen in guard behind the tapestry of his privy closet, expecting the hour of a most cruel revenge: whenas suddenly Thebion knocked at the door and was presently admitted, who had scarcely said, "God save the Emperor," but even in the bending of his knees he was thrust through by Arsadachus, and the others* of the guard, hearing the broil, came and mangled him in pieces, casting the residue to the emperor's lions, according as he had appointed. Protomachus, grudging at the sudden death of Thebion, began to chide Arsadachus for his haste, saying that it was inconvenient for a subject to be punished before he were convicted.

"Convicted?" said Arsadachus. "Why, doth your Grace suspect° his guiltiness? Behold," said he, drawing out the poniard which Thebion had at his back, "the instrument that should have slain you. See," said he, taking the schedule out of his pocket, "the confederacy to betray you. And should such a wretch live then to justify? No, mighty Emperor, my soul abhors it; the care I have of you will not suffer it; the love I bear Margarita will not endure it."

The emperor, overreading the writing and seeing the poniard, gave credible belief, and with tears of joy embracing Arsadachus, he said thus: "Ah, my son, the gods have blessed us in sending us such a friend, who hath saved me from imminent danger and will make me fortunate by marriage. Hold, take thee," said he,

suspect doubt.

"my Margarita, and with her enjoy my empire; and more, take thou my love, which is so rooted in me toward thee, that death may not untwine it."

Arsadachus thanked the emperor for this favour and recomforted Margarita with sweet words, being almost dead to see the stratagem passed. Meanwhile the emperor gave present direction to hang all the other conspirators and put them to other tortures, who presently, without knowing why or licence to answer, were tyrannously executed. So great is the tyranny of princes which are subject to light belief and led by subtile suggestions.

The rumour of this accident spread through the court, moved sundry imaginations in men's minds; some praised Arsadachus, some suspected the practice, all feared; for whereas justice sleepeth being overborne with tyranny, the most secure have cause to fear. Among the rest, Arsinous wept bitterly, knowing in himself the virtue of Ctesides, and remembering him of the murther of his dear Philenia, he could not cease but, well-nigh bedlam,◊ to cry out on the heavens, whose tragedy we must now prosecute, and leave Arsadachus and his Margarita to their merry conceits and discourses.

Protomachus, after that this late treason had been discovered, began to be more wary, to keep greater guard, and to use Arsinous and the rest of the nobility with less familiarity, who, good old man, having before time been shrewdly hurt, took this unkindness to the heart, for where greatest love is, there unkindness is most grievous. For that cause almost desperate, he sought out the emperor, and finding opportunity, he, humbling him on his knees, began thus:

"As Trajan,[76] dread Monarch, was commended in Rome for hearing poor men's complaints, so art thou condemned in Mosco for shutting thy gates against all kind of suitors, so as nowadays thou hearest by others' ears, workest by others' hands, and speakest by others' mouths, wherethrough justice is made a nose of wax warmed and wrought according to all men's pleasures[77] and

bedlam mad.

the poor are left to complain, the which the gods, if thou repent not, will shortly punish in thee. Believe me, good Emperor, such as shut their gates against their subjects cause them not to open their hearts willingly to obey them; and they that nourish fear in their bosoms without cause make themselves guilty of some crime by their suspect. Wherefore fliest thou the sight of those that love thee, shutting thy ears lest thou hear those complaints that have already deaffed the heavens for equity? O Prince, look abroad, it behooveth thee; do justice, for it becometh thee, and hear old Arsinous, a hapless father. Father do I say, being thus robbed of my children? Nay, a desolate caitiff, and do me right. That justice becometh thee, mark these reasons: Homer, desirous to exalt it, could not say more but to call kings the children of the god Jupiter, and not for the naturality they have, but for the office of justice which they minister.[78] Plato saith that the chiefest gift that the gods have bestowed on man is justice;[79] that therefore thou may seem rightly descended of the gods, vouchsafe me audience, and to the end thou may boast thyself to enjoy the least gift of the gods, succour me. Thou knowest my Philenia is slain, but by whose hands thou knowest not; thou hearest Minecius is murthered, but by whom thou enquirest not; thou hast rubbed the gall,[80] but not recured the wound; thou hast tempered the medicine, but hast not ministered it; yea, thou hast refreshed the memory of my griefs very often, but remedied them never. Three months are past since thou hast made inquiry of my daughter's death, and she that I nourished up twenty years and better is forgotten of all but her old father, lamented of none but Arsinous, and can be revenged by none but Protomachus. O Emperor, I hear their discontented grief crying out in mine ears and appealing to thee by my tongue for justice; methinks bloodless Minecius standeth by thy throne upbraiding thee of his services and convicting thee of ingratitude. Philenia crieth justice, Protomachus, justice, not against Brasidas, who was but agent, but against Arsadachus, the principal, that wretched Arsadachus, who in her lifetime assayed to move her to lust and wrought her death in that she would not consent to his lust; against Arsadachus, the viper nourished in your bosom[81] to poison your own progeny, the locust dallied in Margarita's lap to deprive her of life. Ah, banish such a bewitched race of the Cuscans; I mean not out of your kingdom, but out of life; for he deserveth not to behold the heavens that conspireth against the gods; root out that bloodthirsty youngman,⁰ root out that murtherer, root out that monster from the face of nature, that the poor deceased ghosts may be appeased and their poor father pacified. Show thyself a prince now, Protomachus; the surgeon is known, not in curing a green wound, but in healing a grievous fistula; the warrior is known, not by conquering a little village, but a great monarchy; and a prince is perceived in preventing a capital pestilence, not a private prejudice. That I accuse not Arsadachus wrongfully, behold my witnesses:" (which said, he brought out Philenia's page, who confidently and constantly avowed all he had told his master in the presence of the emperor) "wherefore, noble Monarch, have compassion of me, and by punishing this tragic tyranny make way to thine own eternity."

Protomachus, hearing this accusation, was sorely moved, now thinking all truth which Arsinous had said by reason of that virtue he had approved in him in times past, now deeming it false, in that Arsadachus, as he supposed, had lately and so luckily preserved him from death. For which cause, calling the young prince unto him, he urged him with the murther before the old man and the young lad his accuser, who shook off all their objections with such constancy that it was to be wondered.

"What saith he, Protomachus, am I, who have lately manifested my zeal in saving your life, made subject to the detraction of an old doting imagination with his prattling minister? I hope your Majesty," saith he, "measureth not my credit so barely, nor will overslip this injury so slightly,* since you know that when the murther was done I was in my bed; when the tragedy was published, I was the first that prosecuted the revenge; and more, the friendship twixt Minecius and me should acquit me of this

youngman used insultingly to mean servant or yeoman.

suspicion. But it may be that this is some set match of Thebion's confederates that seek my death, which if it shall be here countenanced, I will return to Cusco, where I dare assure myself against all such subtilties."

This said, Arsadachus angrily departed, for which cause Protomachus, fearing his speedy flight, sent Margarita to pacify him; and causing the tongue of the guiltless lad to be cut out and his eyes to be pricked out with needles, both which were guilty, as he said, the one of pretended seeing, the other of lewd uttering. He banished the old Duke of Volgradia, who, for all his faithful services had this lamentable recompense, and removed himself, his court, and daughter to Mosco, where we will leave him a while.

Arsinous thus banished from the court, after he had furnished himself of necessaries convenient for his journey, travelled many a weary walk towards the deserts of Russia, crying out and exclaiming on the heavens for justice; his hoary locks and bushy beard he carelessly suffered to grow, like to those Moscoes who are in disgrace with their emperors, seeming rather a savage man than a civil magistrate, as in time past he had been. Long had he not travelled among many barren rocks and desolate mountains, but at last he arrived in a solitary grove encompassed with huge hills, from the tops whereof, through the continual frosts that fell, a huge river descended, which circling about a rock of white marble made it, as it were, an island, but that to the northward there was a pretty passage of twelve foot broad, decked with ranks of trees, which gave a solitary access to the melancholy mansion; mansion I call it, for in the huge rock was there cut out a square and curious chamber, with fine loops° to yield light, hewn thereout, as might be supposed, by some discontented wood-god wedded to wretchedness. Here Arsinous seated himself, resolving to spend the residue of his days in studies, praying to the gods continually for revenge; and to the end, if happily any should pass that way, that his deep sorrow might be

loops openings.

discovered, he with a puncheon[◊] of steel in a table of white alabaster engraved this over the entrance of his cave:

Domus doloris.[◊]

Who seeks the cave* where horrid Care doth dwell,
  That feeds on sighs and drinks of bitter tears:
Who seeks in life to find a living hell,
Where he that lives all living joy forbears:
  Who seeks that grief that Grief itself scarce knows it,
  Here let him rest, this cave shall soon disclose it.

As is the mite unto the sandy seas,
  As is the drop unto the ocean streams,
As to the orb of heaven a silly pease,[◊]
  As is the lamp to burning Tichius'⁸² beams:
Even such is thought that vainly doth endeavour
  To think that* Care lives here, or count it ever.

Here Sorrow, Plague, Despair, and fierce Suspect,
  Here Rage, here Jealousy, here cursed Spite,
Here Murther, Famine, Treason, and Neglect,
  Have left their stings to plague a woeful wight
    That lives within this tomb of discontent
    Yet loathes that life that Nature hath him lent.

In this solitary and uncouth receptacle Arsinous lived, turning off[◊] his steed to shift for food amid the forest, and ascending every day to the height of the rock, he shed many salt tears before the image of Minecius and Philenia, whose pictures he had brought with him from his castle and erected there. And after his devotions to the gods for revenge and to the ghosts to manifest his grief, he accustomed himself to walk in that desolate coppice[◊] of wood, where sighing, he recounted the unkindness of his prince, the wretchedness of his thoughts and life, melting away in such melancholy as the trees were amazed to behold it

puncheon pointed chisel.   *Domus doloris* House of pain.   **pease** pea.   **turning off** sending away.   **coppice** thicket.

and the rocks wept their springs to hear it, as the Poet[83] saith; on
a desolate and leafless oak he wrote this:

> Thine age and wasteful tempests thee,
> Mine age and wretched sorrows me defaced,
> Thy sap by course of time is blent,◇
> My sense by care and age is spent and chased.
> Thy leaves are fallen away to dust,
> My years are thralled by time unjust.
> Thy boughs the winds have borne away,
> My babe's fierce murther did decay.
> Thy roots are firmed in the ground,
> My roots are rent, my comforts drowned; showers cherish
> Thy barren bosom in the field; I perish,
> Since nothing may me comfort yield.
>
> Storms, showers, age wear, waste, daunt, and make thee dry;
> Tears, cares, age, ice waste, wring, and yet live I.

In these melancholies leave we the desolate Duke of Volgradia till occasion be ministered to remember him, and return we
to Margarita and her lover. Arsadachus, resiant◇ now in Mosco,
whom Protomachus, by reason of the forepassed tragedies,
thought to refresh with some pleasant triumphs: for which cause
he proclaimed jousts* throughout all the empire, assembling all
the dukes, lords, and governors of his provinces to dignify the
open court he meant to keep. Thither also repaired all the fair
ladies of Moscovia; among the rest Margarita, as one of most
reckoning, made not the least expense, for whatsoever, either
to dignify her person or to set out her beauty or to present her
beloved, could either be bought from India, trafficked in Europe,
or merchanded in Asia was sought out, and especially against the
day of the tilt and tourney, at which time, like a second Diana,[84]
having her goldilocks tied up with loose chains of gold and diamonds, her body apparelled in cloth of silver, over which she had

blent rendered turbid, spoiled (*OED* cites line as example: *blend*, v.², 2.).
resiant resident.

cast a veil of black and golden tinsel through which her beauty appeared as doth the bright Phoebus[85] in a summer's morning, leaving our hemisphere, our fair Hecate[86] chasing away baleful darkness with her bright beams, she was mounted on a high arch of triumph covered with cloth of gold.

Near unto her sat her old father in his sovereign majesty; about her a hundred damsels in white cloth of tissue, overcast with a veil of purple and green silk loosely woven, carrying gold and silver censers in their hands, from whence issued most pleasant odours, such as in the pride of the year breathe along the coast of Arabia Felix[87] or drop* from the balmy trees of the East.

Thus seated, the challengers with their several devices◇ entered the tilt-yard, each striving to exceed other in expense and excellence, whose trumpets cleared the air with their melody. After these, the defendants entered, among whom Arsadachus was chief, whose pomp in that exceeded all others I have seen, and the others* are ordinarily matched in our courts of Christendom, I will set down unto you. First, before the triumph entered the tilt-yard, there was a whole volley of a hundred cannons shot off; the noise whereof somewhat appeased,◇ a hundred knights having their horses*, arms, crests, feathers, and each part of them covered with green cloth of gold, with lances of silver, trotted about the yard, making their steeds keep footing according to the melodious sound of an orb, which by cunning of man and wonderful art was brought into the presence of the prince, which whilst it continually turned, presented all the shapes of the twelve signs,◇ dancing as it were to the harmony which the enclosed music presented them. After these marched a hundred pages apparelled in white cloth of silver with crownets of silver on their heads, leading each of them in their right hands a brave courser trapped in a caparison◇ purple and gold, in their left a scutcheon◇ with the image of the princess in the same. After these, Arsadachus in his triumphant chariot drawn by four white unicorns entered the

devices emblematic figures, usually with mottoes.   **appeased** diminished.   **signs** i.e., of the Zodiac.   **caparison** harness and/or apparel.   **scutcheon** shield bearing a coat of arms.

tilt-yard, under his seat the image of Fortune, which he seemed to spurn, with this posy,◊ *Quid haec*?;◊ on his right hand Envy, whom he frowned on, by her this posy, *Nec haec;*◊ on his left hand the portraiture of Cupid, by whom was written this posy, *Si hic;*◊ over his head the picture of Margarita with this mot, *Sola haec.*◊ These arms were of beaten gold far more curious than those that Thetis gave her Achilles before Troy[88] or Meriones bestowed on Ulysses when he assaulted Rhesus,[89] being full of flames and half-moons of sapphires, chrysolites, and diamonds. In his helm he bore his mistress's favour, which was a sleeve of salamander's skin richly perfumed and set with rubies. In this sort he presented him before the emperor and his daughter, who was not a little tickled with delight to behold the excellency of his triumph. The trumpets were sounded and the judges seated, Arsadachus mounted himself on a second Bucephalus[90] and, taking a strong lance, overbore Stilconos, the Earl of Garavia, breaking his arm in the fall; in the second encounter he overthrew Asaphus of Tamirae horse and man; neither ceased he till twenty* of the bravest men-at-arms were unhorsed by his hardiness. All this while with blushes and sweet smiles Margarita favoured every encountery,◊ seeming with the eagerness of eye to break every push of the lance that levelled at Arsadachus. His races being at end, Plicotus of Macarah entered the lists, who behaved himself like a brave prince, conquering as much with the sword as the other with the lance.

In this sort, this day, the next, and that which followed were overpassed, wherein Arsadachus* made evident proofs of great hope: so that Protomachus at the last cried out to his other princes: "See, ye Moscovites, the hope of the empire, whose endings, if they prove answerable to his beginnings, Europe may perhaps wonder, but never equal."

posy short verse.   *Quid haec* What is this (woman)?.   *Nec haec*
Not this (woman).   *Si hic* If here (or, this man).   *Sola haec* This
(woman) alone.   **encountery** shock of encounter.

The third day being ended and the honours bestowed on them that best deserved them, the emperor in the chiefest of the festival caused the tables to be removed and the music to be called for, thinking by this means to give love more fuel, in hope it should burn more brighter; whereupon the princes betook them to dance, and Arsadachus as chief led Margarita the measures.[◊]

And after the first pause, began thus with her: "Princess," said he, "by what means might love be discovered if speech were not?"

"By the eyes, my Lord," said she, "which are the keys of desire, which both open the way for Love to enter and lock him up when he is let in."

"How hap then," said he, "that Cupid among the poets is feigned blind?"

"In that, my Lord," quoth she, "he was masked to poets' memory, and you know that falcons, against they fly, are hooded to make them more fierce and clearer sighted; and so perhaps was Love, which was blindfold at first, in the opinion of poets, who never could see him rightly until they felt his eye in their hearts."

"Why sticketh he his eye in their hearts? I had thought, Madam, it had been his arrow," said Arsadachus.

"Why, his eyes are his arrows," quoth the princess, "or I mistake his shooting; for the last time he levelled at me he hit me with a look."

"I beshrew[◊] him," said the prince and then sounded the next measure, when Arsadachus continued his discourse in this manner: "Madam, if Love wound by the eye, how healeth he?"

"By the eye, my Lord," said she, "having the property of Achilles' sword[91] to quell and recure.[◊]"

"Then, gracious Lady," quoth the prince, "since Love hath wounded me by your looks, let them recover me; otherwise shall I blame both Love's cruelty and your judgment."

the measures in the dance.   **beshrew** invoke evil upon, curse.
recure restore to health.

Margarita replied thus: "Great Prince, if mine eyes have procured your offence, I will pluck them out for their folly; and if Love have shot them for his shafts, I beshrew him, for the last time they looked on you, they left my heart in you."

"In me, Mistress?" quoth Arsadachus.

"Yea, in you, my Lord," quoth Margarita.

"Can you then live heartless?" said the prince.

"Yea, since hopeless," replied she.

This said, the music cut off their merry talk; and the sudden disease of the emperor brake up the pastimes. Whereupon every prince and peer, lord and knight, taking leave of their mistresses, betook them to their rest. Only Margarita, in whose bosom Love sat enthroned, in whose heart affections kept their watch, being laid in her bed, fared like Orlando sleeping in that bed his Angelica had lain with Medor;[92] each feather was a fur[◊] bush; now turned she, now tossed she, now grovelling on her face, now bolt upright, hammering ten thousand fancies in her head; at last, breaking out into a bitter sigh, she began thus.

"Alas, unkind Love, that seasonest thy delights with delays, why givest thou not poor ladies as great patience to endure as penance in their durance? Why are not thy affections like the figs of India, which are both grafted and green of themselves, and no sooner sprung to a blossom but spread in the bud? Why givest thou Time swift wings to begin thee, and so long and slow ere he seize thee? I beseech thee, Love," (oh how she sighed when she besought him) "proine[◊] thou the wings of Time lest he punish me, for thy delay is so great that my disease is unsufferable. Alas, poor wretch that I am, why prate I to Love? Or pray I for relief, being assured that the beginning of Love's knowledge is the ending of human reason; love is a passion that may not be expressed, conceived beyond conceit, and extinguished beside custom; stay thy mind, therefore, foolish Margarita, for it began first in thee beyond expectation, and must end in thee beyond hope. For, as there are no reasons but

fur furze, an evergreen shrub.   **proine** prune.

nature to prove why the swan hateth the sparrow,[93] the eagle the trochilus,[94] the ass the bee,[95] and the serpent the hog,[96] so likewise in love there can no cause but nature be alleged, either of his sudden flourish or vehement fall, his speedy waxing and slow waning. Temper thyself, therefore, though Love tempt thee, and wait thine opportunity; for the wanton, if you fawn on him, will fly you, and setting light by him will leap upon you. Fond that I am, why talk I thus idly, seeming with the prating soldier to discourse of the fortress I have never conquered, and of the fancies I shall never compass? Why doth not Arsadachus smile on me? As who knoweth not that the aspis◇ tickleth when she pricketh, and poisons that are delightful in the swallow are deadly in the stomach? Why hath he not courted me these five months? Fond that I am, the more near am I to my fall; for as the philosopher saith, men are like to the poison of scorpions, for as the sting of the one killeth in three days, so the pride and cruelty of the other quelleth a kind heart in less than a moment. Woe is me; I had rather need Philoxenus[97] to cure me of love by his lays than Anippus to continue love in me; better were it for me to hear Terpander[98] play than Arsadachus preach."

In these thoughts and this speech Love sealed up her eyes till on the morrow; but what she dreamed I leave that to you ladies to decide, who, having dallied with Love, have likewise been acquainted with his dreams. On the morrow, the day being far spent and the court replenished with attendants, Margarita arose, and scarcely was she attired but that a messenger came unto her in the behalf of the Earl Asaphus, beseeching her presence to grace his feast that day, for that he had entertained and invited Arsadachus and the best princes and ladies in court, by the emperor's consent, to make a merry festival; whereunto Margarita quickly condescended and thought every hour two till noontide, at which time, royally attended, she repaired to Asaphus' house, where were assembled of princes Arsadachus, Plicotus, and Stilconos; of ladies, beside herself, Calandra, Ephania, and Gerenia. All these Asaphus entertained heartily, placing them

aspis asp.

according to their degrees, and feasted them with as great pomp and pleasure as he could imagine.

But when he perceived their appetites quelled with delights, their ears cloyed with music, and their eyes filled with beholding, he, being a prince of high spirit, began thus: "Princes and Ladies, I have invited you to my house, not to entertain you with the pomp of Persia or the feast of Heliogabalus,[99] but to dine you according to the direction of the physicians, which is to let you rise with an appetite, which both whetteth your memories and helpeth your stomachs; and for that the after-banquet may as well please your humours as the former appeased your hunger, I must beseech you to rise from this place and repair unto another, where, because the weather is hot and the time unfit for exercise, we will spend the time in pleasant discourse, feeding our fancies with pleasant talk as we have feasted our fast with curious cates.°

To this motion all the assembly easily consented, in that for the most part they had been buzzing in their ears and baiting their hearts, whereupon he brought them into a fair arbor covered with roses and honeysuckles, paved with camomile, pinks, and violets, guarded° with two pretty crystal fountains on every side, which made the place more cool and the soil more fruitful. They all being entered this arbor, Asaphus, being both learned and pleasant witted, began thus.

"My guests," said he, "for name of princes I have sent them lately unto palaces; now let each of you bethink him of mirth, not of majesty. I will have no stoical° humour in this arbor, but all shall be either lovers or love's well-willers. And for that each of us may be more apt to talk of Venus, we will taste of her friend Bacchus,[100] for a draught of good wine, if Lamprias in Plutarch[101] may be believed, whets the conceits, and he, when he had drunk most, debated best. Aeschylus,[102] therefore, ere he had dipped his pen in the ink to write tragedies, dived into the bottom of a wine pot to find terms; for as, where the wolf hath bitten most soundest, the flesh is most sweetest,[103] so whereas wine hath

cates choice foods, dainties.   **guarded** ornamented.   **stoical** indifferent to pleasure and pain.

warmed most hotly, the tongue is armed most eloquently.[104] I therefore carouse to you, my familiars, and as I give you liquor to warm, so will I crown you with joy and roses to allay; then have at Love who list, for methinks I am already prepared for him."

This said, he drank unto them, and all the rest gave him the pledge; and being crowned after the manner of the philosophical banquets, they sat down.

And Arsadachus spake thus: "Asaphus, I have heard that the motion is vain unless the action follow, and delights that are talked of before such as like them, except they grow in force, breed more discontent in their want than pleasure in their report. As therefore you have hung out the ivy bush,◊ so bring forth the wine; as you have prefixed the garland, so begin the race; as you intimated delight, so bring it to entrance."

Asaphus, smiling, replied thus: "Do then all these ladies and brave lovers give me the honour and direction to govern these sports?"

"They do," said Margarita.

"Then sit aside," quoth he, "and give place to your commander."

Whereupon all the assembly laughed, and Asaphus smilingly sat down in the highest room, placing the ladies opposite against their lovers, and himself, seated in his sovereignty, began thus: "Since in banquets the place is not to be given for the majesty but the mirth, be not displeased though I prefer myself, my subjects, since I know this, that I have crotchets in my head[105] when I have tasted the cup, and no man is more apt to talk than I when I have trafficked with good wine, and were it not so, you had no cause to wax wroth◊ with my presumption, for as the mason preferreth not the attic◊ stones in his building for nobility, neither the painter his precious colours in limning for their liveliness, neither the shipwright his Cretan cedar in framing

hung out the ivy bush hung out the sign of a tavern.   **wroth** angry.
attic classically elegant, refined (Athenian).

for the sweetness, so in festivals the guests are not to be placed according to the degrees, but their dispositions, for their liveliness, not their livelihoods, for where pleasures are sought for, the person is smally regarded; which considered, I am justified. But to our purpose, since Love is the affection that leadeth us, at him we will level our fancies, canvassing this question amongst us, whether he so best worketh by the eye, the touch, or the ear, for of the five senses I think these three are most forcible. Now, therefore, we will and command you, our masculine subjects," said Asaphus, "to begin to our feminine philosophers, and since you, Arsadachus, are of greatest hope, *incipe.*◊"

After they had all laughed heartily at the majestical utterance of Asaphus and his imperious manner, the young Cuscan said thus: "The Thibaeans in time past, who confined upon Pontus,[106] begat such children who, when they beheld their parents, killed them by their looks; as it fared with them, so falleth it out with me, who bethinking myself of those thoughts which I have conceived in respect of Love, am confounded in thinking of them, such power hath fancy, where it hath hold-fast. I must, therefore, as they quelled the one, kill the other, or I shall die by thoughts as they did by looks; but since to die for Love is no death but delight, I will adventure to think, talk, and discourse of him, and rather perish myself than suffer these pastimes to be unperformed. Our question is of Love, fair Ladies, whereat you blush when I speak, and I bow when I think, for he giveth me words to discourse and courage to decide: for as Plato saith,[107] Love is audacious in all things and forward in attempting anything; he yieldeth speech to the silent and courage to the bashful; he giveth industry to the negligent and forwardness to the sluggard, making a courtier of a clown; and lighting on a currish Menippus,[108] he softeneth him as iron in the fire and maketh him a courtly Aristippus[109] under his safe conduct. Therefore, I will talk of him, and with your patience I will satisfy you that Love hath soonest entrance by the eye and greatest sustenance by the sight; for sight, whereas it is stirred up by many motions, with that spirit which it darteth

incipe begin.

out from itself, doth likewise disperse a certain miraculous fiery force, by which mean we both do and suffer many things; and as among all the senses, the eye extendeth his power furthest, so is his working most forcible; for as the clay petrol[110] draweth fire, so the looks do gather affection. And that the forcible working of the eye may be proved to exceed all other the senses, what reason can be greater, since according to every affection of the heart or distemperature of the mind, the radiations of the eye are correspondent; if the heart be envious, the looks dart out beams of fierce envy, as may be considered by that of Eutelidas in Plutarch:[111]

> Quondam pulcher erat crinibus Eutelidas,
>   Sed sese ipse videns placidis in fluminis undis:
> Livore infamis perdidit invidiae
>   Facinus attraxit morbum, formamque perdidit.

For it is reported that this Eutelidas, taking a delight in his own lively beauty and beholding the same in a spring, grew in envy against the same, and by that means fell into a sickness whereby he lost both health and beauty. Narcissus,[112] neither by taste nor the ministry of speech nor the office of scent affected his own form, but his sight bereft him of his senses and the eye drew fancy to the heart; for this cause the poets call ladies' eyes Cupid's coach, the beams his arrows, placing all his triumph and power in them as the chiefest instrument of his seigniory; and that the eye only, beside the ministry of other senses, procureth love, you may perceive by these examples following.

"Xerxes,[113] who despising the sea and scorning the land, found out new means to navigate, and armies to choke the earth, yet fell in love with a tree; for having seen a plantain in Lydia of huge greatness, he stayed under it a hot day, making him a shelter of his shadow, a lover of his loves; and afterwards departing from the same, he adorned it with collars of gold and jewels, as if that that tree had been his enamoured, over which he appointed a guardian to assist it, fearing lest any should do violence unto the branches thereof. And what, I pray you, moved this affection in

Xerxes but the eye? A noble young man of Athens loved so much the stature° of good Fortune erected near unto the Prytaneum[114] that he embraced it, and kissed it, and offered a great sum of money to the Senate to redeem° the same, and not attaining his suit, he slew himself; and what wrought this in this noble young man but the eye? For this marble image had neither scent to delight the scent, speech to affect the ear, nor other means to move affection; it was then the sole force of the eye which conducteth to the heart each impression and fixeth each fancy in the same. What resteth there then but to give the honour to the eye, which as it is the best part in a woman, so hath it the most force in love?"

"Soft," said Plicotus, "claim not the triumph before you hear the trial; for if virtue and the whole praise thereof, as the philosophers say, consisteth in act, let the touch have the first place and the eye the second, for looks do but kindle the flame, where the touch both maketh it burn and, when it listeth, quencheth the fury."

"Such as behold anter[115] are healed of the falling-sickness," saith Arsadachus, "and they that sleep under sinilan[116] at such time as the plant swelleth and beareth his flower are slain."

Quoth Plicotus, "Saffron flowers[117] procure sleep; the amethyst[118] stayeth drunkenness, by which reasons you ought to ascribe as much power to the scent as to the sight. But hear me, you detractors from the touch; the herb alyssum,[119] taken in the hand, drives sighs from the heart."

"Yea, but," said Arsadachus, "the mad elephant beholding the rain groweth wild."

"Yea, but the wild bull tied to the fig tree, and tasting thereof, is no more wrathful," said Plicotus. "Ascribe therefore to the touch far more than the sight; heap all the argument that can be for the eyes, it breedeth the sickness: but we rather commend the herb that purgeth the disease than the humour that feedeth it, the salve that healeth the wound than the corrosive that grieveth it, the

stature effigy, statue.   **redeem** purchase.

flower that comforteth the brain and not that which cloyeth the same. The touch, therefore, in love should have the prerogative which both reareth it and restraineth it; and that the touch hath greater power than the sight, what greater reason may be alleged than this, that we only see to desire, especially to touch? The furniture of all delight is the taste, and the purgatory in love is to touch and want$^{\diamond}$ power to execute the affection, as may appear by this example. In the days of Apollonius Tyaneus,[120] who by every man was held for the fountain of wisdom, there was an eunuch found out in Babylon who had unlawfully conversed with a paramour of the king's; for which cause the king demanded of Apollonius what punishment the eunuch ought to have for that his rash and bold enterprise. 'No other,' answered Apollonius, 'save that he live to behold and touch without further attempt.' With which answer the king being amazed, demanded why he gave this answer. To whom Apollonius replied, 'Doubt not you, O King, but that love shall make him feel exceeding pains and martyrdoms; and like a simple fly, he shall play so long with the flame until he fall to cinders.' And for further proof the Egyptians, as Orosius[121] reporteth, whenas they would represent Love do make a net: and the Phoenicians describe him in a hand laid in fire, approving them by the touch which of all senses suffereth most and hath greatest power in the body."

Asaphus, that was still all this while, suddenly brake off the discourse, saying thus: "What sense, I pray you, was that, ye philosophers, that persuaded Ariston of Ephesus to lie with an ass and to beget a daughter, which was afterwards called Onoselino? What sense had Tullius Stellus to be in love with a mare, of whom he begat a fair daughter which was called Sponano? What made Cratis the Iloritan shepherd to love a goat?[122] Pasiphae to fancy a bull?"[123]

Stilconos, hearing that question, replied thus: "Truly a senseless desire, which, having no power of love but instinct of life, ought neither to be mentioned by modest tongues nor uttered in chaste hearing. That love which is gathered by the eye and

want lack.

grounded in the heart, which springeth on the uniformity of affection, having in itself all the principles of music, as Theophrastus[124] saith, as grief, pleasure, and divine instruct, that love which the Grecians call *Ghiciprion*, which is as much to say as bittersweet, of that we talk and no other, which sacred affection I have both tasted with the eye and tried by the touch, and have found so many effects in both, that as the sea ebbs and flows by the motion of the moon, the tropi of Egypt[125] wax and wane according to the floods and fall of Nilus, so have I by smiles, and lovers' pleasures, and repulses found such a taste in love, that did not the ear claim some greater pre-eminence, I should subscribe to you both. But as Love beginneth by the sight and hath pleasure in the touch, so gathereth he his eternity from hearing; by hearing Cupid a boy is made Cupid a god, by hearing Cupid, scarce fledged,* gathereth store of feathers; for even as breath extinguisheth fire in the beginning, but when it is increased both nourisheth and strengtheneth it, so Love that is covered in embers by the air, and scarce enabled and fashioned by the touch, is angry with those that discover him; but when he flies abroad and braggeth in his wrings,◊ he is fed with sweet words and laughs; at pleasant languish if he faint, kind words do relieve him; if he be sick, persuasions purge him; if he misdeem, reasons recover him. In brief, by the ear Love sucketh, by the ear Love thriveth, and by the ear all his essence is fashioned; and for that cause Melpomene and Terpsichore, the Muses,[126] are governors of our hearing, whereas not any Muse or godhead hath any affection to the eye or touch: for delight and gladness in love proceedeth from eloquent persuasion, which, received by the ear, changeth, moveth, altereth, and governeth all the passions of the heart."

Margarita, blushing in that her turn was next, drove Stilconos out of his text in this sort: "My Lord," said she, "if Love were gathered by the ear, old men for their wise discourses should win more credit than young men for their worthy comeliness, or if by the touch Love had his trial, the divinity of Love would

wrings gripes, pinches, turnings (*OED*, sb 2.b).

be wronged by too much inhumanity. It must be the eye, then, which can discern the rude colt from the trained steed, the true diamond from the counterfeit glass, the right colour from the rude, and the perfect beauty from the imperfect behaviour; had not the eye the prerogative, Love should be a monster, no miracle. And were the touch only judge, the soft ermine for daintiness, the seal for his softness, the marterne◇ for his smooth sweetness would exceed both ladies' best perfections and the finest skin of the choicest lover. If by the ear Love were discerned, the Siren[127] by her sweet song should win more favour than Sibylla[128] for her science, and the flatterer should be held for the best favourite. Let the eye, therefore, have the prerogative, which is both curious to behold and imperious to conquer. By it the heart may discover his affections as well as fine phrases, and more sweet hath oftentimes been gathered by a smile than a touch: for by the one we gather a hope of succeeding pleasure, by the other a joy in suspect for fear we be deceived, which beginneth in a minute and endeth in a moment."

"All cats are grey in the dark,"[129] said Calandra, "and therefore, good Madam, you do well to prefer the eye."

"Yea, but," said Ephania, "the eye had need of a candle to light it, or else, perhaps, the fat were in the fire."[130]

"Well," said Gerenia, "I will trust mine ear then, for where neither the eye seeth, nor the touch feeleth, certainly by dark let me hear the words, for they are the tell-troths."

"Ah, Gerenia," said Stilconos, "trust them not, for they that are false for the most part by day will, perhaps, fail you in the night."

"Leave your talk," quoth Asaphus, "and shut me all these three senses in one, and then tell me the felicity when the eye shall give earnest of the heart, the heart take comfort by the ear, the words we have heard and the sights we have seen confirmed by touch; this is the love I had rather have in mine arms than hear it in this place discoursed by argument. Since therefore, my Subjects, you are at my obeisance, and upon my direction are to do homage to Love, I give you free licence to discourse,

marterne marten.

free liberty to look, the sweets whereof, after you have gathered, come to me; and after the priest hath hand-fasted° you, come touch and spare not, you shall have my patent° to take your pleasure."

"It is a dangerous matter," said Arsadachus, "to enter those lists where women will do what they list."

"Well," said Margarita, "devils are not so black as they be painted,[131] my Lord, nor women so wayward as they seem."

"A good earnest penny,°" quoth Asaphus, "if you like the assurance."

With that they brake up the assembly, for it was suppertime, and the prince entreated them to sit down, where they merrily passed the time, laughing heartily at the pleasant and honest mirth wherein they had passed that afternoon.

The supper ended, each lover took his mistress apart, where they handled the matter in such sort that Margarita, which was before but easily fired, now at last grew altogether inflamed, for the night calling them thence and the company taking their leave, she, with a bitter sigh and earnest blush, took her leave of Arsadachus thus: "My Lord," said she, "if time lost be hardly recovered and favours won are to be followed, have a care of your estate, who may brag of that fortune that no one in Mosco can equal." Which said, she in all her period° of sighs, ending as abruptly as she had begun, and so departed.

Arsadachus, that knew the tree by the fruit,[132] the cloth by the list, the apple by the taste, feigned not to see what he most perceived, and taking his leave of Asaphus departed to his lodging, where, in a careless vein as if cloaking and smothering with love, he wrote these verses.

Judge not my thoughts, ne measure my desires
    By outward conduct of my searching eyes,
For stars resemble flames, yet are no fires:
    If under gold a secret poison lies,[133]

hand-fasted married.   **patent** licence, permission.   **earnest penny** down payment.   **period** highest point.

If under softest flowers lie serpents fell,[134]
    If from man's spine bone vipers do arise,[135]
So may sweet looks conceal a secret hell,
    Not love in me, that never may suffice.
The heart that hath the rules of reason known,
    But love in me which no man can devise,
A love of that I want and is mine own,
    Yet love and lovers' laws do I despise.
How strange is this judge you that lovers be,
    To love, yet have no love concealed in me.

And other he wrote in this manner, which came to the hands of his mistress, who prettily replied, both which I have underwritten.

I smile to see the toys[◊]
    Which I in silent see,
The hopes, the secret joys,
    Expected are from me:
The vows, the sighs, the tears are lost in vain
    By silly love through sorrow well-nigh slain.

The colour goes and comes,
    The face now pale, now red,
Now fear the heart benumbs,
    And hope grows almost dead.
And I look on and laugh, tho' sad I seem,
    And feign to fawn, altho' my mind misdeem.

I let the fly disport
    About the burning light,
And feed her with resort,
    And bait her with delight.
But when the flame hath seized her wings, adieu,
    Away will I, and seek for pleasures new.

Smile not, they are no toys
    Which you in silent see,

toys amorous sport, dallying.

Nor hopes, nor secret joys,
  Which you behold in me:
But those my vows, sighs, tears are serious seals,
  Whereby my heart his inward grief reveals.

My colour goes and comes,
  My face is pale and red,
And fear my heart benumbs,
  And hope is almost dead:
And why? To see thee laugh at my desert,
  So fair a man, and yet so false a heart.

Well, let the fly disport,
  And turn her in the light:
And as thou dost report,
  Still bait her with despite:
Yet be thou sure, when thou hast slain the first,
  Thou fliest away, perhaps, to find the worst.

Thus passed the affairs in Mosco till such time as the emperor, growing more and more in sickness, by the consent of his nobles hasted on the marriage. The rumour whereof being spread abroad made everyone rejoice; but among the rest, Margarita triumphed, who, called into open assembly by the emperor, was betrothed to Arsadachus in the presence of the nobility, who by his louring looks at that time showed his discontents. Yet will he, nill he, the day was appointed, the sixteenth of the Calends◇ of March, next ensuing, against which time there were high preparations in court and throughout all the provinces for pastimes. But since it is a most true axiom among the philosophers, that whereas be many errors, there likewise must needs follow many offences, it must needly follow that, since Arsadachus was so fraught with corrupt thought, he should practise and perform no less ungracious, corrupt, and ungodly actions. For no sooner was he departed from the presence of the emperor, but he presently began to imagine how to break off his nuptials, forcing

Calends first day of a Roman month.

in himself a forgetfulness of Margarita's virtues, her love and good deserts, so that it may evidently be perceived and approved that which Ammonius[136] saith, that things concluded in necessity are dissolved by violence; and truly not without reason was love compared to the sun, for as the sun thrusteth forth his purer and warmer beams through darkness and the thickest cloud, so love pierceth the most indurate[◊] hearts, and as the sun is sometime inflamed, so likewise is unstable love quickly kindled. Moreover, as the constitution of that body which useth no exercise endureth not the sun, so likewise an illiterate and corrupt mind cannot entertain love, for both of them after the same manner are disturbed from their estates and attainted with sickness, blaming not the force of love, but their own weakness. But this difference is between love and the sun, for that the sun showeth both fair and foul things to those that look on upon the earth: love only taketh care of the beauty of fair things and only fixeth the eyes upon such things, enforcing us to let slip all other. By this may be gathered that Arsadachus, being vicious, could not justly be attainted with love but with some slight passion, such as affect the greatest tyrants in beholding the pitiful massacre of the innocent, as shall manifestly appear by the sequel.

For after long debating in his restless mind sometime to fly the court, and by that means to escape the bondage which he supposed was in wedlock, sometime to make the princess away by poison, ridding himself thereby of suspect and Artosogon of hope, Fortune is as well the patroness of injuries as the protector of justice, the scourge of the innocent as the favourer of the nocent,[◊] who is rightly blind in having no choice and worthily held for bedlam in that she respecteth no deserts, so smiled on him that in depth of his doubts a remedy was ministered him beyond his imagination, which fell out after this manner. Artosogon, his father, being so tired with years as he must of force yield speedy tribute to death, so loaden with sickness that he seemed well-nigh past all succours, bethinking him of his

indurate hard, callous.   **nocent** guilty.

succession and like a kind father, desirous before his death to behold his son, not without the earnest entreaty of the empress and his nobility, sent present messengers to Mosco, beseeching the emperor Protomachus presently to dispatch Arsadachus unto him, assuring him of the perilous estate of his life and the desire he had to stablish his son before his death; for wherefore* the emperor of Mosco, though loathly, dismissed his pretended triumphs and gave Arsadachus licence to depart for Cusco. The ungodly young prince, seeing his purposes fall out so happily, sacrificed to Nemesis,[137] clearing his brows of those cares wherewith discontent had fraught them: and having with all expedition furnished himself to depart, he thought good to cast a fair foil on his false heart, to colour his corrupt thoughts with comfortless throbs;◇ and coming to Margarita, who was almost dead to hear the tidings, with a feigned look and false heart he thus attempted her.

"Madam, were I not assisted with my sighs and succoured by my tears to disburthen the torments of my heart, I fear me it should even now burst, it is so fraught with bitterness. Alas, I must now leave you, being the bark to the tree, the blossom to the stalk, the scent to the flower, the life to the body, the substance to the shadow; I must now leave you, being the beautiful whom I honour, the chaste whom I adore, and the goddess of all my glory; I must now leave you to live in sorrow without comfort, in despair without solace, in tears without rescouse,◇ in pains without ceasing; I must now leave you as the dam her young kid, the ewe her dear lambkin, the nightingale her prettiest nestling, fearing lest the cuckoo hatch those chickens which I have bred, the callax[138] bring up those young fish I have got, and foreign eyes feed on those beauties which only fasten life in me. Ah Margarita, so fair as none so fair, more virtuous than Virtue herself; if these troubles attaint me, in what temper shall I leave you, being the mirror of beauty, and even the miracle of constancy? Methinks I see those injurious, though fair, hands

throbs lamentations.   **rescouse** rescue, assistance.

beating those delicate breasts, these eyes surfeiting with tears, these lips with blasting their roses with sighings. But ah, dear Lady, let not such follies be your familiars; for as the thorn pricking the dead image in wax pierceth the lively substance indeed, so every light fillip° you give this breast will fell this body, every light tear that trickleth from these eyes will melt me to water, the least sighs steaming from these lips will stifle me. Have therefore patience, sweet Lady, and govern your passions with discretion; for as the smallest kernel in time maketh the tallest tree,[139] so in time these shadows of sorrow shall turn to the substance of delight: yea, in short time my return shall make you more happy than my present depart now maketh you heavy."

With these words, Arsadachus was ready to take his leave, when Margarita, presaging the mischief that was to follow, casting her arms about his neck, gave him this sorrowful adieu.

"Since my misgiving mind assureth me of my succeeding harm, ah suffer me, sweet Prince, to embrace that which I never hereafter shall behold, and look upon that with my weeping eyes which is the cause of all my wasteful envies. Ah my soul, must thou leave me when thou wert wholly incorporate in this body? Ah my heart, must thou forsake me to harbour in this happy bosom? What then shall remain with me to keep me in life, but my sorrow? Being the bequest of misery shall assist me in my melancholy. Ah dear Arsadachus, since thou must leave me, remember thou leavest me without soul, remember thou leavest me heartless; yea, I would to the gods thou mightst leave me lifeless, for then, disburthened of this body, I might in soul accompany thee, uniting our parts of fire. Since our fleshly persons must be parted, farewell, dear Lord, farewell, ever dear Lord, but I beseech thee, not for ever, dear Lord. Remember thou hast conquered and art to triumph, thou hast gotten the goal and art to reap the garland, thou hast taken the captive and mayest enjoy the ransom: hie thee, therefore, oh hie thee lest heaviness overbear me; return to her that shall live in terror till thou return.

fillip flick of the finger.

But if some angry Fates,[140] some untoward fortune, some sinister planet detain thee, and with thee my soul, heart, life, and love, now, now, oh now, ye Destinies, end me."

This said, she fell in a swoon, and her ladies could hardly recover life in her. Meanwhile, by the direction of the emperor, who heard her impatience, Arsadachus was called away, to whom Protomachus presented many gifts, swearing him in solemn manner before the whole assembly of his nobility to make a speedy return to Mosco to accomplish the marriage. In the meantime, Margarita was revived, who, seeing her Arsadachus absent, demeaned° herself in the most pitiful manner that ever poor lamentable lady did: at last, remembering her of a rich jewel which Arsinous had given her, which was a precious box set with emeralds, the which at such time as he gave it her, he charged her to keep until such time as he she loved best should depart from her. She sent the same for a present to Arsadachus, beseeching him, as he loved her, never to open the same box until such time as he began in any sort to forget her, for such counsel Arsinous had given her. This present was delivered the prince when he mounted on horse, who promised carefully to keep it, and with his retinue rode on his way towards Cusco. Where we leave him to return to Margarita, who no sooner heard of the departure of Arsadachus, but laying apart her costly jewels, her rich raiment, and princely pleasures, closed herself up in a melancholy tower, which through the huge height thereof beheld the country far and near, on the top whereof each hour she diligently watched for the return of her beloved Arsadachus. Her lodging was hanged about with a cloth of black velvet embroidered about with despairs; before her bed hung the picture of her beloved, to which she often discoursed her unkindness conceived, offering drops of her blood daily to the deaf image. Such a fondling° is Love when he groweth too fiery; no day, no night passed her wherein she spent not many hours in tears, and many tears every hour; neither could the authority of her father, the

demeaned conducted.   **fondling** foolish person.

persuasions of his counsel, nor the entreatings of her attendants alter her resolution.

In which melancholy a while I will leave her to discourse the damned treasons of Arsadachus, who, arriving at last in Cusco after long journeys, was after many hearty welcomes conducted to his father, who received such sudden joy at the sight of him that he recovered strength and cast off his sickness; so that, calling his nobility unto him, he ordained a time wherein Arsadachus should be invested in the empire, publishing the same through all his provinces. In the meantime, with much mirth and festival, the young prince lived in his father's court, dearly tendered by the empress, Lelia his mother, and duly attended by the best of the nobility, among whom Argias, the Duke of Moravia, being a prince of deep reach and of great revenues, following the custom of such who desire to grow in favour with princes, entertained Arsadachus with huge feasts and banquets; and among the rest, with one most especial, wherein as he had employed all what-soever the country could afford to delight the taste, so spared he no cost to breed pastime and triumph. Among all other, after the supper was solemnized, he brought in a masque of the god-desses, wherein his daughter, being the mirror and the *A per se*◇ of the whole world for beauty, was apparelled like Diana, her hair scattered about her shoulders, compassed with a silver crownet, her neck decked with carcanets◇ of pearl, her dainty body was covered with a veil of white net-work wrought with wires of silver and set with pearl, wherethrough the milk-white beauties of the sweet saint gave so heavenly a reflexion that it was suffi-cient to make Saturn[141] merry and mad with love, to fix his eye on them. Among all the rest that had both their parts of perfec-tion and beauty, and great lovers to like them, Arsadachus made choice of this Diana, who not only resembled her in that show but indeed was called by the name of Diana, on whose face when he had fixed his eyes, he grew so inflamed as Montgibel[142] yieldeth

A per se "the first, chief, most excellent, most distinguished, or unique person or thing; one who is *facile princeps*, or in modern phrase, A1" (*OED*, A.iv.).   **carcanets** necklaces.

not so much smoke as he sent out sighs. To be brief, he grew so suddenly altered, that as such as beheld the head of Medusa[143] were altered from their shapes, so he that saw the heaven of these beauties was ravished from his senses; to be brief, after he had danced the measures, passed the night, and was conducted by Argias and his attendants, he took no rest, but tossing on his bed grew so altered that on the morrow all the court was amazed to behold his melancholies. It cannot be reported how strangely he demeaned himself, for his sleeps fled him, his colour changed, his speech uncertain, his apparel careless; which Argias perceiving as being marvellous politic, ministered oil to the lamp, fuel to the fire, flax to the flame,[144] increasing his daughter's beauty with cost and Arsadachus' love by her company; for he ceased not to invite him, hoping that at the last the clouds would break out and rain him some good fortune. Diana was trained by him to the lure and taught her lesson with great cunning, who was as apt to execute as her father to counsel. Arsadachus one day among the rest, finding the opportunity and desirous to discover his conceits, was stricken so dumb with her divine beauty as he could not disclose his mind. Whereupon calling for pen and ink, he wrote this, thrusting it in Diana's bosom, walked melancholy into a fair garden on the back side of Argias' palace, where he wept so bitterly that it was supposed his heart would burst.

> I pine away expecting of the hour,
>   Which through my wayward chance will not arrive;
> I wait the word, by whose sweet sacred power
>   My lost contents may soon be made alive:
> My pensive heart, for fear my grief should perish,
>   Upon fallacious hope his fast appeaseth;
> And to myself my frustrate thoughts to cherish,
>   I feign a good that flits before it ceaseth:
> And as the ship far scattered from the port,
>   All well-nigh spent and wrecked with wretched blast,
> From East to West, midst surging seas is tossed,
>   So I, whose soul by fierce delay's effort

Is overcome in heart and looks defaced,*
Run here, run there, sigh, die, by sorrow crossed.

Diana took no days to peruse this ditty, but having overread it, gave it her father to judge of, who, feigning a severity more than ordinary and glad of the opportunity, entered the garden where the prince was well-nigh forspent with sorrow and taking occasion to interrupt his meditations, he began thus.

"Most royal Prince, I think the heavens lour on me, that labouring by all endeavours to procure your delights, I rather find you more melancholy by my motions than merry by my entertainment. Alas, my Lord, if either my actions do displease, my entertainment be too base, or if in anything I have defaulted wherein I may make amends, I beseech you let me know of you, and you shall find such readiness in me, your humble servant, as no hazard, danger, or discommodity whatsoever shall drive me from the accomplishment of your pleasures and behests."

Arsadachus, seeing Argias so pliant, began to recover hope, whereupon fixing his eyes upon him a long while, at last he brake his mute silence thus: "Argias, thy courtesy cannot bode my discontents, for thy kindness is such as binds me unto thee and breeds me no melancholy; and for I see thee so careful for my good, I will first therefore show thee of what importance* secrecy is, and declare unto thee those punishments antiquity bestowed on those that revealed secrets. Lastly, upon thy faithful oath, I may venture further, but so as thy silence may make thee happiest man in Cusco. To be of fair words, Argias, becometh a man of much virtue; and no small treasure findeth that prince* who hath a privy and faithful secretary in whose bosom he may pour his thoughts, on whose wisdom he may repose his secrets. Plutarch writeth[145] that the Athenians, having war with King Philip of Macedon, by chance lighted upon certain letters which he had written to Olympias, his wife, which they not only sent back sealed and unsearched, but also said that, since they were bound by their laws to be secret, they would neither see nor read other men's private motions. Diodorus Siculus[146] writeth that among the Egyptians it was a criminal act to open secrets, which he proveth to be true by example of a priest who had unlawful company with a virgin of the goddess Isis, both which trusting their secrecy to another priest, and he having little care to keep their action concealed, suddenly cried out, wherethrough the offenders were found out and slain, and he banished. And whereas the same priest complained against the unjust sentence, saying that whatsoever he had revealed was in favour of religion, he was answered by the judge, 'If thou alone hadst known it without being privy to them, or hadst thou had notice without corrupt consent, thou shouldst have reason to be aggrieved; but suddenly whereas they trusted their secrecy unto thee which they had in hand, and thou promisedst them to keep silence, hadst thou remembered thee of thy bond and promise, and the law which we have to be secret in all things, thou hadst never had the courage to publish it.' Plutarch, in his book of banishment,[147] saith that an Athenian sought under the cloak of an Egyptian, asked him what he carried hid, to whom he answered: 'Thou showest thyself smally read and worse nurtured, O thou Athenian, sith thou perceivest not that I carry this hid for no other respect but that I would have no man know what I carry.' Many other are the examples of Anaxilas, Dionysius,[148] Plato, and Bias,[149] which were too long for me to report and too tedious for thee to hear; my only desire is to let* thee know the weight of secrecy and the punishment that, knowing the one and the other, my Argias, thou mightst in respect of thy life keep silence with the tongue."

Argias, that knew the bird by the feather[150] and the eagle by the flight,[151] the leopard by his spot[152] and the lion by his claw,[153] cut off his circumlocutions with this discourse: "Aristarchus the philosopher,[154] most noble Prince, was wont to say that by reason of their instability, some* knew not that which the most* men ought to desire, nor that which they should fly, because that every day changeth and swift Time flieth: Eubeus the philosopher was wont many times to talk this at the table of great Alexander: 'By nature everyone is prompt and sharp witted to give counsel and to speak his opinion in other men's affairs, and fond and slow in his own purposes.' Truly this sentence was both grave and learned, for many there be that are discreet in other men's causes and judge rightly, but among ten thousand there is not one that is not deceived in his own causes.* This considered, your Grace doth most wisely to seek to disburthen your thoughts in a secret bosom and to ask counsel of another in your earnest occasions, for by the one you shall benefit your grief, by the other conquer it. Histories report that the valiant captain Nicias[155] was never mistaken in anything which achieved by another man's counsel, neither ever brought anything to good effect which he managed according to his own opinion. It is therefore virtue in you, good Prince, if in imitation of so great a chieftain you rather trust other men's wisdom than your own wit; and since it pleaseth you to grace me with the hope of secrecy, your Excellency shall not need to* misdoubt, for by all those gods whom I reverence, by this right hand which I lay on thy honourable loins, so may my pastures be plentiful, my barns filled, my vines burthened, as I vow to be secret, resolved to seal my faith with such assurance as death itself shall never be able to dissolve it."

Arsadachus, hearing his zealous promises and weighing his wise answers, by the one assured himself of his loyalty, by the other gathered his great wisdom and learning; whereupon taking Argias by the hand and withdrawing himself into a very secret and close arbor in the garden, he, after he had a while rested himself and meditated on that he had to say, with a bitter sigh brake out into these speeches: "Oh Argias, had the Destinies made us as prone to endure the assaults of love as they have made us prompt to delight in them, if they had favoured us with as much power to pacify the fury of them as they have given us will to persevere in the folly, I could then be mine own physician, without discovering my grief, and salve that with discretion which I now sigh for through despair. But since they have denied us that grace in their secret wisdom, to have will to relieve our own weakness, purges to expulse our poisons, and constancy to endure love's conflicts, I must have recourse unto thee, in whom consisteth the source of all my safety, beseeching thee, dear Argias, if thou hearest that thou shouldst not, consider that I suffer that I would not, and so temper my defects by the force and effects of thy wisdom, that I may be relieved and thou nothing grieved. Thou knowest, sweet friend, the contract I have passed with Margarita, thou knowest the resolution of my father wholly bent to accomplish it, thou knowest the expedition is required to accomplish the marriage: all which shall no sooner be accomplished, but I shall perish; and that day I shall become the bridegroom of Margarita, I wish to be buried in my grave. This is the first mischief must be anticipated, this the first sore must be salved, this the first consumption must have a cordial.◇"

"Mighty Prince," said Argias, "those conditions that consist on impossibilities may be broken, and marriage, which by an inviolable law of nature was ordained to knit and unite souls and bodies together, cannot be rightly solemnized between such whose good likings have not the same limits, whose affections are not united with self-like faculties; for as to join fire and water, moist and dry, were a matter impossible, especially in one subject, and more, in that they be contraries; so to couple love where there is hatred, affinity where there is no fancy, is a matter against right, repugnant to reason, and such a thing as, since nature doth impugn it, the gods, if it be broken, will easily dispense withal, whereas therefore you are a prince in your waxing years, your father in his waning, in your pride of wit, your father is impoverished in his understanding. Since the cause concerneth you in act, him but in words; since this damage is but the breach of a silly vow, if the marriage be broken; your detriment the misery of an age without all manner of content, you may, good Prince, in reason to prevent your own harm, in justice, since you cannot affect, break off those bands. And if Protomachus shall threaten, let him play the wolf and bark against the sun,[156] he cannot bite; you have power to resist him and friends to assist you."

"Aye,* but my father, Argias, how shall we pacify him?"

consumption must have a cordial wasting disease must have a restorative medicine.

"Either by persuasions, good Prince," said Argias, "or by impulsion; by the laws of Solon,[157] old men that dote must be governed by young men that have discretion. If he gainsay you, there are means to temper him; better he smart than you perish; my shirt is near me, my Lord, but my skin is nearest;[158] the cause concerneth you and must not be dallied."

Arsadachus, having found a hawk fit for his own lure[159] and a counsellor agreeable to his own conceit, with a smiling regard he greeted Argias again in this kind of manner: "Dear friend, thou hast rid me of my doubts and wert only reserved me by the gods to redress my damage. Thou hast complotted the means to displace Margarita, to appease Artosogon; now, if to pacify that raging affection that subdueth me thou find me a remedy, I will make thee the chiefest man in Cusco, of most authority in court. Yea, thou shalt be my second heart, my Argias, and yet this which I require of thee, though it be the difficultest in me, is the easiest in thee; for if it be lawful for me, as thou provest, to break my first marriage, to bridle my father, and work also whatso is mine own will, what letteth° my second wedlock with which thy favour shall be solemnized between thy angelical Diana and me, wherethrough I shall have peace and thou pre-eminence?"

Argias, that had already caught the fox in the snare, now laid hands of him and with a pleasing countenance began thus: "O Prince, this last doubt is your least danger, for where you may command my life, where you are lord of my wealth, can I be so forgetful of duty, think you, to deny you my daughter, whose worth is of too great weakness to entertain such dignity? But since it pleaseth your Excellence to deign it her in virtuous sort, command me and her to our utmost powers, we are yours."

Arsadachus, thinking himself in heaven, thanked Argias for his courtesy, who at last wholly discovered unto him how secret he was to his affections, showing him his sonnet: to be brief, it was so complotted that without further delay Arsadachus should be presently wedded to Diana, which was effected so that

letteth stands in the way of.

both these two married couples, in the height of their pleasures, passed their time in wonderful delight in Argias' castle. But as nothing is hidden from the eye of Time, neither is anything so secret which shall not be revealed.[160] The emperor Artosogon, by reason of Arsadachus' continual abode at Argias' house, discovered at last both the cause and the contract; whereupon, storming like the ocean incensed with a north-east breeze, he presently sent for Argias, and without either hearing his excuses or regard of his entreaties, presently caused him to be torn in pieces at the tails of four wild horses. Then, casting his mangled members into a litter, he sent them to Diana in a present, vowing to serve her in the same sauce her father had tasted, that durst so insolently adventure to espouse with the sole heir of his empire. The poor lady, almost dead to see the dead body of her father, but more moved with her own destruction which was to follow, fell at Arsadachus' feet, beseeching him with brinish tears, which fell in her delicate bosom, to be the patron of her fortunes. Arsadachus, who loved her entirely, comforted her the best he might, assuring her safety in spite of his father's tyranny; whereupon he levied a guard of his chiefest friends to the number of three thousand men and, shutting Diana in a strong fortress, left her, after many sweet embraces, in their custody. And for that the time of his coronation drew near, he assembled four thousand such as he knew most assured; he repaired to the court, vowing in his mind such a revenge on his father, as all the world should wonder to hear the sequel. Being arrived in court, he cloyed the gates thereof with armed men, placing in every turning of the city sufficient routs° of guard to keep the citizens from insurrection. Then, ascending the royal chamber where the emperor his father with his nobility were resident, he proudly drew him from his seat royal, in which action those of the nobility which resisted him were slain; the rest that tremblingly beheld the tragedy heard this which ensueth. Arsadachus, proudly setting him in his father's seat, was ready to speak unto the assembly, when the

routs companies, troops.

old emperor that had recovered his fall, awaking his spirits long dulled with age and weakness, began in this sort to upbraid his ungracious heir.

"Viper villain and worse, avaunt,[◊] and get thee out of my presence. How darest thou lay hands on thy lord? Or stain the imperial seat with thine impure and defiled person? Canst thou behold thy father without blushes, whom thou hast perjured by thy perverseness, making my oaths frustrate through thine odious follies? Ah, caitiff as thou art! More depraved than Caligula,[161] more bloody indeed than Nero,[162] more licentious than Catiline: would God either thou hadst been unborn or better taught. Thou second Tarquin[163] fostered by me to work tragedies in Cusco; thou proud youngman, thy beauty thou hast employed in riot, thy forces in tyranny. Oh, unkind wretch, I see, I see with mine eyes the subversion of this empire, and that which I have kept forty years thou wilt lose in less than thirty months. How can thy subjects be obedient to thee that despisest thy father? How can these nobles hope for justice at thy hands, that hast injuriously attempted me, an old man, thy father that bred thee, thy lord that cherished thee, the emperor that must inherit thee. What may strangers trust in thee, that hast broken thy faith with Protomachus, abused the love of Margarita, and all for a fair-faced minion, whom, if I catch in my claws, I will so temper as thou shalt have little lust to triumph? O what pity is it, thou perverse man, to see how I have bought thee of the gods with sighs; how thy mother hath delivered thee with pain; how we both have nourished thee with travels; how we watched to sustain thee; how we laboured to relieve thee; and after, how thou rebellest and art so vicious that we thy miserable parents must not die for age, but for the grief wherewith thou dost torment us! Ah, woe, woe is me that beholdeth thy lewdness, and wretched art thou to follow it. Well did I hope that thy courage in arms, thy comeliness in person, thy knowledge in letters were virtues enough to yield me hope and subdue thy follies: but now I say and say again, I affirm and affirm again, I swear and swear

avaunt be off, go.

again, that if men which are adorned with natural gifts do want requisite virtues, such have a knife in their hands wherewith they do strike and wound themselves, a fire on their shoulders wherewith they burn themselves, a rope on their necks to hang themselves, a dagger at their breasts to stab themselves, a stone to stumble at, a hill to tumble down. Oh, would to God that members wanted in thee so that vice did not abound; or would the loss of thine eyes might recompense the lewdness of thine errors. But thou laughest to hear me lament, which showeth thy small hope of amends; thou hast no touch of conscience, no fear of the gods, no awe of thy parents; what then should I hope of thee? Would God thy death, for that were an end of detriment; if thy life, I beseech the gods for mine own sake close mine eyes by death, lest I see thy unjust dealings."

In this state, Arsadachus, that was resolved in his villainy, without any reply, as if scorning the old man, caused his tongue by a minister to be cut out, then commanded his right hand to be struck off, wherewith he had signed the writ of Argias' death. Afterwards, apparelling him in a fool's coat and fetching a vehement laughter, he spake thus: "Cuscans, wonder not, it is no severity I show, but justice; for it is as lawful for me to forget I am a son as for him to forget he is a father; his tongue hath wronged me, and I am revenged on his tongue; his hand hath signed to the death of my dear Argias, and it hath paid the penalty. And since the old man doteth, I have apparelled him according to his property and impatience, wishing all those that love their lives not to cross me in my revenges nor assist him in his sinister practices."

This said, he made all the nobility to swear loyalty unto him: and Diana laughing incessantly at the old man, who continually* pointed with his left hand and lifted his eyes to heaven for revenge; sometimes he embraced the nobles, inciting them by signs to revenge, but all was in vain; fear subdued their affections.

In the meanwhile, the news of these novelties were spread through the city, so that many took arms to revenge the old emperor, who were presently and incontinently slain by the soldiers.

In brief, as in all conflicts, the weak at last went to the wall,[164] and necessity enforced such as misdeemed of Arsadachus' proceedings to allow of them in show. The day of coronation drew on, against which time Lelia, the empress, little suspecting that which had fallen out, arrived in Cusco, who, hearing of the hard measure, was offered her husband by her ungracious son, for Artosogon was shut up all the day till meal times, when Arsadachus called for him forth to laugh at him. She entered the palace with such cries as might have made the hardest heart melt to hear them, where clasping of her arms about the neck of the old and aged man, who melted in tears to behold the melancholy of the chaste matron, she cried out and complained in this manner.

"O you just gods, can you see these wrongs without remedy? Are you deaf to hear or pitiless to redress? Ah, look down, look down from your thrones and behold my throbs,◇ witness such wrongs as the sun hath never seen the like; the dog is grateful to his master for his meat, the elephant to his teacher for his knowledge, the serpent to the huntsman for his life; but our untoward son, for relieving◇ him hath grieved us, for giving him sweet milk in his youth doth feed us with bitter aloes in our age, and I, for bearing him with many groans, am now betrayed by him to many griefs. Ah, Artosogon, ah my dear Artosogon, it is enough grief for thee to endure; let me weep" (for the old man, to see her, shed many tears) "because thou sufferest, that, as thou decayest through tyranny, I may die with tears."

This said, sorrow stopped the passage of her speech, and they both swooned, he to behold his Lelia so forlorn, she to see her Artosogon so martyred. He that saw Venus lamenting Adonis,[165] Aurora bewailing Memnon,[166] Myrrha her tossed fortunes[167] saw but the shadow of cares, not the substance of complaints; for this sorrow of the princes was only beyond compare and past belief, wherein so long they demeaned themselves till age and sorrow, after long strife, surrendered to Death, who pitied the old princes, being despised of their lewd son, and ended their sorrows in

throbs heart palpitations; also, lamentations.   **relieving** raising up, feeding.

ending them. The rumour of whose fall was no sooner bruited[◇] in the ears of Arsadachus, but that, instead of solemnizing their funerals, he frequented his follies; instead of lamenting for them, he laughed at them, causing them for fashion sake to have the favour of the grave, not for any favour he bore them.

Then calling for Diana to his court, he honoured her as a goddess, causing his subjects to erect a shrine and to sacrifice unto her; and such was his superstitious and besotted blindness that he thought it the only paradise of the world to be in her presence; no one was better rewarded than he that could best praise her. Sometimes would he, attiring her* like a second Diana ready to chase, disguise himself like a shepherd, and sitting apart solitarily, where he might be in her presence, he would recount such passions as gave certain signs in him of an excellent wit, but matched with exceeding wickedness; among which these ten, as the most excellent for variety sake, after his so many villainies, I thought good to set down in this place.

I see a new-sprung sun that shines more clearly,
   That warms the earth more blithely with her brightness,
That spreads her beams more fair and shines more cheerly
   Than that clear sun that glads the day with lightness.

For but by outward heat the one offends me,
   The other burns my bones and melts their marrow:
The one when he sets on further blends[◇] me,
   The other ceaseless makes her eye Love's arrow.

From that a shower, a shadow of a tree,
   A foggy mist may safely me protect;
But this through clouds and shades doth pass and pierce me,
   In winter's frosts the other's force doth flee.
But this each season shines in each respect,
   Each where, each hour my heart doth plague
                              and pierce me.

bruited sounded.   **blends** makes blind; dazzles.

This other for the strange form thereof, though it have the second place, deserves the first, which howsoever you turn it backward or forward, is good sense, and hath the rimes and cadence according, the curiousness and cunning whereof the learned may judge: the first stands[◊] is the complaint, the second the counsel, both which he wrote in the entrance of his love with Diana.

Complaint.

132	Tears, cares, wrongs, grief feel I,	1132
221	Woe, frowns, scorns, crafts nill cease,	4241
314	Years, months, days, hours do fly;	3314
443	From me away flieth peace.	2423
1	Oppressed I live, alas, unhappily,	2
2	Rest is exiled, scorned, plagued, thus am I.	1

Answer.

132	Mend her, or change fond thought,	1132
221	Mind her, then end thy mind,	4241
314	End thee will sorrow sought,	3314
443	Kind if thou art, too blind.	2423
1	Such love fly far, lest thou perceive and prove,	2
2	Much sorrow, grief, care, sighing breeds such love.	1

The third, though short for the method, is very sweet, and is written in imitation of Dolce the Italian,[168] beginning thus: *Io veggio, &c.*[◊]

> I see with my heart's bleeding
> Thus hourly through my pain my life desires,
> I feel the flames exceeding,
> That burn my heart by undeserved fires.
> But whence these fires have breeding,
> I cannot find though great are my desires.
> O miracle eterne!
> That thus I burn in fire, and yet my fire cannot discern.

stands stanza.   *Io veggio, &c* I see.

The fourth, being written upon a more wanton subject, is far more poetical and hath in it his decorum as well as the rest.

Whenas my pale to her pure lips united,
    (Like new-fallen snow upon the morning rose)
Suck out those sweets wherein my soul delighted,
    Good Lord, how soon dispersed were my woes!
And from those gates whence comes that balmy breath
    That makes the sun to smile when he ariseth,
I drew a life-subduing nearing death,
    I sucked a sweet that every sweet compriseth.

There took my soul his hand-fast to desire,
    There chose my heart his paradise on earth,
There is the heaven whereto my hopes retire,
    There pleasure bred, and thence was Cupid's birth:
        Such is their power that by a touch they sever
        The heart from pains that liv'd in sorrows ever.

Another time, at such time as in the entrance of love he despaired of all succour, he desperately wrote this, and that very prettily.

Even at the brink of sorrow's ceaseless streams,
    All well-nigh drowned through dalliance and disdain,
Hoping to win the truce in my extremes,
    To pierce that marble heart where pride remains.

I send salt tears, sad sighs, and ruthful lines,
    Firm vows (and with these true men) my desire,
Which in his lasting sufferance scarce repines,
    To burn in ceaseless Aetna[169] of her ire.

All which (and yet of all, the least might serve)
    If too too weak to waken true regard,
Vouchsafe, O Heaven, that see how I deserve,
    Since you are never partial in reward,
        That ere I die she may with like success,
        Weep, sigh, write, vow, and die without redress.

This other in the self-like passion, but with more government, he wrote, which for that cause I place here consequently.

> Heap frown on frown, disdain upon disdain,
>   Join care to care, and leave no wrong unwrought,
> Suppose the worst, and smile at every pain,
>   Think my pale looks of envy, not of thought.
>
> In Error's mask let Reason's eye be masked,
>   Send out contempts to summon Death to slay me,
> To all these tyrant woes tho' I be tasked,
>   My faith shall flourish tho' these pains decay me.
>
> And tho' repining love to cinders burn me,
>   I will be famed for sufferance to the last,
> Since that in life no tedious pains could turn me,
>   And care my flesh, but not my faith could waste.
>   Tho' after death for all this life's distress,
>   My soul your endless honours shall confess.

Another melancholy of his, for the strangeness thereof, deserveth to be registered, and the rather in that it is in imitation of that excellent poet of Italy, Ludovico Paschale,[170] in his sonnet beginning *Tutte le stelle havean de'l ciel l'impero.*

> Those glorious lamps that heaven illuminate,
>   And most incline to retrograde aspects,
> Upon my birth-day shone the worst effects,
>   Thralling my life to most sinister fate.
>
> Wherethrough my self estranged from truth a while,
>   Twixt pains and plagues, midst torments and distress,
> Supposed to find for all my ruth° redress,
>   But now belief, nor hope, shall me beguile.
>
> So that (my heart from joys exiled quite),
>   I'll pine in grief through fierce disdains accursed,
> Scorned by the world, alive to nought but spite:
>   Hold I my tongue? 'Tis bad; and speak I? Worst.

ruth sorrow.

Both help me noughts; and if perhaps I write,
    'Tis not in hope, but lest the heart should burst.

Another in imitation of Martelli,[171] having the right nature of an
Italian melancholy, I have set down in this place.

O shady vales, O fair enriched meads,
    O sacred woods, sweet fields, and rising mountains,
O painted flowers, green herbs, where Flora[172] treads,
    Refreshed by wanton winds and watery fountains.

O all you winged quiristers° of wood,
    That perched aloft your former pains report,
And straight again recount with pleasant mood
    Your present joys in sweet and seemly sort.

O, all you creatures whosoever thrive
    On Mother Earth, in seas, by air or fire,
More blessed are you than I here under sun;
    Love dies in me, whenas he doth revive
In you; I perish under Beauty's ire,
    Where after storms, winds, frosts, your life is won.

All other of his having allusion to the name of Diana and the
nature of the moon I leave, in that few men are able to second the
sweet conceits of Philippe Desportes,[173] whose poetical writings
being already for the most part englished and ordinarily in every
man's hands, Arsadachus listed not to imitate; only these two
others which follow, being his own invention, came to my hand,
which I offer to your judgment, Ladies, for that afterward I mean
to prosecute the history.

Twixt reverence and desire, how am I vexed?
    Now prone to lay ambitious hands on beauty,

Now having fear to my desires annexed,
    Now haled on by hope, now stayed by duty.

quiristers choristers.

Emboldened thus, and overruled in striving,
  To gain the sovereign good my heart desireth,
I live a life, but in effect no living,
  Since dread subdues desire that most aspireth.

Tho' must I bide the combat of extremes,
  Fain to enjoy, yet fearing to offend,
Like him that strives against resisting streams
  In hope to gain the harbour in the end:
    Which haven her grace, which happy grace enjoyed,
    Both reverence and desire are well employed.

The conclusion of all his poetry I shut up with this his hyperbolical praise, showing the right shape of his dissembling nature.

Not so much borrowed beauty hath the stars,
  Not so much bright the mighty eye of day,
Not so much clear hath Cynthia[174] where she wars
  With Death's near niece in her black array.

Not so true essence have the sacred souls
  That from their natural mansions are divided,
Not so pure red hath Bacchus in his bowls
  As hath that face whereby my soul is guided.

Not so could Art or Nature if they sought
  In curious works themselves for to exceed,
Or second that which they at first had wrought,
  Nor so could Time, or all the gods, proceed
    As to enlarge, mould, think, or match that frame,
    As I do honour under Dian's name.

Now leave we him in his dalliance, making all things in a readiness for his coronation, and return we to the constant Margarita, who, living in her solitary seat, minding nothing but melancholies, triumphing in nothing but her tears, finding at length the prefixed time of Arsadachus' return almost expired, and her impatience so great as she could no longer endure his absence, in a desperate fury setting light by her life, she resolved privily to fly from her father's court to find out Arsadachus in his own country. For which cause she brake° with a faithful follower of hers called Fawnia, by whose assistance, without the knowledge of any other, in the disguise of a country maid, she gate° out of the city, attended only by this trusty follower, about the shutting in of the evening, at such time as her train without suspect intended their other affairs, and by reason of her melancholy little suspected her departure out of doors. And so long she travelled, Desire guiding her steps and Sorrow seating herself in her heart, that she got into an unpeopled and huge forest, where, meeting with a poor shepherd, she learned sure tidings of her way to Cusco, keeping in the most untrodden and unfrequented ways for fear of pursuit, weeping as she walked incessantly, so that neither Fawnia's words nor the hope she had to revisit her beloved could rid her of ruthfulness. Three days she so walked, feeding her thoughts on her own wretchedness, till on the fourth about the break of the day when Phoebus had newly chased the Morn, crowned with roses, from the desired bed of her beloved paramour, she sat her down by a fair fountain, washing her blubbered face in the clear spring and cooling her thirst in the crystal waters thereof. Here had she not long rested herself, talking with her Fawnia in what manner she would upbraid Arsadachus in Cusco of his unkind absence, whenas suddenly a huge lion, which was accustomed to refresh himself at that spring, brake out of the thicket behind their backs. Fawnia, that first spied him, was soon surprised,° then she cried and was rent* in pieces, in that she had tasted too much of fleshly love, before she feared. Margarita, that saw the massacre, sat still attending her own tragedy, for nothing was more welcome to her than death, having lost her friend, nor nothing more expected. But see the generosity and virtue of the beast: instead of renting her limbs, he scented her garments; in the place of tearing her piecemeal, he laid his head gently in her lap, licking her milkwhite hand and showing all signs of humility instead of

brake revealed what was in her mind.   **gate** walked.   **surprised** attacked.

inhumanity. Margarita, seeing this, recovered her senses, and, pitifully weeping, spake thus.

"Alas, ye gods, why yield you sorrows to those that despise fancy and betray you them by death who desire to flee detriment? Woe is me; how fortunate were Margarita to have been dismembered. How forlorn was Fawnia to be thus mangled. Ah, tyrant beast, hadst thou spared her, her virtue had deserved it; hadst thou spoiled me, why I was reserved for it, for what care have not I part in? Or from what joy am not I parted? Love, that is a lord of pity to some, is pitiless to me; he giveth others* the rose, but me the thorn; he bestoweth wine on others, and me vinegar; he crowneth the rest with laurel in respect of their flourishing fortune, but me with cypress, the tree dedicated to funeral. Out, alas, that I live or that I have time to speak; I live, in that I have had time so long to love with neglect and to pine in the delay. Ah, courteous beast," said she, "why executest thou not that which my sorrow doth prosecute? Let thy teeth, I beseech thee, rid me of Love's tyranny."

This said, she pitifully wept; but the lion ceased not to play with her, stroking her with his rough paw, as if willing to appease her, but all was in vain, till that sleep by reason of her sorrow seized her and settled herself in the lion's eyes, where we leave them, returning to Mosco, where the day no sooner appeared but Protomachus, according to his custom coming to visit his daughter, found her suddenly fled; whereat storming incessantly, he presently put all her attendants to most bitter and strange death, sending out espials through all the country to find out Margarita, who by reason of her solitary walks was free from their search. At last, looking among her secret papers, he found a letter, wherein the princess had written to Arsadachus that if he presently returned not, she would shortly visit him. By reason whereof, being a wise prince, he gathered some circumstance of her flight and levying a power° of soldiers, with as much expedition as he might, he set forward towards Cusco, where I leave him to return to Arsinous, who, studying magic in his

power force.

melancholy cell, found by reason of the aspect of the planets that the hour of his revenge was at hand. Whereupon being resolved of the place, which was Cusco, and the manner, with all other actors in the tragedy, he, being desirous to behold that with his eyes which he had long time longed for with his heart, forsook his melancholy home and set forward toward Cusco. And as he passed on his way, it was his chance to behold where Margarita lay sleeping, having the lion's head in her lap, whereat being amazed and affrighted, in that he heartily loved the princess, he with his staff awaked her, who, seeing a man so overgrown in hairs and years, yet carrying as much show in his countenance of honour as discontent, softly stole from the lion and left him sleeping there.

Suddenly seizing Arsinous by the hand, she said thus: "Father, thank Fortune that hath given thee time to escape death if thou list, and follow me who hath both need of thy counsels and of such a reverend companion as thou art."

Which said, they both withdrew them out of the way, hasting two long hours without ever looking back till at last, when Arsinous saw her and himself in safety, he courted her thus: "Country lass by your coat but courtly dame by your countenance, whither travel you this ways, or for what cause are you so woeful?"

"Forlorn man by thy apparel but honourable sir by thy behaviour, I am travelling to Cusco, where both remaineth the cause of my woe and the means to cure it."

"May I be so bold," said Arsinous, "to know of you what you are and what you ail?"

"It neither pertaineth to you that I tell it," quoth Margarita, "neither pleaseth it me to discover it, for the one will seek my harm, the other yield you little help."

"Then," quoth Arsinous smiling, "I will try mine own cunning to cross a woman's resolution."

Whereupon entreating Margarita to set her down under a palm tree to avoid the heat of the sun, which being at his noontide flamed very fiercely, he drew a book out of his bosom and read so long till suddenly there appeared one in selflike shape and substance as Arsadachus was wont to be, whom Margarita no sooner espied but that she ran fiercely towards him that hastily fled.

She cried out, "Oh stay thee, my Arsadachus, stay thee; behold thy Margarita that hath left her father's court, hazarded her honours, adventured all dangers for thy love, for thy sake, oh stay!"

This said, the vision suddenly vanished and she, striving to embrace him, caught his shadow, whereupon vehemently weeping, she exclaimed on the gods over Love and his laws, renting her hairs and beating her breasts in such sort as it was pity to behold it, and had died in that agony had not Arsinous recomforted her in this sort.

"Fie, Margarita, doth this beseem your wisdom, to demean sorrow without cause and seek your death through a delusion? Why, Princess, whatever you saw was but an apparition, not the substance, devised only by your servant Arsinous to discover you."

She, hearing the name of Arsinous, presently started up, and clasping her arms about his aged neck whom she suddenly had discovered, she spake thus: "Ah, my Father, pardon my folly, that sought to keep that secret which is discovered by your science."

"Tut, Madam, the pardon is to be granted by your hands," said he, "who are most injured. Was it ever seen," quoth he smilingly, "a lady to be so besotted on a shadow?"

"Ah, pardon me," said Margarita, "I held it for the substance:[175] but Father, I pray you, tell me whither you intend your journey."

Arsinous, desirous in short words to satisfy her, told her that he pretended his course to Cusco, forsaking his melancholy cell of purpose to meet her whose danger he had perceived in private, being in his study; further he told her many things touching the emperor's search after her, not pretermitting° anything to content her, but concealing that which tended to her ruin, which with erneful° heart he inwardly perceived. Margarita, somewhat

pretermitting omitting.   **erneful** compassionate.

rejoiced with the company of such a guide, sat her down, seeking some herbs in the forest to relieve her hunger.

Arsinous that perceived it said thus: "See, Madam, what love can do, that fashioneth courtly stomachs to homely acates;◇ the gods grant you may speed well, for I see you can feed well." Hereon he opened his book and read, and suddenly a pavilion was pitched, the table was reared, the dishes served in with all kind of delicates, the music exceeding pleasant, so that Margarita was ravished to behold this; but being animated by Arsinous, she fell to her meat, certifying him at dinnertime of such things as had passed in her father's court in his absence. Thus in jollity appeased they their hungry stomachs and eased their sorrowful hearts, till occasion called them forth to travel, at which time the pavilion, servitors, and all things vanished, and only Arsinous and Margarita were left alone, having two squires attending on them, with two rich jennets◇ bravely trapped fit for their managing, which they speedily backed,◇ talking merrily as they rode of such strange things as Arsinous had wrought by his art. And so long they travelled towards Cusco that they arrived within two leagues of the same, understanding by the great troops that rode that way that the coronation was the next day following. Margarita, by Arsinous' counsel, stayed in the castle of an aged knight,* where he wrought so by his art that, although Margarita had a desire to hear tidings of Arsadachus, yet made she no question of him all the time of her abode there.

And here let us leave them and return to Cusco, to the accursed and abominable tyrant, Arsadachus, who, as soon as the day began to break, the birds to hale forth the sun, the sun to haste his course, arose from his bed, apparelling himself in rich and princely robes; about which hour Diana was not idle, for whatso of excellence could be bought for money or had for friendship, she wanted◇ nothing thereof to set out her beauty. The courtiers, to grace their emperor, spared no cost, the citizens

acates foreign viands, delicacies.   **jennets** small Spanish horses.
backed mounted.   **wanted** lacked.

no triumphs, so as the triumph of Antigonus Epiphanus,[176] in comparison hereof, was but a trifle, the manner whereof, since it was miraculous, I have thought good to mention in this place.

First came five thousand of the youngest Cuscans out of the palace, trotting along the streets unto the temple armed, according to the Roman fashion; after them as many Tartars armed after their manner, who were followed with three thousand Thracians and Plessians,[177] all of which carried silver lances and shields, having their headpieces decked with ostrich plumes and emeralds. After them marched two hundred and fifty sword-players, who followed the brave cavaliers that marched before, after whom trotted the horsemen, of which one thousand, together with their horses, were all pompously garnished with gold and silver, with a garland of gold upon their heads. After them rode another thousand horsemen, decked with gold and purple, with lances of gold headed with pointed diamonds; next them rode those which were called the emperor's minions, clothed in cloth of tissue, their horses trapped in green cloth of gold, their stirrups of silver. After them came the emperor's guard on horseback, having their caparisons studded with iron and brass, wearing upon their armours a certain curious stole wherein, with gold and silver, silk, and gossampine◇ thread of many colours, were woven the images of those gods which the Cuscans most worshipped; after whom came one thousand five hundred armed chariots, the most part drawn by two white jennets, but forty of them by four. After them there came a chariot drawn by elephants and attended by six and thirty elephants, with eight hundred young men attending them as their keepers, attired with ornaments of gold and having their temples encompassed with wreaths of roses and silver bends.◇ After them came eight hundred young lads leading many fat oxen with gilded horns* to be sacrificed to the gods; next unto them eight hundred ministers bearing platters of gold with precious stones, unicorns' horns,

gossampine cotton-like fibre.   **bends** bands, coronets.

and elephants' teeth to be sacrificed for the health of the emperor; next which an infinite number of statues were carried, not only of their gods but also of those fiends they feared; likewise the images of all their kings deceased, according as every one deserved for his excellence, apparelled in goodly garments of gold and silver, and other precious and inestimable jewels, each of them having a table° at his feet in which all his noble and worthy actions were written. There were likewise other semblances of the day, the night, of heaven, of the morning and mid-day, with an infinite number of vessels likewise forged out of gold and silver and borne by the slaves of the empire; after these came six hundred pages of the emperor apparelled in gold, after whom came three hundred virgins in white cloth of tissue, burning with censers in their hands of silver and agate spreading sundry sorts of sweet perfumes, followed by five hundred coaches of silver wherein Diana's damsels were carried, after which came fourscore of beaten gold wherein all the princely heirs of the empire were royally seated. After all these the emperor with his Diana rode in one coach attended with one hundred attired in beaten cloth of silver, casting rich cloth before the coach, whereon the horses that drew the emperor should tread. It were a vain thing for me to set down the riches of Arsadachus' garments, or the attire of his goddess; sufficeth it that it exceeded that which is past, and all was beyond belief. In this solemn sort entered they the temple, where, according to the custom, they were sacred,° anointed, and enthroned, receiving homage of the princes.

And after, in self-like pomp returned they to the palace, where having many rich delicates prepared for them with sweet and melodious music they sat them down to eat, where, after they had somewhat refreshed their stomachs and whetted their wits with costly wines, Arsadachus, remembering him of his Margarita, called for his box, merrily jesting with Diana and saying that the empress of Mosco deserved so small a remembrance. Which was no sooner brought unto him and opened but—see

table tablet.   **sacred** consecrated to office (from *sacre*, v. obs. *OED*).

the judgment of just heaven — a sudden flame issued thereout, which with a hideous odour so bestraught Arsadachus of his senses that, thrusting the tables from him and overthrowing whatsoever encountered him, he brake out from his seat, cursing the heavens, renting his embalmed◇ hair, tearing his royal vestures. His nobility that saw this became amazed, and among the rest Brasidas, who fled for the murther in Mosco and was at that time in great favour with him, came to pacify him; who no sooner espied him, but taking a huge bowl of wine and crying out, "Brasidas, I drink to Philenia whom thou murtheredst," he tasted the wine, and with the cup took him such a mighty blow on the head that he pashed out all his brains. All they that beheld this sat still; some for fear stole secretly out of his presence; among the rest, woeful Diana, rather like the statue of Venus raised in Paphos than the lovely Lucina[178] that gave light to all Arsadachus' delights, sat still quaking and trembling, as one ready to depart this life; whom, when the emperor espied where she sat, he hastily ran unto her, crying out, "Ah, tyrant that hast robbed me of my heart, my hope and life, let me sacrifice to Nemesis; I will sacrifice."

Which said, with the carving knife he slit up the poor innocent lady's body, spreading her entrails about the palace floor; and seizing on her heart, he tore it in pieces with his tyrannous teeth, crying, "*Sic itur ad astra.*"[179] By this time the rumour was spread throughout the palace, and from the palace through the city; by which means the triumphs which were commenced were turned to mournings, for Arsadachus used such cruelties every way that the Numantines[180] for all their inhumanity could never be able to match him. And in this fit continued he for the space of six hours, at which time he entered the secrets of his palace, and finding there a young son which his Diana had bred and he begotten, he took it by the legs, battering out the brains thereof against the walls, in such sort as the beholders were amazed to see him. This done, he flung it on the ground among the dead members of his

embalmed perfumed.

mother, calling on the name of Artosogon and Lelia, his father and mother, and telling them that in some part he had yielded them revenge.

By this time Arsinous and Margarita were entered the city, who, hearing the turmoil through the city, questioned the cause thereof and were certified by those that passed by in what estate the emperor was at that present. Margarita, hearing the cause, began woefully to exclaim till she was pacified by Arsinous, who told her that the nature of the medicine which he gave her was such that, if Arsadachus were constant to her, it would increase his affection; if false, it would procure madness: to which effect, since the matter was brought, it could not be but the young emperor had wronged her. With these persuasions he drew her to the palace, where thrusting through the prease° Arsinous thought himself happy to see such a revenge wrought on his enemy. Margarita was heartless° to behold the doleful estate of Arsadachus, so that forgetting the honour of his name and the modesty of her sex, she brake through the guard and ran to Arsadachus, where he sat embrewed in the blood of innocents, and with tears spake thus unto him.

"Is this the joy of my love?" said she. "Are these thy welcomes to thy beloved, instead of triumphs to feast her with tragedies, in lieu of banquets with blood? Why speaketh not my dear spouse? Why lookest thou so ghastly? O, if it be thy pleasure to show cruelty on me, make it short by a death, not lingering by life."

Arsadachus all this while sat mute, ghastly staring on Margarita; at last fiercely flinging her from his neck, his rage revived and he cried out, "Diana, ah Diana, by thy bright looks, by thy beautiful locks, let not thy ghost be displeased; thou shalt have blood for blood;[181] here is the sacrifice, here is the instrument."

Whereupon drawing a rapier out of the sheath of one of those who ministered fast by him, he ran Margarita quite through the body: and in this sort with bedlam madness fled out of the presence to his privy chamber. The poor princess, even when

prease crowd of people.   **was heartless** lacked the heart, could not endure.

Death began to arrest her, pursued him, and as she endeavoured to utter her moans, fell down dead on the floor, whom Arsinous woefully bewept, and in the presence of the princes* of Cusco discovered what she was. Then began each of them to imagine a new fear, doubting◇ lest the emperor of Mosco should revenge her death at their hands. For which cause they consulted how to shut up Arsadachus till Protomachus were certified,◇ which they effected suddenly in that they found him laid on his bed and soundly sleeping, enforced thereunto by the industry and art of Arsinous. Who, after he perceived the whole assembly of princes dismayed, caused the ministers to gather up the mangled members and cover them with a rich cloth of gold, and afterwards seeing all the courtiers attentive, he began in this manner.

"Thales,[182] ye worthy Princes, after he had travelled long time and at last returned home, being asked what strange or rare thing he had seen in his voyage, answered: an old tyrant; for certain it is that such as practise open wrong live not long, for the gods yield them shortest life that have the wickedest ways. Muse not therefore to see your young emperor in these passions, whose sins, if they be ripped up,◇ exceed all sense, whose tyrannies surpass the belief of any but such as have tried them. What, know you not of his disobedience, who spared not his own father that begat him, his dear mother that bred him? What, know you not of his perjury, that hath falsified his faith to Protomachus, betrayed and murthered Margarita, and at one time frustrated the hope of both these empires? What, know you not of his murthers, where these in sight are sufficient to convict him, but those I sigh for are more odious, who through his lewd lust bereft me, poor Arsinous, of my daughter, and her of an husband? But the just gods have suffered me to behold the revenge with mine eyes, which I have long wished for with my heart. Truly, ye Cuscans, ye are not to marvel at these chances if you be wise, neither to wonder at your emperor's troubles if you have discretion; for as unity, according to Pythagoras,[183] is the father of number, so

doubting fearing.   **certified** informed.   **ripped up** brought up again for notice or discussion.

is vice the original of many sorrows. When the fish tenthis[184] appeareth above the water, there followeth a tempest: when evils are grown to head, there must needly follow punishment; for as the gods in mercy delay, so at last in justice they punish. Hear me, ye men of Cusco, and consider my words: if never as yet any tyrant lived without his tragedy, what should you expect? In faith, no other thing but the confirmation of Plato's reason, who said that it is unnecessary for him to live that hath not learned how to live well.[185] The tyrant of Sicily, Dionysius,[186] of whom it is said that he gave as great reward to those that invented vices as Rome did to those that conquered realms, died a private man and in misery. Now, what in respect of this man can you hope of Arsadachus, who hired not men to invent, but did himself in person practise? Believe me, believe me, your sufferance of such a viper in your realm is a heinous sin in you; and as Dion[187] saith, it is but meet they be partakers to the pain who have winked at the fault. Caligula, the emperor of Rome, was so disordered in his life that, if all the Romans had not watched to take life from him, he would have waited to take life from them; this monster bore a brooch of gold in his cap, wherein was written this sentence: *Utinam omnis populus unam praecise cervicem haberet, ut uno ictu* omnes necarem*◊.[188] And what was this man in regard of Arsadachus? Truly almost innocent; for the one pretended kindness to those that gently persuaded him, but the other neither feared the gods, neither spared his friends, neither regarded justice, and can such a monster deserve life? The Romans, when the tyrant Tiberius was made away, sacrificed in their open streets, in that the gods had reft them of such a troublesome wretch.[189] Why cease you then, you Cuscans, to sacrifice to your gods to the end they may deliver you of this trouble-world*? It was a law among the Romans that that child which had disobeyed his father, robbed any temple, injured any widow, committed any treason to a stranger should be banished

---

Utinam omnis . . . omnes necarem Would that all people had precisely one brain/neck, so that with one blow I could have killed everyone.

from Rome and disinherited of his father's possessions; and what hath not Arsadachus done of these things? And why is not Arsadachus punished? Scedasus' daughters[190] being violated in Lacedemon and unrevenged by the magistrates of the city, the gods afflicted* both the guilty and unguilty with plagues, in that they inflicted* not punishment on the offenders. And what can you hope, ye Cuscans, that suffer this sink of sin to triumph in your palaces? You will perhaps say that no man is to be punished afore he be convicted. And, I pray you, for what should ill men plead, since, as Chrysippus[191] saith, nothing is profitable unto them? You see testimonies of his murther before your eyes, tokens of his perjury I ring in your ears, his lust the gods abhor, and shall he yet live?"

This said, there grew a great muttering among the nobility, and the noise thereof awaked the emperor, whose sleep had stayed the working of the enchantment, who, finding himself wholly imbrued with blood, his doors fast locked unto him, began to misdeem: whereupon calling and exclaiming on his attendants, some of them at last fearfully opened the doors. The nobility, hearing of his freedom, presently fled, but whenas the fatal fruits of his fury were discovered unto him and his ruthful eyes beheld what his hands had executed, Lord, what pitiful exclamations used he! How he rent his breast with fury, how he tore his face. At last, laying him down upon the mangled members of Diana and embracing the dead body of Margarita, he washed both of them in his tears and demeaned himself so woefully, as it was wonder to behold. At last, with a bitter sigh, he brake out into these bitter words, whilst his nobles, hearing of his recovery, began to re-enter the palace.

"True it is that Plutarch saith," quoth he, "that life is a stage-play, which even unto the last act hath no decorum: life is replenished with all vices and impoverished of all virtue.[192] Sooth spake Chrysippus when he alleged this, that the evils of this life are so many that the gods cannot invent more, neither a living man endure half; so that rightly I may say with Hercules:

Plenus malorum sum iam, nec superest locus
  Aliis novis recipiandis◇————193

But why philosophy◇ I of life, complaining on it where I ought only to convict myself? It is not the wretchedness but the wickedness of life that maketh it odious. Then hast thou occasion, wretched man as thou art, to learn thee, who, having sinned in the excess, oughtest rightly to have thy comforts in defect. Yea, I have sinned, O ye heavens, first in beguiling this chaste Margarita with hope, in wronging my dear parents in their age, in slaughtering this poor infant with his mother. Oh, Aetna of miseries that I see! Oh, ye Cuscan Princes, why suffer you me alive that have stained your empire with such infamies? Why unsheath you not your swords? For pity delay not, for pity rid me of life. Alas, why crave I pity that have been altogether pitiless? Ah, ye flocks of flatterers, where are you now that fed me with follies? Come now and punish my follies in me. None heareth me, all forsake me, despised of the gods, hated of men. Ah, just heavens, I honour you that have left me occasions in myself; you cursed eyes of mine that have glutted yourselves in vanity, since you reft me of my senses, I will be revenged on your sight."

Which said, he drew out his eyes weeping piteously in so erneful manner, that the whole assistance became compassionate: at last some one of his nobles, labouring to pacify him, alleging reasons of great weight, which in a man of government were sufficient to qualify the fury of sorrow, he replied thus: "Friends and Princes, the force of reason, as the Stoics say, is not to be used in those things that are not; it concerneth not me, Lords, that I live. Persuade me not for that cause to entertain and think of life, for if it be odious to those that through infirmities of their flesh grow in hate with it, what should it be to me who have not only a body aggrieved with sorrows, but a soul sweltered in sins? Lament me not, therefore, neither relieve me; for as the dew causeth leprosy in man though it yieldeth life to flowers, so tears

Plenus . . . recipiandis So great is the evil I now have that I have no room to receive any more.   **philosophy** philosophize.

rather torment those that despair than relieve them; and though they comfort the distressed, yet they are tedious to the desperate. I feel my forlorn heart, you nobles, cloyed with thoughts and longing to be disburthened. I see with mine inward eyes the ghosts of these poor slaughtered souls calling for justice at my hands; stay me not therefore from death, but assist me to die, for by this means you shall rid your country of a plague, the world of a monster. Such as are wounded with brazen weapons are, according to Aristotle's opinion,[194] soon healed; so likewise are they that are tainted◊* with easy sorrow: but whereas the passions exceed reason, they have no issue but death; the instrument that woundeth is deadly. Ah, my heart, I find Plutarch's reason of force; for as the sun is to the heaven, so is the heart to the man;[195] and as the one eclipseth, the other cloudeth; when the one danceth, the other dieth. I feel thee, poor heart, dispossessed of all joy, and shall I continue possessed of life? No, you ghosts, I will visit you."

This said, he grappled about the floor among the dead bodies, and at last he griped that weapon wherewith he slew Margarita, wherewith piercing his hated body, he breathed his last, to the general benefit of all the Cuscans, who, in that they would pacify the Emperor Protomachus, who as they understood had levied a huge army, after they had interred their slain emperor with his fair love, bestowed honourable funeral on the Princess Margarita, on whose sepulchre, as also on that of Diana's, Arsinous wrote these epitaphs.

Margarita's Epitaph.

A blessed soul from earthly prison loosed,
   Ye happy heavens, hath Faith to you conveyed;
The earthly hold within this tomb enclosed,
   White marble stones, within your womb is laid.

The fame of her that soul and body lost
   Survives from th'isle to the Bactrian coast.[196]

tainted hurt, impaired.

A precious pearl° in name, a pearl in nature,
   Too kind in love unto too fierce a foe,
By him she lov'd, she died. O cursed creature,
    To quite° true faith with furious murther so!
      But vain are tears for those whom Death hath slain,
      And sweet is fame that makes dead live again.

Diana's Epitaph.

Thy babe and thou, by sire and husband's hand,
   Belov'd in stayed sense were* slain in rage,
Both by untimely death in native land
    Lost empire, hope, and died in timeless age,
      And he whose sword your blood with fury spilt
      Bereft himself of life through cursed guilt.

All ye that fix your eyes upon this tomb,
   Remember this, that beauty fadeth fast,
That honours are enthralled to hapless doom,
    That life hath nothing sure, but soon doth waste;
      So live you then, that when your years are fled,
      Your glories may survive when you are dead.

In this sort were these murthered princes both buried and honoured with epitaphs, by which time the emperor of Mosco arrived in Cusco, who, certified of that which had ensued, with bitter tears lamented his daughter, and upon the earnest submission of the Cuscans spoiled not their confines, but possessing himself of the empire, he placed Arsinous governor of the same, whom, upon the earnest reconcilement and motion of the princes, he took to favour, being certified of his wrong and innocency. Which done, he returned to Mosco, there spending the remnant of his days in continual complaints of his Margarita.

FINIS

pearl margarite is a kind of pearl.   **quite** requite.

Textual Notes

In the preparation of this text of Thomas Lodge's *A Margarite of America*, the three known extant copies were collated: Bodleian Malone 569(3) [Bod], British Library C.14.a.2 [BL:C], and British Library G.10441 [BL:G]. The Bodleian copy was used as the source text. Numerous substantive and accidental variants were detected during the course of collation, indicating that some revision of the text had occurred during printing. Typographical errors and obvious misprints have been silently corrected, as have misspellings of proper names, such as "Aeschylus," "Menippus," and others; only the substantive variants and the editorial emendations are noted in the following list. In the case of emendations, the designation "orig." denotes an original reading common to all of the copies.

p. 73. clothed] orig. clothe

p. 77. travail] orig. travel

p. 77. are] orig. is

p. 78. difference] orig. different

p. 78. yourselves] orig. your self

p. 80. with] orig. which

p. 81. reigneth] orig. raineth

p. 83. were] orig. was

p. 83. were] orig. was

p. 87. beasts] orig. beast

p. 92. delude] orig. deluded

p. 92. others] orig. other

p. 97. many] orig. a many

p. 99. Arsadachus] orig. Arsinous

p. 107. yea] orig. ye

p. 107. all] orig. each

p. 107. others] orig. other

p. 109. had written] orig. had wrote

p. 110. murther] orig. murthered

p. 110. dispossess] orig. dispossessed

p. 111. near] Bod, BL:G; new BL:C

p. 112. others] orig. other

p. 115. nor will overslip this injury so slightly] Bod, BL:G; neither
will overslip this injury slightly BL:C

p. 117. cave] Bod, BL:G; care BL:C

p. 117. that] orig. the

p. 118. jousts] orig. a justs

p. 119. drop] orig. drops

p. 119. others] orig. other

p. 119. horses] orig. horse

p. 120. twenty] orig. 20

p. 120. Arsadachus] orig. Arsadach

p. 130. fledged] orig. fligd

p. 136. wherefore] BL:C, BL:G; therefore Bod

p. 141. defaced] orig. desast

p. 141. importance] orig. important

p. 141. that prince] Bod, BL:C; that that prince BL:G

p. 142. is to let] Bod, BL:C; is to to let BL:G

p. 142. some] omitted in orig.

p. 142. which the most] Bod, BL:C; which they most BL:G

p. 143. his own causes] Bod, BL:C; his owns cause BL:G

p. 143. need to] Bod; to need to BL:C, BL:G

p. 144. Aye] orig. I

p. 148. continually] orig. continual

p. 150. her] orig. him

p. 156. and was rent] orig. and rent

p. 157. others] orig. other

p. 160. an aged knight] orig. Aged knight

p. 161. horns] Bod; herse BL:C, BL:G

p. 165. princes] orig. princesse

p. 166. *ictu*] Bod, BL:G; *actu* BL:C

p. 166. trouble-world] Bod, BL:G; troubled world BL:C

p. 167. afflicted] BL:C; inflicted Bod, BL:G

p. 167. inflicted] orig. afflicted

p. 169. tainted] Bod; taunted BL:C, BL:G

p. 170. were] orig. was

Commentary

1. Lady Russell] Elizabeth Cooke (1528–1609) was an author, who married first Sir Thomas Hoby (June 27, 1558) and, after his death in 1566, John, Lord Russell (December 23, 1574). See *DNB* , Vol. 17, p. 431, and Vol. 9, pp. 949–50.
2. Sappho] Greek lyric poet, born c. 600 B.C. in Lesbos. She was for a time the head of a school for girls devoted to the study of poetry and music.
3. Magellan] Ferdinand Magellan (c. 1480–1521) was a Portuguese navigator who received Spanish support for a western voyage to the East. He sailed through the Strait of Magellan separating the mainland of South America from Tierra del Fuego and on into the Pacific Ocean.
4. Patagones] Inhabitants of Patagonia, a region comprising southern Argentina, extreme south-east Chile, and northern Tierra del Fuego.
5. Oppian . . . Theodosius] Oppian was a Greek poet of Cilicia in the late 2nd century A.D.; Theodosius could be any one of numerous individuals, for there were many men with that name in the ancient world.
6. the Muses] In classical mythology, these were the daughters of Jupiter and Mnemosyne (Memory), each one being assigned as patron in some area of art, literature, or science: Calliope, epic poetry; Clio, history; Erato, lyres or lyric poetry; Euterpe, flutes or music; Melpomene, tragedy; Polyhymnia, sacred song; Terpsichore, dance; Thalia, comedy; Urania, astronomy.
7. M. Candish] Thomas Cavendish (1560–92) was a pirate and a circumnavigator of the globe. See *DNB* , Vol. 3, pp. 1267ff.

8. Sanctum] Santos, a city on a small island just off the coast of Brazil at São Paulo. It was founded c. 1545.

9. Cephalus] In classical mythology, Cephalus, an Attic hero and hunter, was loved by Aurora, goddess of the dawn, but he rejected her in favour of his wife Procris. Aurora gave Cephalus an ominous warning, which led him to doubt his wife's faithfulness. His suspicion caused him to test her fidelity, but her innocence was confirmed. Later, however, Procris' own suspicion was aroused by someone who had overheard the resting Cephalus talking to the cool air; she followed her husband into the woods one day to spy on him and his supposed lover, and she was killed when Cephalus, mistaking her for a beast, threw his hunting spear at her. George Sandys, in his commentary on the story in Ovid's *Metamorphoses*, Book 7, makes the point that Procris' error lay "in taking a name for a substance" (p. 350), which is also Margarita's problem in taking "a shadow . . . for the substance" with respect to Arsadachus in Lodge's romance. See George Pettie's *A Petite Pallace of Pettie His Pleasure* for another version of the story.

10. Mantinea] This was a "small city-state in the south-east of Arcadia, north of Tegea, created by the unification of five villages c. 500 B.C." (*OCCL*, p. 345). It suffered the misfortunes of being the site of major battles involving Sparta and its enemies, at various times Athens, Argos, and Thebes.

11. what Plutarch saith] Lodge may have drawn upon Plutarch's brief essay "Virtue and Vice" for this. See *Plutarch's Moralia*, Vol. 2, pp. 95–101.

12. Plato . . . thus: 'If I commend . . . realms.'] See Book 1 of Plato's *Laws* for a discussion of issues such as are raised here. He does not there, however, specifically mention the Lydians.

13. cast more water . . . drown it] Proverbial; cf. Tilley W106: To cast water into the sea (Thames). See also Whiting W80, Apperson 84, and *Oxford* 870.

14. Aristotle . . . covetousness] In *Politica*, Aristotle says about the middle-class: "And this is the class of citizens which is most secure in a state, for they do not, like the poor, covet their neighbours' goods; nor do others covet theirs, as the poor covet the goods of the rich; and as they neither plot against others, nor are themselves plotted against, they pass through life safely" (4.11.1295b.30ff). I don't know how Lodge came by his version of what Aristotle is supposed to have said.

15. Alexander] Presumably Alexander III, "The Great" (356–323 B.C.), king of Macedon and son of Philip II. He was the greatest general of

ancient times, conquering nations from Greece and Egypt to India. See his story in *Plutarch's Lives*, Vol. 7, pp. 223–439, and in Arrian's *Anabasis of Alexander*. The reference to his weeping seems to derive from Plutarch's essay "On Tranquillity of Mind," sec. 4, in which he writes: "Alexander wept when he heard Anaxarchus discourse about an infinite number of worlds, and when his friends inquired what ailed him, 'Is it not worthy of tears,' he said, 'that, when the number of worlds is infinite, we have not yet become lords of a single one?' " (*Moralia*, Vol. 6, pp. 177–79).

16. Zeno] This is probably Zeno of Citium (335–263 B.C.), founder of Stoicism, which emphasized the power of reason over emotion or passion and taught a detachment from the world of ambition and strife. Thus, a Stoic would avoid putting himself into Alexander's position.

17. Octavius Caesar's time] Octavius Caesar, or Augustus, lived from 63 B.C. to A.D. 14. He established a period of peace and stability at home and abroad, the so-called *Pax Romana*.

18. faithfully counselled him] See Machiavelli's observation in Discourse 54, Book 1, on "How Great an Influence a Grave Man may have in restraining an Excited Crowd" (*Discourses*, Vol. 1, p. 332).

19. Drusus Germanicus] Nero Claudius, son of Tiberius Claudius Nero and Livia Drusilla, was born in 38 B.C. and died at the age of 30. He had a brilliant military career, and was granted the surname of Germanicus in honour of his victories over the Germans.

20. the seven sages of Greece] "Under this name were included in antiquity seven men living in the period from B.C. 620–550. They were distinguished for practical wisdom, and conducted the affairs of their country as rulers, lawgivers, and councillors, and were reputed to be the authors of certain short maxims in common use, which were variously assigned among them; the names also of the seven were differently given. Those usually mentioned are: Cleobulus, tyrant of Lindus in Rhodes ('Moderation is the chief good'); Periander, tyrant of Corinth, 668–584 ('Forethought in all things'); Pittacus of Mitylene, born about 650, . . . ('Know thine opportunity'); Bias of Priene in Caria, about B.C. 570 ('Too many workers spoil the work'); Thales of Miletus, 639–536 ('To be surety brings ruin'); Chilon of Sparta ('Know thyself'); Solon of Athens ('Nothing in excess,' i.e. observe moderation)" (*Harper's Dictionary*, p. 1459). F.C. Babbitt, one of Plutarch's translators, points out that "Plutarch names, as the seven wise men, Thales, Bias, Pittacus, Solon, Chilon, Cleobulus, and Anacharsis [in 'Dinner of the Seven Wise Men,' *Moralia*, Vol. 2]. Plato (*Protagoras*, 343A)

puts Myson in place of Anacharsis, and in other lists Periander is found in his stead. Pherecydes, Epimenides, and Peisistratus are the other candidates for a place in the list" ("Introduction," *Moralia*, Vol. 2, p. 347).

21. goddess of chastity] Diana/Artemis.

22. Acteon] In classical mythology, Acteon was a hunter who came upon the naked Diana bathing. Offended at being seen, she turned him into a stag, which was then chased down and killed by his own hounds. In commenting on this story as given in Ovid's *Metamorphoses*, Book 3, George Sandys says:

> But this fable was invented to shew us how dangerous a curiosity it is to search unto the secrets of Princes, or by chance to discover their nakednesse: who thereby incurring their hatred, ever after live the life of a Hart, full of feare and suspicion: not seldome accused by their servants, to gratulate the Prince, unto their utter destruction. For when the displeasure of a Prince is apparent, there commonly are no fewer Traitors then servants, who inflict on their masters the fate of *Actaeon*. (p. 150)

23. Cupids of Anacreon] Anacreon was a famous Greek lyric poet, born c. 570 B.C. at Teos in Ionia, whose poetry spoke of love, wine, and merry company. Lodge has created an intriguing and evidently original emblem of "well-shaped" Modesty attempting to restrain the exuberant cupids.

24. Eternity . . . with a golden trumpet] In Renaissance iconography it was Fame, a female figure winged like an angel, that normally blew the trumpet for honour and tribute: see Whitney, p. 196, Wither, p. 146, Peacham, p. 35, and *Emblemata*, col. 1536. The idea of Eternity, on the other hand, has traditionally been represented by a circle, most commonly in the form of the Ouroboros, the circular figure of a serpent with its tail in its mouth: see examples in *Emblemata*, cols. 652–57, and Wither, pp. 45, 102. The circular snake was sometimes combined with other symbols to signify virtues like Prudence, Wisdom, and Self-knowledge. A different emblem of Eternity is given by Ripa, p. 152: a maiden from the waist up, with the lower body and legs flowing together to form the body of a serpent which encircles her completely. The maiden's body is sprinkled with stars, and in each hand she holds a golden ball. See also Peacham, p. 141. Lodge's emblematic image is unique, it seems.

25. Orpheus] In classical mythology, he was the most famous musician, whose music charmed man, beast, and plants. For the story of Orpheus and Eurydice, see Ovid's *Metamorphoses*, Book 10; for his death at the hands of the Thracian maidens, see Book 11.

26. Hebrus] The river into which the murderous Thracian maidens cast Orpheus' head and lyre. See Ovid's *Metamorphoses*, Book 11.

27. Dolce] Lodovico Dolce, Venetian poet, playwright, translator and treatise writer (1508–68), is best known for his five comedias, a treatise on memory, another on the dignity of women, and several tragedies, including *Giocasta* (1549), translated into English by George Gascoigne and Francis Kinwelmershe. Alice Walker has shown that the quoted poem, "If so those flames I vent," was really a translation of a poem by Ludovico Paschale, not by Dolce. In her article, she discusses Lodge's misattributions in detail.

28. Echo] In classical mythology, Echo was a nymph whose incessant chatter displeased Juno, who rendered her speechless except for purposes of reply. But she could only mimic what had been said to her. She fell in love with Narcissus, but was spurned by him like all the other maidens. See Ovid's *Metamorphoses*, Book 3.

29. Ganymede] In classical mythology, a Trojan boy whom Jupiter, in the form of an eagle, seized and carried off to be his cup-bearer and catamite. See Ovid's *Metamorphoses*, Book 10, for a brief account.

30. quake . . . leaves] Proverbial; cf. Tilley L140: He trembles (quakes, shakes) like an aspen leaf. See also Whiting A216, Apperson 18, and *Oxford* 21.

31. alcatras] Spanish and Portuguese name for the pelican; but albatross or perhaps the frigate bird may be meant (*OED*).

32. ephemerus] The plant *ephemeron*, which "has the leaves of a lily, but smaller, a stem of the same length, a blue flower, a seed of no value, and a single root of the thickness of a thumb, a sovereign remedy for the teeth if it is cut up into pieces in vinegar, boiled down, and used warm as a mouth wash. And the root also by itself arrests decay if forced into the hollow of a decayed tooth" (Pliny, *Natural History*, Book 25, sec. 107). Important to the context of Lodge's reference, of course, is the ephemeral nature of the plant.

33. trifolium] "A large genus of leguminous plants, with trifoliate leaves, and flowers mostly in close heads; including many valuable fodder-plants, known as *clovers* or *trefoils*" (*OED*). Pliny asserts: "It is also a well-ascertained fact that trefoil bristles and raises its leaves against an approaching storm" (*Natural History*, Book 18, sec. 89).

34. unicorn] Aelian, in his *On the Characteristics of Animals*, Book 3, sec. 41, writes:

> India produces horses with one horn, they say, and the same country fosters asses with a single horn. And from these horns they make drinking-vessels, and if anyone puts a deadly poison in them and a man drinks, the

plot will do him no harm. For it seems that the horn both of the horse and of the ass is an antidote to the poison.

Flavius Philostratus also makes mention of this in his *Life of Apollonius of Tyana*, Book 3, chap. 2, and the Spanish physician Nicholas Monardes expands on Philostratus' comment in his *Joyfull Newes Out of the Newe Founde Worlde* (Vol. 2, pp. 67–68).

35. anthias] This is a fish thought to be the Mediterranean barbier by some, the great sea-perch or mérou by others, or the albacore, a kind of tunny (Thompson, *Fishes*, pp. 14–15). Aristotle identifies it with the "aulopias, which . . . spawns in the summer" (*Historia Animalium*, 6.17.570b) and later says: "Wherever an anthias-fish is seen, there will be no dangerous creatures in the vicinity, and sponge-divers will dive in security, and they call these signal-fishes 'holy-fish'" (9.37.620b). It is described by Pliny in his *Natural History*, Book 9, sec. 85, and discussed by Plutarch in "Whether Land or Sea Animals are Cleverer" ("The Cleverness of Animals"), sec. 32, *Moralia*, Vol. 12, pp. 453–55. Aelian in parts of his *On the Characteristics of Animals* also mentions it, as does Oppian in his *Halieutica, or Fishing*. I don't know why Lodge calls it a fowl unless, as is likely, he has confused it with "the anthus, a bird about the size of a finch" (Aristotle, *Historia Animalium*, 8.3.592b). It is an enemy of the horse (9.1.609b), as well as of the acanthis and the aegithus. Aristotle affirms "that the blood of the anthus will not intercommingle with the blood of the aegithus" (9.1.610a). It seems from our various sources that the anthus is a titmouse and the aegithus is a yellow wagtail, although there is sometimes confusion in the namings.

36. nibias] Not identified.

37. Augustus] See note 17. Born September 23, 63 B.C. as Gaius Octavius, he was the first Roman emperor, having received the title "Augustus" on January 16, 27 B.C. He died at Nola on August 19, A.D. 14.

38. Plato saith: 'To be a king . . . following.'] Lodge seems to be in error here, for the ideas do not appear in this form in Plato's dialogues. However, see *The Statesman* (or, *Politicus*) for his ideas on kingship.

39. Hannibal] Hannibal (247–183 B.C.) was a Carthaginian general who crossed the Alps to invade Italy in the Second Punic War.

40. lenca] Not identified.

41. acanthis] Aristotle reports that "[t]he ass and the acanthis are enemies; for the bird lives on thistles, and the ass browses on thistles when they are young and tender" (*Historia Animalium*, 9.1.610a). Croll and Clemons identify the acanthis as the goldfinch, which is

"sometimes known as the 'thistle-finch' " (p. 219, n. 1). Lodge's spelling with "-us" probably comes from Aelian, who writes: "Those who know about birds say that the bird Acanthus derives its name from the acanthus which provides it with food" (*On the Characteristics of Animals*, Book 10, sec. 32). The latter acanthus is a plant with medicinal qualities described by Pliny in *Natural History*, Book 22, sec. 34. According to Scholfield, Aelian's acanthus is the linnet or the siskin.

42. Catiline] Roman patrician known for his cruelty and involvements in conspiracies against civil authorities in Rome. He died in battle in 62 B.C. See Ben Jonson's treatment of his story in *Catiline his Conspiracy* (1611).

43. gold . . . glistered] Proverbial; cf. Tilley A146: All is not gold that glisters (glitters); and Whiting G282: All is not gold that shines. See also Apperson 6 and *Oxford* 316.

44. the stone precious . . . fair foil] Proverbial? Apperson quotes Fuller, *Holy War*, 3.4 (1639): "So true it is, none can guess the jewel by the casket" (333). Cf. the dilemma of Portia's suitors in Shakespeare's *Merchant of Venice*, 2.7, 2.9, and 3.2.

45. water shallow . . . silence] Proverbial; cf. Tilley M78: Beware of a silent man (dog) and still water; and Whiting W63: Believe not still standing water. See also *Oxford* 58.

46. Machevil's prince] Niccolo Machiavelli (1469–1527), Florentine statesman and political philosopher, wrote *The Prince* (*Il Principe*) in 1513 and published it in 1532. It was published in English in 1640, although a number of English translations were in MS circulation long before then. The variant spelling "Machevil" is an example of the Elizabethan association of Machiavelli with evil and villainy. See Introduction, footnote 2.

47. mother Nana] Nanna is a major figure in Pietro Aretino's *The Ragionamenti* (1534), in which she describes herself as follows: "as long as I lived a whore, I acted like a whore" (p. 160). Part one's complete title, translated, is "Conversation of Nanna and Antonia carried on at Rome under a fig-tree; composed by the divine Aretino as a whim, for the improvement of the three states of women" (p. xv). The states are nuns, married women, and courtesans. Part two, published in 1535, deals with Nanna's instructions and warnings to her daughter Pippa (p. xv).

Lodge mentions her again in *Wit's Misery* (1596): "And if he require further insight into the filthy nature of this fiend [Scurrility], in Aretino in his mother Nana, Rabelais in his Legend of Ribaldry, and Bonaventure de Perriers in his novels, he shall be sure to lose his time, and no doubt corrupt his soul" (pp. 88–89; quotation mod. ed.).

48. feather . . . thunder] "The Eagle being the bird of Jove, its feathers were regarded apparently as having special power to withstand thunder" (Gosse, p. 34). Indeed, Pliny writes: "It is stated that this [eagle] is the only bird that is never killed by a thunderbolt; this is why custom has deemed the eagle to be Jupiter's armour-bearer" (*Natural History*, Book 10, sec. 4).

49. therbis] Not identified.

50. his mother at Paphos] Venus/Aphrodite. One of her major temples was located at Paphos on the island of Cyprus.

51. bdellium] A tree yielding a myrrh-like resinous gum. Both the tree and the gum are described by Pliny in *Natural History*, Book 12, sec. 19.

52. You do speak Greek] Proverbial; cf. Tilley G439: It is Greek to me. See also Apperson 273 and *Oxford* 336.

53. Aesculapius] In classical mythology, the god of medical arts. In Book 2, "The Origin of Error," of his *Divine Institutes*, Lactantius, referring to the actions of "Dionysius, the tyrant of Sicily, when he had gained possession of Greece," writes: "Likewise, when he took the gold beard from Aesculapius [i.e., the statue], he said it was unfitting and unfair (since Apollo, the god's father, was still unbearded and smooth), for the son to be seen bearded before the father." In a note, McDonald explains that "the beard referred to . . . may have been of gold braid" (p. 108). The story is repeated by Sandys in his commentary to Ovid's *Metamorphoses*, Book 15 (p. 713).

54. Philostratus] Philostratus II, or L. Flavius Philostratus "the Athenian," born c. A.D. 172 and died 244–49. He was the author of the *Life of Apollonius of Tyana*, *Lives of the Sophists*, and *Love Letters*. Although Letter 28 [47] mentions "my petition" and urges "hearkening to lovers' words," most of the Love Letters present roses and eyes as means of advancing love. For a discussion of the vexing question of identity and attribution among the Philostrati, see the Introduction to *Love Letters*, pp. 387–94.

55. Tiberius] Tiberius Julius Caesar Augustus, Roman emperor A.D. 14–37, born November 16, 42 B.C. and died March 16, A.D. 37. He was the older brother of Drusus Germanicus; see note 19.

56. Cicero] Marcus Tullius Cicero, the greatest of the Roman orators and rhetoricians, was born at Arpinum in 106 B.C. and died in 43.

57. Cato] Styled the "Elder" and also "Censorius," because of the severity with which he fulfilled the office of censor, Marcus Porcius

Cato was born in Tusculum in 234 B.C. and died in 149. His life was marked by a dedication to Roman moral ideals.

58. Apollo's golden bush] Phoebus Apollo, in classical mythology, was the twin brother of Diana and pre-eminently the god of the sun. His "golden bush" is the laurel (*laurus nobilis*), which has yellowish flowers, with the variant *aurea* having yellowish leaves. See the story of Phoebus and Daphne in Ovid's *Metamorphoses*, Book 1.

59. Vulcan] Or Hephaestus, in classical mythology, the god of fire, especially of terrestrial fire, and artificer in metal. He made Achilles' armour, for instance. In order to expose the affair which his wife Venus was carrying on with Mars, he fashioned a net which he used to entrap them in their embraces on his bed. See Ovid's *Metamorphoses*, Book 4.

60. Eurotas] The chief river in Laconia, on which Sparta stood.

61. hyacinth] See Ovid's *Metamorphoses*, Book 10, for the story of the hyacinth.

62. opinion of Aristotle] In *Historia Animalium* (6.18.571b), for example, Aristotle says: "The she-bear is fierce after cubbing, and the bitch after pupping." Oppian, in his *Cynegetica, or the Chase*, describes the situation more fully:

> So also among wild beasts roaring Lionesses and swift Leopards and Tigers of striped back stand forward to defend their children and fight with hunters and for their young ones are prepared to die, joining issue with the spearmen face to face; and in the battle for their offspring they shudder not at the advancing crowd of javelin-throwers, not at the gleaming bronze and flashing iron, nor at the swift cast of shaft and shower of stones, but they are eager either to die first or save their children. (pp. 123–25)

63. no meat . . . mowing] Proverbial; cf. Tilley M832: No meat for mowers (your mowing). See also *Oxford* 521. "Mowing" means "grimacing" or "mocking."

64. Venus . . . Adonis] In classical mythology, Adonis was a handsome youth who was beloved by Venus, but who died of a wound inflicted by a wild boar during a hunt. See Ovid's *Metamorphoses*, Book 10, for their story.

65. Chryses' . . . Achilles] In Homer's *Iliad*, I, Chryses, priest of Apollo, appealed with tears and ransom for the release of his daughter Chryseis, who had been awarded to Agamemnon. Agamemnon refused; Chryses prayed to Apollo, who sent a plague upon the Greeks; Achilles argued on behalf of the girl; and finally Agamemnon relented, but took Achilles' prize, Briseis, for himself. Hence the "wrath of Achilles."

66. Alexander to Campaspe] Pliny tells the story as follows:

> And yet Alexander conferred honour on him [Apelles, the court painter] in a most conspicuous instance; he had such an admiration for the beauty of his favourite mistress, named Pancaspe [Campaspe], that he gave orders that she should be painted in the nude by Apelles, and then discovering that the artist while executing the commission had fallen in love with the woman, he presented her to him, great-minded as he was and still greater owing to his control of himself, and of a greatness proved by this action as much as by any other victory: because he conquered himself, and presented not only his bedmate but his affection also to the artist, and was not even influenced by regard for the feelings of his favourite in having been recently the mistress of a monarch and now belonged to a painter. Some persons believe that she was the model from which the Aphrodite Anadyomene (Rising from the Sea) was painted. (*Natural History*, Book 35, sec. 36.86–87)

67. Pompey . . . prisoner] Pompey the Great (106–48 B.C.) was a Roman general and statesman. He was a member of the First Triumvirate, which also included Julius Caesar and Crassus. He was murdered in Egypt by one of his former centurions now serving the Egyptian king. For a passage describing his treatment of prisoners, see "Pompey," sec. 27–28, in *Plutarch's Lives*.

68. Destinies] In classical mythology, the Destinies (also called the Fates) determined each person's thread of life: Clotho spun the thread, Lachesis measured it out, and Atropos cut it at death.

69. Elysium] In classical mythology, the area of Hades, or the Underworld, reserved for those favoured by the gods; also called the Elysian Fields.

70. the iron hot . . . strike] Proverbial; cf. Tilley I94: It is good to strike while the iron is hot. See also Whiting I60, Apperson 605–06, and *Oxford* 781.

71. under the clear crystal . . . worm] Proverbial; a variation of several proverbial phrases, like Tilley B50: The bait hides the hook; P9: There is a pad [toad] in the straw; S585: Snake in the grass; and the like.

72. under the green leaf . . . serpent] Proverbial; cf. Tilley S585: Snake in the grass. See also Whiting S153, Apperson 583, and *Oxford* 748.

73. in fairest bosoms . . . hearts] Proverbial; cf. Tilley F3: Fair face foul heart; and Whiting H271: A felonious heart under a friendly face. See also Whiting C174, F2, F6; Apperson 200; and *Oxford* 239.

74. Gyges] Herodotus tells the story of how it happened that Gyges, one of the bodyguards of King Candaules of Lydia, came to kill the king, take the throne, and marry the queen (Book 1, sec. 8–15, in *Herodotus*, Vol. 1, pp. 11–19). Plato presents a different, more

exotic, version of the story in his *Republic*, Book 2, *Dialogues*, Vol. 2, pp. 200–01.

75. dreams . . . fancies] Proverbial; cf. Tilley D587: Dreams are lies; and Whiting D387: Dreams are false. See also *Oxford* 202.

76. Trajan] Roman emperor from A.D. 98 to 117, he was born in Italica in Spain on September 18, A.D. 52 or 53, and died in Cilicia in August of 117.

77. nose of wax] Proverbial; cf. Tilley N226: A nose of wax [A thing or person easily molded.], and H531, L104. See also Apperson 451 and *Oxford* 577.

78. Homer . . . justice] In the *Iliad*, Book 16.385ff, Homer writes: "when Zeus poureth forth rain most violently, whenso in anger he waxeth wroth against men that by violence give crooked judgments in the place of gathering, and drive justice out, recking not of the vengeance of the gods"; and in the *Odyssey*, Book 19.109ff: "as does the fame of some blameless king, who with the fear of the gods in his heart, is lord over many mighty men, upholding justice."

79. Plato saith] See Plato's *Protagoras*, *Dialogues*, Vol. 1, p. 147.

80. rubbed the gall] Proverbial; cf. Tilley G12: To rub one on the gall. See also Whiting G7 and Apperson 540. A gall is a sore.

81. viper . . . bosom] Proverbial; cf. Tilley V68: To nourish a viper (snake) in one's bosom. See also Apperson 663 and *Oxford* 747.

82. Tichius] In classical mythology, it was the peak of Mount Oeta (now Banina), which lay between Thessaly and Macedonia, on which mountain the dying Hercules was burned on a pyre. Poets imagined that from behind its height the sun, moon, and stars arose.

83. the Poet] The effects on nature of Arsinous' laments suggest those of Orpheus as described by Ovid, the likely "Poet" in this instance.

84. Diana] In classical mythology, the twin sister of Apollo, associated with virginity and goddess of the moon and of the hunt, although in this latter capacity she was also guardian of wild beasts.

85. Phoebus] Phoebus Apollo; see note 58.

86. Hecate] In classical mythology, she was said, according to Sandys, "to have three heads, of her three denominations; called *Cynthia* in Heaven, *Diana* on Earth, and *Proserpina* in hell: said in her increase to be in Heaven, and to borrow light of her brother; when at full, to impart her owne to the Earth; and when waining, to decline unto Darknesse, and as it were to the infernall mansions; the Moone according to the distance of the Sun assuming severall figures; honoured by witches for her powerfull operations"

(pp. 334–35). She is probably best known as the goddess of sorcery and witchcraft, although Lodge's reference is to her heavenly function.

87. Arabia Felix] Ancient Arabia was divided into three parts: Arabia Petraea, which included the Mount Sinai peninsula and the area to the north and northeast (whose capital was Petra); Arabia Deserta, which encompassed the great Syrian desert and a section of the interior of the Arabian peninsula; and Arabia Felix, which comprised all the rest of Arabia, including the strip of fertile land on the west coast.

88. Thetis . . . Troy] In classical mythology, Thetis was a daughter of Nereus and Doris, hence a goddess of the sea; she married Peleus and thus became the mother of Achilles. The armour that she gave Achilles had been fabricated by Vulcan at her request, and was impenetrable. See Ovid's *Metamorphoses*, Book 11 for her story.

89. Meriones . . . Rhesus] In classical mythology, Meriones was the son of Molus, half-brother to Idomeneus of Crete; he joined the latter in the expedition against Troy, in which assault he was a brave warrior, excelling in archery.

90. Bucephalus] Alexander the Great's horse, so called "either because of its fierce appearance or from the mark of a bull's head branded on its shoulder . . . . This horse when adorned with the royal saddle would not allow itself to be mounted by anybody except Alexander, though on other occasions it allowed anybody to mount" (Pliny, *Natural History*, Book 8, sec. 64). For the account of how Alexander tamed the horse in the first place, see "Alexander," sec. 6, in *Plutarch's Lives*.

91. property of Achilles' sword] In the *Iliad*, Book 19.372–73, we read that "about his shoulders . . . [Achilles] cast the silver-studded sword of bronze." Bronze was supposed to have a medicinal power to heal cuts; for more on this, see note 194.

92. Orlando . . . Angelica . . . Medor] See Ariosto's *Orlando Furioso*, Book 23, stanzas 91–98 (trans. Harington [1591]) for the account of Orlando's sad plight. Compare Lodge's description of Margarita's distress with stanzas 96 and 97:

> And as it were enforst he gives the raine
> To raging griefe upon his bed alone.
> His eyes do shed a verie showre of raine
> With many a scalding sigh and bitter grone.
> He slept as much as if he had then laine
> Upon a bed of thornes and stuft with stone,
> And as he lay theron and could not rest him,
> The bed it selfe gave matter to molest him.

Ah wretch I am (thus to him selfe he sed)
Shall I once hope to take repose and rest me
In that same house, yea ev'n in that same bed
Where my ungratefull love so lewdly drest me?
Nay, let me first an hundred times be ded,
First wolves devour and vulturs shall digest me.
Straight up he starts, and on he puts his cloths,
And leaves the house, so much the bed he loaths.

93. swan hateth the sparrow] The hostility between swan and eagle is well documented, as in Pliny, *Natural History*, Book 10, sec. 95; Aristotle, *Historia Animalium*, 9.1.610a; and Aelian, *On the Characteristics of Animals*, Book 5, sec. 34. How does Lodge arrive at a swan-sparrow enmity? There was in ancient times some confusion between the various kinds of hawks and eagles. Thompson points out an Egyptian word and a couple of Greek words applying to both birds (*Birds*, pp. 101 and 213, 255); Aristophanes includes "kestrel, buzzard, vulture, great owl, eagle" under the designation "Hawk Archers" (*Birds*, l. 1181); and Pliny describes "the hawk-eagle, also called the mountain stork, which resembles a vulture" (Book 10, sec. 3). Aelian states that "Falcons are excellent at fowling and are no whit inferior to eagles; . . . in size they are as large as eagles." He also affirms that a falcon will fight with an eagle (Book 2, sec. 42). Thompson (*Birds*, p. 6) refers to "Hawking with trained Eagles in India" and to "Eagles trained for falconry in Afghanistan, Turkestan, &c." It seems that, with so much confusion about the identification of these birds, it would be no great leap for Lodge to move from eagle to hawk to sparrow-hawk to sparrow.

94. the eagle the trochilus] Pliny in his list of animal hostilities includes *aquila et trochilus*, which Rackham translates as "eagle and the goldcrest" (*Natural History*, Book 10, sec. 95). Aristotle comments on the hostility between the eagle and the wren (*Historia Animalium*, 9.1.609b and 9.11.615a), and in 8.3.592b he describes the wren as being "golden-crested"; in 8.3.593b he identifies the trochilus with the sandpiper, and later goes on to say:

> When the crocodile yawns, the trochilus flies into his mouth and cleans his teeth. The trochilus gets his food thereby, and the crocodile gets ease and comfort; it makes no attempt to injure its little friend, but, when it wants it to go, it shakes its neck in warning, lest it should accidentally bite the bird. (9.6.612a)

95. the ass the bee] Accounts of the ass's enmity with the aegithus, the wolf, the raven, the lizard, and the acanthis (Aristotle, *Historia*

Animalium, 9.1.609a–610a), the blue tit (Aelian, *On the Characteristics of Animals*, Book 5, sec. 48), the raven (Aelian, Book 2, sec. 51), and the wolf (Aelian, Book 8, sec. 6), and so on are easy to find. But I have not yet come across a reference to an ass-bee hostility.

96. the serpent the hog] Aristotle says that "[t]he snake is at war with the weasel and the pig; . . . with the pig for preying on her kind" (*Historia Animalium*, 9.1.609b).

97. Philoxenus] A Greek poet (435–380 B.C.) of Cythera, famous for his dithyrambs. According to Athenaeus, he was "excessively fond of fish" (*Deipnosophists*, Vol. 4, pp. 47–49; see also Vol. 1, p. 27).

98. Terpander] An outstanding poet and musician from Lesbos (early 7th century B.C.) who composed and performed, winning several musical competitions.

99. Heliogabalus] The name of a god worshipped by the Phoenicians. The name has also been applied to the debauched Emperor Elagabalus (early 3rd century A.D.), a worshipper of the sun.

100. Bacchus] In classical mythology, the Roman name of Dionysus, the god of wine, son of Jupiter and Semele.

101. Lamprias in Plutarch] The name "Lamprias" is mentioned in various places in Plutarch's writings. For example, in "Antony," sec. 28 (*Lives*), and in "Table-Talk," Book 5 (*Moralia*, Vol. 8, pp. 407, 437), Lamprias is Plutarch's grandfather; in "The E at Delphi" (*Moralia*, Vol. 5, p. 205) and in "Table-Talk," Book 1 (*Moralia*, Vol. 8, p. 83 et seq.), the name refers to Plutarch's brother.

102. Aeschylus] The earliest of the great Athenian tragic dramatists, c. 525–456 B.C. The others were Sophocles and Euripides.

103. where the wolf . . . is most sweetest] For an explanation of this, see Plutarch's "Question 9" in "Table-Talk," Book 2, *Moralia*, Vol. 8, pp. 181–83. It seems that "the wolf's temper is so very hot and fiery that . . . the flesh of sheep bitten by wolves decomposes more quickly than that of others."

104. wine hath warmed . . . eloquently] Proverbial; cf. Tilley W491: Wine whets the wit (valor); and Apperson 693: Wine is a whetstone to wit. See also *Oxford* 895. But Lodge's source is more Plutarchan than proverbial; compare the passage "And for that each of us . . . armed most eloquently" with the following from Plutarch:

> Furthermore, it was said that love is like drunkenness, for it makes men hot, gay, and distraught, and when they get in that condition, they are carried away into song-like and quite metrical speech: Aeschylus allegedly wrote his tragedies while drinking, indeed thoroughly heated with wine. My grandfather Lamprias was his most ingenious and eloquent self when drinking, and it was his habit to say that, much as incense is volatilized by heat, so was he by wine. ("Table-Talk," Book 1, *Moralia*, Vol. 8, p. 65)

105. crotchets in my head] Proverbial; cf. Tilley C843: He has crotchets
     in his head. See also Apperson 123. Crotchets are whimsical
     fancies.
106. Thibaeans . . . Pontus] The Thibaeans, who were a mythical people
     "who anciently lived near the Pontus [south coast of the Euxine
     (Black) Sea], were, according to Phylarchus, deadly not only to
     children but to adults. He says that those who were subjected to
     the glance [the evil eye], breath, or speech of these people, fell ill
     and wasted away" (Plutarch, "Table-Talk," Book 5, *Moralia*, Vol. 8,
     p. 419). Pliny also discusses the evil eye, and cites Phylarchus on
     "the Thibii tribe and many others of the same nature in Pontus,
     whose distinguishing marks he records as being a double pupil in
     one eye and the likeness of a horse in the other" (*Natural History*,
     Book 7, sec. 2.17).
107. as Plato saith] See Plato's *Symposium, Dialogues*, Vol. 1, pp. 503 ff.
108. Menippus] A Cynic writer from Gadara (early 3rd century B.C.)
     who specialized in satire.
109. Aristippus] He was "from Cyrene, an associate of Socrates, [and
     he wrote] . . . dialogues and historical works . . . . Much of the
     ancient evidence concerns his worldly and luxurious mode of life"
     (*OCD*, p. 161). Athenaeus, for example, describes him as an avid
     "fish-eater" (*Deipnosophists*, Vol. 4, p. 57).
110. petrol] A "kinde of Marle or Chaulky Clay, or rather a substance
     strained out of the natural *Bitumen*: It is for the most part white,
     but sometime black, and being once set on fire, can hardly be
     quenched" (Thomas Blount, *Glossographia* . . . [London, 1656], sig.
     Gg3$^\mathrm{v}$).
111. Eutelidas in Plutarch] Max Nelson informs me in a letter that
     "[t]hese lines . . . are clearly a Latin translation of a fragment
     of dactylic hexameter poetry of Euphorion of Chalcis from the 3rd
     C. B.C. which survives in the 2nd C. A.D. author Plutarch . . . .
     This mythological episode of Eutelidas, who is so beautiful that he
     gives himself the evil eye when looking at his reflection, is known
     only in antiquity in Euphorion's fragment and in Plutarch's sub-
     sequent discussion ["Table-Talk," Book 5, *Moralia*, Vol. 8, pp. 427–
     31]. Scholars have often connected this story to the Narcissus
     myth (see especially C. Zimmerman, *The Pastoral Narcissus*, 1994:
     pp. 39–73) but I have denied the link (M. Nelson, "Narcissus: Myth
     and Magic," *The Classical Journal* 95 [2000] 363–389, especially 364,
     n. 7)." Nelson offers the following translation of the text quoted by
     Lodge: "Eutelidas was once beautiful with respect to the locks of
     his hair, but he himself seeing himself in the calm flowing waves,

disgraceful, destroyed [himself] by the taint of envy. The evil eye attracted death and destroyed beauty." He adds: "Note that Plutarch cites the Eutelidas story specifically to show that people can die because of the evil eye even if there is no envious gaze but simply stunning beauty, while the Latin adaptor retains the usual concept of the evil eye working through envy (*invidia*)."

112. Narcissus] In classical mythology, Narcissus was a beautiful but conceited young man who rejected many nymphs and mocked many men. Finally, Nemesis, responding to the prayer of one scorned youth, condemned Narcissus to fall in love with his own reflection in the water and consequently to pine away from unrequited love. See Ovid's *Metamorphoses*, Book 3.

113. Xerxes] Son of Darius the Great, he was king of Persia from 485 to 465 B.C. The story of Xerxes and his love for a plane-tree (sycamore) is told by Aelian in his *Historical Miscellany*, Book 2, sec. 14.

114. Prytaneum] A public building dedicated to Hestia, goddess of the hearth, and the place where hospitality was offered to foreign dignitaries and to Athenians who had performed distinguished service to the state. The story of the young Athenian and his love for the statue is told by Aelian in his *Historical Miscellany*, Book 9, sec. 39.

115. anter] Anteros, "a precious Stone, the best sort of Amethyst" (John Kersey, *Dictionarium Anglo-Britannicum* [London, 1708], sig. F^r). Gosse explains it as "Perhaps the same as the Anterotes, or Amethyst, which was supposed to cure or prevent drunkenness" (p. 14). It might be of interest to note that Anteros, in classical mythology, was the name of a son of Venus and Mars; as brother of Eros (Cupid), he was associated with requited love and also with the anti-love impulse. If "falling-sickness" is read as sexual desire instead of epilepsy, then perhaps this latter significance is what Lodge has in mind here. *Emblemata* shows an emblem of a blind-folded Eros, without wings, sitting and holding his arrows while Anteros, winged, stands before him breaking his bow. The caption reads: "Anteros zerbricht Amors Bogen" (col. 1767).

116. sinilan] This word is undoubtedly a misprint for "smilax"; evidently the compositor misread Lodge's "smi" as "sini" (minim confusion) and his "x" as "n". Lodge wrote in a neat, predominantly Italic hand (see Greg, *English Literary Autographs*, plate XIX); he was one of those "writers who made their *x*'s of two addorsed curves sometimes . . . [leaving] a little space between them and sometimes . . . [trying] to make them without a pen-lift, giving us such *x*'s as . . . are easily mistaken for *n*" (Tannenbaum,

Handwriting, p. 85). Lodge does, in his preface, apologize to "the Gentlemen Readers" for "those faults, . . . , escaped by the printer in not being acquainted with my hand, and the book printed in my absence." Furthermore, the word "sinilan" has nowhere, as far as I know, been identified; on the other hand, "smilax" is the name of a couple of well-known plants. It refers to a species of yew tree about which Pliny writes the following: "The fruit of the male yew is harmful — in fact its berries, particularly in Spain, contain a deadly poison; even wine-flasks for travellers made of its wood in Gaul are known to have caused death. Sextius says that the Greek name for this tree is *milax*, and that in Arcadia its poison is so active that people who go to sleep or picnic beneath a yew-tree die" (*Natural History*, Book 16, sec. 20). The smilax is perhaps better known as a species of ivy, and in this connection Ovid and Sandys are helpful. Ovid mentions "*Crocos* and *Smilax*, chang'd to pretty flowres" (*Metamorphoses*, Book 4, c. line 290) and Sandys comments: "The *Smilax* resembles Ivy, bearing a flowre like our violet; some white, some yellow, some purple, some white and black, with variety of mixtures. These flowres in regard to the infortunity of those lovers; were consecrated to the *Eumenedes*: nor worne in garlands by any, as ominous and fatall" (p. 206). In either case, the smilax/sinilan is a dangerous plant.

117. saffron] "An orange-red product consisting of the dried stigmas of *Crocus sativus* . . . formerly extensively used in medicine as a cordial and sudorific" (*OED*). Pliny discusses saffron in *Natural History*, Book 21, sec. 81, and points out that "It induces sleep, has a gentle action on the head, and is an aphrodisiac."

118. amethyst] From the Greek meaning "not drunken," this word was "applied subst. to this stone (as also to a herb), from a notion that it was a preventive to intoxication" (*OED*). The *OED* also cites the passage from *Margarite*.

119. alyssum] Nicholas Monardes tells a story which may be of interest here:

> In the yere of 1562, when the Earle of Nieba was in the Peru, he had there a gentlewoman whiche was maried that served hym, and her housbande waxed sicke of a grevous desease, and an Indian of greate reputation seeyng her to be in much sorrowe: saied to her, if she would knowe whether her housband would live or die of that desease, that he would sende her a Bowe [bough] of an hearbe, that she should take it in her lefte hande, and that she shoulde holde him faste, for a good while, and if he shoulde live, that then she should showe muche gladnesse, with holdyng the Bowe in her hande, and if he should die that then she should showe muche sadnesse. And the Indian sent her the Bowe, and she did as he

had willed her to doe: and the bowe being put into her hande, she tooke so muche sadnesse and sorrowe, that she put it awaie from her, thinking that she shoulde have died, and so he died within a fewe daies. I was desirous to knowe if that it were soe, and a gentleman of the Peru that had been there many yeares, did certifie and saied unto mee that it was of trueth, that the Indians did this with their sicke people, it hath put mee in admiration, and in muche consideration. (*Joyfull Newes*, Vol. 2, pp. 21–22)

120. Apollonius Tyaneus] The most celebrated of the Neo-Pythagoreans of Cappadocia, living c. A.D. 50 and regarded by many as a god and rival to Jesus Christ. The story of the eunuch is told by Flavius Philostratus in his *Life of Apollonius of Tyana*, Book 1, chap. 36.

121. Orosius] "[A] Spanish writer, A.D. 416, who published a universal history, in seven books, from the creation to his own time, in which, though learned, diligent, and pious, he betrayed a great ignorance of historical facts and of chronology" (Lemprière, p. 430).

122. Ariston of Ephesus . . . Cratis the Iloritan shepherd] I have not yet been able to identify this Ariston, but the story of a groom falling in love with a mare is told by Aelian in *On the Characteristics of Animals*, Book 4, sec. 8, and that of the goatherd Crathis and his goat in Book 6, sec. 42.

123. Pasiphae] In classical mythology, the wife of Minos II of Crete. She fell in love with a bull that Neptune had sent Minos for a sacrifice; the offspring of Pasiphae and the bull was the Minotaur. See Ovid's *The Art of Love*, Book 1, pp. 33–35, and George Pettie's *A Petite Pallace of Pettie His Pleasure*.

124. Theophrastus] Theophrastus (c. 370–287 B.C.) was born at Eresus in Lesbos. He studied under both Plato and Aristotle, and on the latter's retirement he assumed the headship of the Peripatetic School. He was a very prolific writer, best known for his advancement of Aristotelian thought and for his *Characters*, which exerted a strong influence in Renaissance literature.

125. tropi of Egypt] According to Pliny, the *tropaei* are the so-called "turning winds" which blow back again from the sea to the land, as opposed to the offshore winds (*Natural History*, Book 2, sec. 44).

126. Melpomene and Terpsichore] In classical mythology, Melpomene was the Muse of tragedy and Terpsichore of dance; see note 6.

127. Siren] In classical mythology, Sirens were sea nymphs, daughters of the river god Achelous, who, by their seductive singing, tried to entice seafarers to leap to their deaths in the sea as their ship passed by the Sirens' island. At some point, they were transformed into creatures with the bodies of birds, but with their human faces and voices preserved. For the story of their transformation, see Ovid's

Metamorphoses, Book 5.551–63; for the account of their attempt on Ulysses, see Homer's *Odyssey*, Book 12.1–72, 153–200.

128. Sibylla] Originally, that is by the 5th century B.C., it was the name of a single prophetic woman; but eventually the term became generic and referred to various oracular Sibyls, with the one connected with Rome being of particular importance to pagans and Christians alike.

129. All cats are grey] Proverbial; cf. Tilley C50: When candles be out (At night) all cats be gray. See also Apperson 85 and *Oxford* 111.

130. the fat . . . fire] Proverbial; cf. Tilley F79: The fat (All the fat) is in the fire. See also Whiting F71, Apperson 205, and *Oxford* 247.

131. devils . . . be painted] Proverbial; cf. Tilley D255: The devil is not so black as he is painted. See also Whiting D189, Apperson 147, and *Oxford* 182.

132. knew the tree . . . fruit] Proverbial; cf. Tilley T494: Such as the tree is such is the fruit; and T497: The tree (fruit) is known by the fruit (tree). See also Whiting T465, Apperson 263 and 607, and *Oxford* 837. Also biblical: cf. Matthew 12: 33.

133. under gold . . . poison lie] Proverbial; cf. Tilley P458: Poison is hidden in golden cups. See also Apperson 504 and *Oxford* 637.

134. under softest flowers lie serpents] Proverbial; see note 72. In his fourth eclogue, Alexander Barclay writes: "Oft under flowers vile snakes have I found" (*The Eclogues of Alexander Barclay*, ed. Beatrice White, Early English Text Society [London: Oxford University Press, 1928], p. 143; quotation modernized ed.). Lady Macbeth advises her husband to "look like th'innocent flower,/ But be the serpent under't" (Shakespeare, *Macbeth*, 1.5.63–64).

135. from man's spine . . . arise] Pliny states: "We have it from many authorities that a snake may be born from the spinal marrow of a human being" (*Natural History*, Book 10, sec. 86).

136. Ammonius] There are various individuals of this name in antiquity, but Lodge has probably drawn on Ammonius (A.D. c. 440–525), son of Hermias and a native of Alexandria. He was a disciple of Proclus and taught philosophy in his native city. He writes in his commentary on Aristotle's *Categories*: "for contraries are more violently opposed. Indeed, they destroy one another, and if one exists the other always perishes" (p. 114) and "contraries are destructive of one another, and when one of them exists the other would never exist in the subject in the same part at the same time" (p. 125). The relationship involving Arsadachus and Margarita gives evidence of this.

137. Nemesis] In classical mythology, the daughter of Night. She embodied the righteous anger and vengeance of the gods, especially toward the arrogant, the insolent, and the criminal.

138. callax] This may be the fish charax of the Red Sea, which Aelian describes in *On the Characteristics of Animals*, Book 12, sec. 25: "It has fins, and the lateral ones are like gold in appearance, and so are all its dorsal fins. On the lower part of its body are rings of purple, but the tail, believe me, is golden, while purple dots colour beautifully the centre of its eyes." In a note to his translation of Oppian's *Halieutica, or Fishing*, A.W. Mair states that "such evidence as we have points to a Sea-bream" (p. 223 [j]).

139. as the smallest kernel . . . tallest tree] Proverbial; cf. Tilley S211: Of little seeds grow great cedars (trees); and Whiting K12: Of a little kernel comes a mickle tree.

140. Fates] Destinies; see note 68.

141. Saturn] In classical Roman mythology, he was originally a king of Italy who introduced agriculture and civilization to the people. The Romans associated him with Cronos and saw him as the father of the major gods; the association with the Greeks' Demeter, mother of Persephone and provider of fertility and plenty, is also strong. Here, Lodge may have in mind a saturnine disposition: morose and gloomy.

142. Montgibel] A volcano perhaps named after Gibil, the Mesopotamian god of fire. Gosse identifies it as Mount Aetna (p. 50).

143. Medusa] In classical mythology, Medusa (or Gorgo) was a monstrous individual with snakes instead of hair on her ugly head. A glance from her eyes could turn people and animals to stone. See Ovid's *Metamorphoses*, Book 4.

144. oil . . . flame] All three expressions are proverbial; cf. Tilley O30 and O32 (oil), F785 (fuel), F278 and F351 (flax).

145. Plutarch writeth] See "Demetrius," sec. 22, in *Lives*.

146. Diodorus Siculus] A historian "of Agyrium, Sicily, . . . [he] is the author of . . . a universal history from mythological times to 60 B.C. Only 15 of the original 40 books survive fully . . . ; the others are preserved in fragments" (*OCD*, p. 472). He lived in the 1st century B.C. It would seem that the story referred to by Lodge has not survived into modern editions of Diodorus Siculus.

147. Plutarch, . . . banishment] See "On Being a Busybody" in *Moralia*, Vol. 6, p. 481, for the story.

148. Anaxilas, Dionysius] Anaxilas was a Greek middle-comedy poet in the 4th century B.C. He and his works are frequently referred to by Athenaeus in *The Deipnosophists*. There are too many ancients

by the name of Dionysius to make identification certain, although the Syracusan general and ruler Dionysius (c. 430–367 B.C.), who was "a dramatist perhaps no worse than the generality in an age of decline" (*OCD*, p. 477), might be meant.

149. Bias] One of the seven sages of Greece; see note 20.

150. bird . . . feather] Proverbial; cf. Tilley B369: Every bird is known by his feather.

151. eagle . . . flight] Proverbial; cf. Tilley E4: You cannot fly like an eagle with the wings of a wren. See also Apperson 173.

152. leopard . . . spot] Proverbial; cf. Tilley L206: A leopard (panther) cannot change his spots. See also *Oxford* 456.

153. lion . . . claw] Proverbial; cf. Tilley L313: A lion is known by his paw (claw).

154. Aristarchus] Probably Aristarchus of Samothrace (c. 216–144 B.C.), a scholar who wrote textual criticism of Homer, Hesiod, and other authors; commentaries on Homer, Pindar, Sophocles, and others; and critical treatises on the *Iliad* and the *Odyssey*. See *OCD*, p. 159.

155. Nicias] A moderate politician and general of Athens, living c. 470–413 B.C. For his story, see *Plutarch's Lives*, Vol. 3.

156. play the wolf . . . sun] Proverbial?; cf. Tilley M1123: To bark against the moon. See also Whiting M654.

157. Solon] An Athenian poet, lawgiver, and politician of the 6th century B.C. He was one of the seven sages of Greece; see note 20.

158. my shirt . . . skin is nearest] Proverbial; cf. Tilley S356: Close fits (sits) my shirt (coat) but closer my skin. See also Whiting S256, Apperson 437, and *Oxford* 556.

159. a hawk . . . lure] Proverbial; cf. Whiting H198: As ready as any (a) hawk to lure (that is lured). See also Tilley H230 and Apperson 291.

160. nothing is hidden . . . Time] Proverbial; cf. Tilley T333: Time reveals (discloses) all things; and N330: There is nothing so secret but it may be discovered. See also Whiting T326, Apperson 634–35, and *Oxford* 823.

161. Caligula] Gaius Julius Caesar Germanicus, who served as Roman emperor A.D. 37–41; he was born in A.D. 12 in Antium.

162. Nero] Nero Claudius Caesar was Roman emperor A.D. 54–68.

163. Tarquin] Lucius Tarquinius Superbus, last of the early Roman kings (534–510 B.C.), killed his father-in-law, Servius Tullius, and usurped his throne. See Shakespeare's *The Rape of Lucrece* for the story of his son Sextus' rape of Lucretia, wife of Lucius Tarquinius Collatinus.

164. the weak . . . the wall] Proverbial; cf. Tilley W185: The weakest goes to the wall. See also Whiting W130, Apperson 671, and *Oxford* 873.
165. Venus . . . Adonis] See note 64.
166. Aurora . . . Memnon] In classical mythology, Memnon, son of Aurora and Tithonus, was an Ethiopian king who fought on the Trojan side in the Trojan War. He was slain by Achilles. See Ovid's *Metamorphoses*, Book 13, for his story.
167. Myrrha] In classical mythology, the mother of Adonis through an incestuous relationship with her father, Cinyras. She was transformed into a myrrh tree, from an opening in which Adonis was born. See Ovid's *Metamorphoses*, Book 10, for her story.
168. imitation of Dolce] "This poem too was translated not from Dolce but from a madrigal of Paschale's 'Io veggio apertamente' " in his *Rime Volgari*, published in Vinegia in 1549 (Walker, p. 76).
169. Aetna] The active volcano in eastern Sicily.
170. Ludovico Paschale] "An obscure Italian poet of the first half of the sixteenth century, from whose *Rime Volgari* [1549] Lodge had borrowed" the quoted sonnet (Walker, p. 76). The quoted line *Tutte le stelle* . . . is translated "All the stars have dominion (rule, power) of the sky."
171. Martelli] Ludovico Martelli, a Florentine author (1499–1527). His *Works* were published in 1548.
172. Flora] In classical mythology, the goddess of flowers.
173. Philippe Desportes] French poet (1546–1606), born at Chartres. His *Amours* (1573) for a time were "very popular, eclipsing the fame of Ronsard" (Rachum, p. 140). Lodge translated several of his poems, including those published in *Rosalind* (1590), *Phillis* (1543), and *Scilla's Metamorphosis* (1589).
174. Cynthia] Diana.
175. I held it . . . substance] Proverbial; cf. Tilley S951: Lose not the substance for the shadow. See also Apperson 560 and *Oxford* 110.
176. Antigonus Epiphanus] A general under Alexander the Great, and later king over much of Asia Minor; he died in battle in 301 B.C.
177. Plessians] Perhaps men of Plestia in Umbria, Italy, a "municipium of the tribus Ufentina in a pass by the Lacus Plestinus, midway from Fulginia to Serravalle . . . . It was the scene of a disastrous defeat of Roman cavalry by Hannibal shortly after the Battle of Trasimene" (*Princeton Encyclopedia*, p. 717).
178. Lucina] In classical mythology, the goddess of childbirth, associated with both Juno and Diana.

179. *Sic itur ad astra*] Thus one may go to the stars (i.e., gain immortal fame). From Virgil's *Aeneid*, Book 9.641.

180. Numantines] Inhabitants of Numantia on the upper Durius (Douro) River in northern Spain. Their defeat by the forces of Scipio Aemilianus in 133 B.C. signalled the end of Iberian military resistance to Rome.

181. have blood for blood] Proverbial; cf. Tilley B458: Blood will have blood. See also Whiting B361 and *Oxford* 69.

182. Thales] One of the seven sages of Greece; see note 20.

183. Pythagoras] Greek intellectual (mid-6th century B.C.) whose theories in religion (transmigration of souls), mathematics (geometry, number theory), music (consonances and harmonics), and astronomy have made him one of the most influential figures in the history of Western thought.

184. tenthis] An Internet website tells us that the tenthis is a "sea porcupine, light brown; a sea fish, *tenthis vermiculata*" (www.hindunet. org/saraswati/Indian%20Lexicon/fish.htm). It may well be a kind of globe-fish, or porcupine fish, which Thompson describes as "A Red Sea fish: it looks like a sea-urchin, and has long, hard spines or prickles: Ael. xii.25" (*Fishes*, p. 263). On p. 185 of the same book, Thompson notes that the globe-fish "was supposed to show how the wind blows," which bears some relevance to Lodge's reference.

185. Plato's reason . . . live well] See Plato's *Gorgias, Dialogues*, Vol. 2, p. 610. Cf. *Republic*, same volume, p. 257.

186. tyrant of Sicily, Dionysius] Dionysius the Elder (430–367 B.C.), tyrant of Syracuse, brought prosperity and firm rule to Syracuse.

187. Dion] This is Cassius Dio (born A.D. 155–164, died after 229), Greek senator and historian who wrote *Roman History*. Numerous incidents that Dio describes in his history of the Caesars and others bear out the truth of this statement.

188. *Utinam omnis populus . . . omnes necarem*] Dio, in his *Roman History*, writes that Caligula, angry that the crowd cheered on opponents of his favourites at an arena event, exclaimed, "threatening the whole people: 'Would that you had but a single neck'" (Book 59, Vol. 7, p. 299). He adds later that, after Caligula's death, bystanders watching the ensuing demonstrations in the streets "recalled the words once addressed by him to the populace, 'Would that you had but one neck,' and they showed him that it was he who had but one neck, whereas they had many hands" (p. 363). Suetonius also mentions Caligula's outburst at the arena, writing that "he

shouted out: 'If only the Roman people had a single neck' " *(Lives of the Caesars*, p. 152).

189. Tiberius . . . troublesome wretch] Suetonius, in his *Lives of the Caesars*, writes: "The people were so delighted at his death that when they first heard the news some ran about shouting 'Into the Tiber with Tiberius!' while others prayed to Mother Earth and the shades that he should be given no place in the underworld except among the wicked" (p. 134).

190. Scedasus' daughters] During the reign of Cleombrotus, king of Sparta in the 4th century B.C., the two daughters of Scedasus, a Boeotian, were raped by two Spartans. For shame, they committed suicide, and Scedasus, unable to gain justice, killed himself on their tomb. This incident is reported by Plutarch in "Pelopidas," 20.3–4, in *Lives*, Vol. 5, p. 391, and by Pausanias in his *Description of Greece*, Book 9: "Boeotia," sec. 13.5–6, in Vol. 4, pp. 227–29. See also Diodorus of Sicily's version in his *Library of History*, Book 15, sec. 54, in Vol. 7, pp. 103–05.

191. Chrysippus] Chrysippus of Soli in Cilicia (c. 280–206 B.C.) was the third leader of the Stoic school in Athens, after Zeno of Citium, its founder, and Cleanthes of Assos, its second head. Chrysippus' question "for what should ill men plead, since . . . nothing is profitable unto them?" seems to be reflected in Plutarch's critique of Stoic thought in his "On Stoic Self-contradictions," sec. 31, *Moralia*, Vol. 13, Pt. 2, pp. 535–37.

192. Plutarch saith . . . of all virtue] Although Plutarch does occasionally speak of dramatic presentation, as in his comments on tragedy and comedy in "Table-Talk," Book 7, Question 8 (*Moralia*, Vol. 9, pp. 77–91), I have not been able to find this particular comment in his writings. The idea is, of course, a commonplace in literature.

193. Sooth spake Chrysippus . . . *novis recipiandis* ———] This is evidently Lodge's slimmed-down version of this passage in Plutarch: "At any rate, if the gods should change and wish to injure, maltreat, torment, and finally crush us, they could not make our condition worse than now it is, as Chrysippus declares that life admits no higher degree either of vice or of unhappiness, so that, if it should get the power of speech, it would recite the line of Heracles: 'I'm now replete with woes, and there's no room' [Euripides, *Heracles*, 1245]" ("On Stoic Self-contradictions," sec. 31, *Moralia*, Vol. 13, Pt. 2, pp. 537–39). The literal Latin translation of Heracles' line which Lodge quotes is:

> I am already full of evils, nor does the place remain with other new things to be received.

It might be of interest to note that Plutarch quotes Heracles' line again in "Against the Stoics on Common Conceptions," sec. 11, *Moralia*, Vol. 13, Pt. 2, p. 693.

194. Aristotle's opinion] In *Problemata*, 1.35.863a, Aristotle raises the question: "Why is it that, if one is cut with a copper instrument, the wound heals more quickly than if the cut is made with iron?" He gives the answer that "copper has a medicinal power of its own, and 'in all things it is the beginning that is important,' and so the copper, by its immediate action as soon as the cut is made, causes the wound to close up." In Aristotle's time, copper and bronze (copper + tin) were hardly distinguished one from the other. Brass (copper + zinc) was not widely used until Roman imperial times. Richard Caton, in his paper on ancient medicinal and surgical instruments, observes that

> [i]n ancient times knives were either of stone or of bronze. The superstitious fear of iron lingered even into the Christian era. It was unlawful to introduce an iron implement into any Greek temple. Bronze on the other hand had a special purifying virtue. . . . No Roman priest might be shaven by an iron razor or iron scissors. I mention this superstition as possibly explaining a peculiarity to be observed in surgeons' knives: it will be remembered that surgical treatment was related to the worship and ritual of Asklepios. (pp. 114–15)

195. heart to the man] In "Concerning the Face Which Appears in the Orb of the Moon," sec. 15, Plutarch says "the sun in the heart's capacity transmits and disperses out of himself heat and light as it were blood and breath" (*Moralia*, Vol. 12, p. 93).

196. Bactrian coast] Bactria was a region in Asia generally corresponding to present-day Afghanistan. As far as I can tell, it had no access to the sea.

Works Cited or Consulted

Addison, James Clyde, Jr., ed. *And* [sic] *Old-Spelling Critical Edition of Thomas Lodge's* A Margarite of America *(1596)*. Salzburg: Institute für Anglistik und Amerikanistik, Universität Salzburg, 1980 (Diss. University of Tennessee, 1980).

Aelian. *Historical Miscellany*. Ed. and trans. N.G. Wilson. Cambridge, Mass.: Harvard University Press, 1997.

——. *On the Characteristics of Animals*. Trans. A.F. Scholfield. 3 vols. Cambridge, Mass.: Harvard University Press; London: Heinemann, 1958–59.

Albertus Magnus. *The Book of Secrets of Albertus Magnus of the Virtues of Herbs, Stones and Certain Beasts also A Book of the Marvels of the World*. Ed. Michael R. Best and Frank H. Brightman. Oxford: Clarendon Press, 1973.

Ammonius. *On Aristotle Categories*. Trans. S. Marc Cohen and Gareth B. Matthews. London: Duckworth, 1991.

Apperson, G.L. *English Proverbs and Proverbial Phrases: A Historical Dictionary*. London: Dent, 1929.

Aretino, Pietro. *The Ragionamenti*. Ed. Peter Stafford. London: Odyssey, 1970.

Ariosto, Ludovico. *Orlando Furioso*. Trans. John Harington (1591). Ed. Robert McNulty. Oxford: Clarendon Press, 1972.

Aristophanes. *Birds*. Ed. and trans. Alan H. Sommerstein. Warminster: Aris and Phillips, 1987.

Aristotle. *The Works of Aristotle*. Ed. W.D. Ross et al. 12 vols. Oxford: Clarendon, 1928–52.

Arrian. *Anabasis of Alexander* [and] *Indica*. Trans. P.A. Brunt. 2 vols. Cambridge, Mass.: Harvard University Press; London: Heinemann, 1976–83.

Athenaeus. *The Deipnosophists.* Trans. Charles Burton Gulick. 7 vols. Cambridge, Mass.: Harvard University Press; London: Heinemann, 1927–41.

Atlas of the Classical World. Ed. A.A.M. Van der Heyden and H.H. Scullard. London: Nelson, 1959.

Avicenna. *Avicenna's Poem on Medicine.* Trans. and ed. Haven C. Krueger. Springfield, Ill.: Thomas, 1963.

Caton, Richard. "Notes on a Group of Medical and Surgical Instruments Found near Kolophon." *Journal of Hellenic Studies* 34 (1914) 114–18.

Croll, Morris William, and Harry Clemons, eds. *Euphues: The Anatomy of Wit* [and] *Euphues and His England.* By John Lyly. New York, 1916. Rpt. New York: Russell and Russell, 1964.

Dictionary of National Biography. Ed. Leslie Stephen and Sidney Lee. Vols. 3 and 17. London: Oxford University Press, 1937–38. [*DNB*]

Dio, Cassius. *Dio's Roman History.* Trans. Earnest Cary. 9 vols. Cambridge, Mass.: Harvard University Press; London: Heinemann, 1914–27.

Diodorus of Sicily. [Diodorus Siculus]. [*Library of History*]. Trans. C.H. Oldfather et al. 12 vols. Cambridge, Mass.: Harvard University Press; London: Heinemann, 1933–57.

Emblemata: Handbuch zur Sinnbildkunst des XVI. und XVII. Jahrhunderts. Ed. Arthur Henkel and Albrecht Schöne. Stuttgart: J.B. Metzlersche Verlagsbuchhandlung, 1967.

Gayley, Charles Mills. *The Classic Myths in English Literature and in Art.* New ed. rev. Waltham, Mass.: Blaisdell, 1911.

Gerard, John. *The Herball or Generall Historie of Plantes.* 2 vols. London, 1597.

Golding, Arthur. *Shakespeare's Ovid Being Arthur Golding's Translation of the Metamorphoses.* Ed. W.H.D. Rouse. 1961. New York: Norton, 1966.

Gosse, Edmund. "Index and Summary." Vol. 4 of *The Complete Works of Thomas Lodge.* Ed. Gosse. 4 vols. Hunterian Club, 1883.

Greg, W.W., ed. *English Literary Autographs 1550–1650.* Oxford, 1932; rpt. Nendeln, Liechtenstein: Kraus Reprint, 1968.

Harper's Dictionary of Classical Literature and Antiquities. Ed. Harry Thurston Peck. New York: Cooper Square, 1965.

Herodotus. Trans. A.D. Godley. 4 vols. Cambridge, Mass.: Harvard University Press; London: Heinemann, 1920–25 (Vol. 1 rev. 1926, Vol. 2 rev. 1938).

Homer. *The Iliad.* Trans. A.T. Murray. 2 vols. Cambridge, Mass.: Harvard University Press; London: Heinemann, 1924–25.

———. *The Odyssey*. Trans. A.T. Murray. 2 vols. Cambridge, Mass.: Harvard University Press; London: Heinemann, 1953.

Lactantius. *The Divine Institutes Books I–VII*. Trans. Sister Mary Francis McDonald. Vol. 49 of *The Fathers of the Church*. Washington: Catholic University of America Press, 1964.

Lemprière, John. *Lemprière's Classical Dictionary of Proper Names Mentioned in Ancient Authors Writ Large*. 3rd ed. London: Routledge and Kegan Paul, 1984.

Machiavelli, Niccolo. *The Discourses of Niccolo Machiavelli*. Trans. Leslie J. Walker. New introd. Cecil H. Clough. 2 vols. London: Routledge and Kegan Paul, 1975.

Maser, Edward A., trans. and ed. *Cesare Ripa Baroque and Rococo Pictorial Imagery. The 1758–60 Hertel Edition of Ripa's 'Iconologia' with 200 Engraved Illustrations*. New York: Dover, 1971.

Monardes, Nicholas. *Joyfull Newes Out of the Newe Founde Worlde*. Trans. John Frampton. 2 vols. London: Constable, 1925; rpt. New York: AMS Press, 1967.

Oppian. *Cynegetica, or The Chase* [and] *Halieutica, or Fishing* in *Oppian Colluthus Tryphiodorus*. Trans. A.W. Mair. Cambridge, Mass.: Harvard University Press; London: Heinemann, 1928.

Ovid. *The Art of Love, and Other Poems*. Trans. J.H. Mozley. 2nd ed. rev. G.P. Goold. Cambridge, Mass.: Harvard University Press; London: Heinemann, 1979.

———. *Ovid's Metamorphosis* [sic] *Englished, Mythologized, and Represented in Figures*. By George Sandys. 1632. Ed. Karl K. Hulley and Stanley T. Vandersall. Lincoln: University of Nebraska Press, 1970.

Oxford Classical Dictionary. Ed. Simon Hornblower and Antony Spawforth. 3rd ed. Oxford: Oxford University Press, 1996. [*OCD*]

Oxford Companion to Classical Literature. Ed. M.C. Howatson. 2nd ed. Oxford: Oxford University Press, 1989. [*OCCL*]

Oxford Dictionary of English Proverbs. 3rd ed. rev. F.P. Wilson. Oxford: Clarendon, 1970. [*Oxford*]

Pausanias. *Description of Greece*. Trans. W.H.S. Jones. 4 vols. with rev. companion vol. 5. Cambridge, Mass.: Harvard University Press; London: Heinemann, 1918–55.

Peacham, Henry. *Minerva Britanna or a Garden of Heroical Devises, ...* London, 1612.

Philostratus. *The Life of Apollonius of Tyana*. Trans. F.C. Conybeare. 2 vols. Cambridge, Mass.: Harvard University Press; London: Heinemann, 1912.

——. *Love Letters* in *The Letters of Alciphron, Aelian, and Philostratus*. Trans. Allen Rogers Benner and Francis H. Fobes. London: Heinemann; Cambridge, Mass.: Harvard University Press, 1949.

Plato. *The Dialogues of Plato*. Trans. B. Jowett. 4 vols. 4th ed. Oxford: Clarendon Press, 1953.

Pliny [Elder]. *Natural History*. Trans. H. Rackham et al. 10 vols. Cambridge, Mass.: Harvard University Press; London: Heinemann, 1938–62.

Plutarch. *Plutarch's Lives*. Trans. Bernadotte Perrin. 11 vols. Cambridge, Mass.: Harvard University Press; London: Heinemann, 1914–26.

——. *Plutarch's Moralia*. Trans. Frank Cole Babbitt et al. 16 vols. Cambridge, Mass.: Harvard University Press; London: Heinemann, 1927–69.

Princeton Encyclopedia of Classical Sites. Ed. Richard Stillwell. Princeton: Princeton University Press, 1976

Rachum, Ilan. *The Renaissance: An Illustrated Encyclopedia*. New York: Mayflower Books, 1979.

Ripa, Cesare. *Iconologia*. Padua, 1611. Rpt. New York: Garland, 1976.

Sandys, George. Commentary in *Ovid's Metamorphosis* [sic].

Scott, Mary Augusta. *Elizabethan Translations from the Italian*. Boston: Houghton Mifflin, 1916.

Suetonius. *Lives of the Caesars*. Trans. Catharine Edwards. Oxford World's Classics. Oxford: Oxford University Press, 2000.

Tannenbaum, Samuel A. *The Handwriting of the Renaissance*. New York: Columbia University Press, 1930; rpt. New York, Ungar, 1967.

Theophrastus. *Enquiry into Plants and Minor Works on Odours and Weather Signs*. Trans. Sir Arthur Hort. 2 vols. Cambridge, Mass.: Harvard University Press; London: Heinemann, 1916.

Thompson, D'Arcy Wentworth. *A Glossary of Greek Birds*. London: Oxford University Press, 1936.

——. *A Glossary of Greek Fishes*. London: Oxford University Press, 1947.

Tilley, Morris Palmer. *A Dictionary of the Proverbs in England in the Sixteenth and Seventeenth Centuries*. Ann Arbor: University of Michigan Press, 1950.

Wace, Alan J.B., and Frank H. Stubbings, eds. *A Companion to Homer*. London: Macmillan, 1962.

Walker, Alice. "Italian Sources of Lyrics of Thomas Lodge." *Modern Language Review* 22.1 (1927) 75–79.

Whiting, Bartlett Jere, and Helen Wescott Whiting. *Proverbs, Sentences, and Proverbial Phrases From English Writings Mainly Before 1500*. Cambridge, Mass.: Harvard University Press (Belknap), 1968.

Whitney, Geffrey. *A Choice of Emblemes, and Other Devises,* . . . . Leyden, 1586.

Wither, George. *A Collection of Emblemes, Ancient and Moderne* . . . . London, 1635.

The Barnabe Riche Series

This volume of the Barnabe Riche Series was produced using the TEX typesetting system, with Adobe Palatino Postscript fonts and in-house critical edition macros.